Secrets
in the
Water

Secrets
in the
Water

a novel by
Alice Fitzpatrick

A Meredith Island Mystery

Stonehouse Publishing Inc. is an independent
publishing house, incorporated in 2014.
Cover design and layout by Elizabeth Friesen.

Printed in Canada
Stonehouse Publishing would like to thank and acknowledge
the support of the Alberta Government funding for the arts,
through the Alberta Media Fund.

Government

National Library of Canada Cataloguing in Publication Data
Alice Fitzpatrick
Secrets in the Water
Novel
ISBN 978-1-988754-60-4
First edition

For the real George and Lilian, my grandparents
George Terence and Alice May Fitzpatrick,
who supported and encouraged my dreams.

CHAPTER 1

Kate stepped out of the musty church and took a deep breath. The cool air tasted of salt water and damp earth. She reached into her jacket pocket, pulled out a crumpled tissue, and wiped her eyes.

Alex inclined her head against Kate's and took her other hand. "All right, Mum?"

Kate managed a smile, but inside a voice whispered, *how can anything ever be all right again*? Lilian, her grandmother, the woman she'd known all her life, was gone. Except for Alex, there was no one left of her family, no one to whom she was related by blood. And that realization made her feel uncharacteristically vulnerable.

They followed the polished oak casket to where the mourners clustered at the graveside in their bright clothing. Sombre colours and subdued voices had no place at island funerals. Respect was paid through dressing in one's best, whether it be neon pink or lime green, and the islanders had done Lilian proud.

The Reverend Imogen Larkin looked toward Kate and Alex from behind red-framed reading glasses, giving them a comforting smile. As Imogen recited the centuries-old service, it seemed to Kate that she managed to say each phrase with sincerity and affection as if she were creating it just for this occasion. Even though Imogen was a relative newcomer—and to the Welsh islanders that was anyone whose great-grandparents hadn't been born here—she made it sound as though she'd known Lilian all her life.

Surrounding the newly-dug grave were the graves of other Galways—Kate's grandfather, her mother Miriam, and her Aunt

Emma. Wilted irises still lay against the headstones, lovingly placed by Lilian. It must have been one of her final acts.

Irises had been Emma's favourite.

Back on the mainland, entire months would pass without Kate thinking of Emma, but here, it was hard to avoid her memory. When she was first told about the circumstances of her aunt's death, young Kate had envisioned Emma lying on soft sand, her yellow swimsuit clinging to her slim body, a scrap of green seaweed entangled between her fingers. But it was a child's fantasy, created to help Kate deal with something that was beyond her understanding. It wasn't until many years later that she learnt her aunt's body had been found at the back of the island. Emma's pale skin would have been torn and bruised from being battered against the rocks, her fingers and toes bitten and chewed by crabs and fish. It was a horrifying thing to happen to someone you love.

Kate took a deep breath and brought her attention back to the empty grave at her feet.

"We therefore commit her body to the ground; earth to earth, ashes to ashes, dust to dust; in the sure and certain hope of the Resurrection to eternal life..."

Lilian was lowered into the ground. Kate and Alex each threw a handful of earth down onto the coffin, both taking care to avoid the brass nameplate, as if wanting Lilian's name to remain visible in the world, if only for a few more minutes. As the mourners began to leave, Kate hesitated, trying to find an excuse to stay with her grandmother. But finally she joined the others.

Subdued laughter and loud voices speaking in Welsh and English drifted back from the crowds making their way to the wake at the pub. Winifred Lamb, Lilian's next-door neighbour, put her arm through Kate's. She'd been a good friend to Lilian, looking after her in her final weeks.

"Beautiful service, absolutely beautiful. You did her proud." The lines around Winifred's eyes deepened as she smiled. "The hymns were lovely and the sing-along to 'Embraceable You,' obviously in memory of your grandfather. But I'm afraid the island band let us down." Winifred made a *tsk, tsk* sound as if to emphasize her disapproval. "What were they playing? 'Men of Harlech' was it?"

"I thought it was the 'William Tell Overture,'" Alex said.

"I never understood the attraction, but Lilian loved a brass band," Kate said.

They paused for a moment, as if to consider her eccentric taste in music.

"Well, God rest their souls," Winifred continued. "They're all together now."

Kate hoped it was true. At a moment like this, she envied Winifred her faith.

They followed the procession toward the harbour. What few cars there were taxied older residents down the road which ran along the cliff edge, scooters, bicycles, and the odd skateboard weaved their way among groups of walkers. Kate and Alex were offered a lift, but Kate preferred to walk. She wanted to feel the cool sea air against her face.

Today was one of those overcast spring days she remembered so well. It could be warm, but then there'd be a sudden gust of cold wind as if the island was teetering between winter and summer, unsure whether to go forward or to retreat. With the incoming tide had come dense slate-coloured clouds, and from the feel of the heavy air, Kate knew that by the time they reached the pub, it would be raining.

"She was so proud of you—your university degrees, you a teacher. And your Alex a barrister. A teacher and a barrister in the family... and, of course, your James."

Kate didn't bother to correct Winifred. He hadn't been her James for almost ten years.

Her grandmother had always liked James, even after the divorce, and Kate felt he owed it to Lilian to be here. But at least he'd sent an elegant arrangement of white roses in his place. So she said nothing, not wanting to challenge Alex's opinion of her father.

Up ahead were the grey stone cottages that lined the cliff side road leading down to the harbour. Over the years, each house had taken on a character of its own, some with extensions on the back, others with second storeys, like Lilian's and Winifred's with her garden full of daffodils, brilliant yellow in the grey light. Along with some overgrown bushes, flowers of different sizes and colours had taken over Lilian's garden—white crocuses, pink foxgloves, blue anemones and hyacinths, yellow primroses. Like Lilian's home, everything and everyone was welcome.

Winifred left them to fetch the cake she was bringing to the wake, leaving Kate and Alex to carry on alone. Kate stared out over the water where the grey sky met an even greyer sea. That straight line of horizon was something she never saw in the city, hidden by a barricade of concrete and glass, divorcing earth from sky. The island and its people took up such a tiny space on the globe, yet the sea and the sky went on forever. She took some comfort in that.

"You were thinking about Emma at the cemetery," Alex said.

"What makes you think that?"

"You always have such a sad expression on your face when you talk about her. You had it at the cemetery."

"It was the flowers on the graves. I always think of her when I see irises."

"I remember when you told me she'd committed suicide," Alex said softly.

"It was one of the hardest conversations we ever had."

"Do you think the islanders still believe she was murdered?" Alex asked. Her question didn't surprise Kate. After all, the islanders had been quietly speculating about Emma's death for the past fifty years.

"I know that the coroner's verdict was hard for everyone to accept. Emma was beautiful, intelligent, and headed for university. None of us could understand why she would choose to end her life."

"But did she though?"

Kate had no answer, and so much time had passed she'd given up hope of ever learning the truth. But giving up doesn't necessarily bring you peace. "I don't know, love. I honestly don't know."

They were approaching the pub. The Fish and Filly—known as

The Filly—was a large two-storey building. It dominated the harbour amid a row of joined houses, The Sea Breeze restaurant, an art shop, and Craggy's, the island post office and general store, which curved along the road leading to the wharf. The pub offered panoramic views of the sea through large windows on either side of a shiny green door, guarded by wooden tubs of purple and white delphiniums. It was a door that was always open except on the coldest and dampest of days, allowing the laughter, the singing, and the patrons to spill out onto the narrow, paved road. The Filly didn't have the elegant exterior of many of the mainland pubs Kate was familiar with, but that was perfectly fine with the islanders. It was solid and square like their cottages. It was the heart of the island, and one of Kate's favourite places.

Kate forced a smile. "No more talk about Emma. We're here for Lilian."

True to her prediction, it was beginning to rain. Kate exchanged greetings with the hardy souls clustered outside, puffing on cigarettes, their glasses balanced on the stone wall overlooking the harbour. Over by the community centre, the flag with its red dragon on a white and green field was flying at half-mast. Tomorrow it would be raised to its regular position, and the world would go on as normal. But without Lilian.

The conversation was loud when Kate and Alex stepped into the crowded pub. Overhead lights cast a pale glow over people already resting against the polished wooden bar or gathered around tiny round tables, covered with red and blue cloths. Additional chairs lined the walls which were a wash of cream with dark green accents.

A long table was loaded with plates heaped with food brought by the islanders. Kate's mother's Welsh cakes and Lilian's sherry trifle were conspicuous by their absence. Alex must have noticed it too, as she leaned over and softly kissed her mother's damp cheek.

At the end of the bar was a photograph of Lilian and George among the roses in their garden. Next to the picture was a glass of what Kate suspected was Lilian's whiskey of choice. Winifred approached with a glass each for each of them.

The landlord rang the last call bell for everyone's attention, and the room grew silent. Those outside gathered around the door.

"Ladies and gentlemen, silence please," he said.

He raised his glass in one hand, and with the other pushed back his thick, dark hair with an easy motion. "Ladies and gentleman, to one of our own. To a beloved wife, mother," and he looked toward Kate and Alex, their arms wrapped around each other, "grandmother, and great-grandmother, and a dear friend to us all. As eternal as the sea and as beautiful as the sky that bends down to kiss it. To Lilian. *Heddwch i'w llwch.*"

The islanders raised their glasses toward Lilian's picture, echoing Julian's wish for her soul to be at peace, and downed their whiskeys in one swallow.

With the formalities of the funeral behind her, Kate felt herself begin to relax.

A giddy shriek of female laughter drew her attention to a crowd of older women surrounding artist David Sutherland, Meredith Island's most famous native son, and according to Alex, on the A-list of contemporary British artists. Kate reckoned he must have been going on seventy but looked younger with a full head of faded blonde hair. Unlike so many older people whose faces fatten to blur their original features, his face had managed to retain its high cheekbones, deep-set eyes, and a jawline softly rounded yet remarkably unbroken by jowls or creases around his mouth. As a young man, he must have been stunningly attractive.

David looked over at Kate. She lowered her gaze, embarrassed that she'd been caught staring, and quickly scanned the room for her daughter. Alex was being plied with large pieces of Madeira cake by three elderly men known to the islanders as Feebles, Gooley, and Smee, which had always struck Kate as an excellent name for a Dickensian law firm.

Alex excused herself and came to stand beside her mother.

"You'll be struggling to get into those power suits if you eat any more cake," Kate teased.

Alex licked the stray crumbs from her lips and laughed. "Uncle

Gooley says I need some meat on my bones, so he's taken it upon himself to fatten me up."

"I can't say I disagree, but did you tell him you spend thousands of pounds a year to sweat at some posh gym to keep your bony figure?"

"I think he'd be shocked and quite probably disgusted. I'm sure I'd be if I were him." Alex stared at the people in the pub. "God, I love this place."

As a child, Alex had divided her summer holidays between the Galways and James's mother in her Cheshire cul-de-sac whose residents spent their days deadheading roses and taking an inordinate delight in keeping each other informed about any curious goings-on. But it was on Meredith Island that Alex had been free to be herself.

Alex smiled and wiped a tear from her cheek. "I seem to be getting sentimental."

"It's a day for being sentimental." Kate gave her daughter a quick hug. "Right, I think I could do with another drink," and she handed Alex her empty glass.

In Alex's absence, Kate's attention was once again drawn to where David Sutherland continued to hold court. Judging from the expressions on the faces of his female admirers, Kate wasn't the only one who found him easy on the eye. Fiona Caldicott, who looked two sizes smaller than her mauve print dress, stroked David's arm like a woman whose inhibitions had vanished with her last gin and tonic.

Alex returned and handed Kate her whiskey. "Is Fiona flirting with David Sutherland?"

"Oh, it's moved way beyond flirting."

Alex raised her glass in salute. "Well, good for her. I hope I can summon up that much enthusiasm for it when I'm her age." Alex stared intently for a moment. "David's looking good. Do you think he's had work done?"

"Alex!"

"C'mon, Mum. He definitely does something with his hair. As

for the rest, well, he can certainly afford it. I mean, you can't buy a David Sutherland painting for less than £80,000."

"That much?"

David disentangled himself from his ladies and started to approach Alex and Kate.

"Oh God, he saw us," Kate whispered. "That's twice he's caught me staring."

"Well, he must be used to it. You can't deny it's a nice view."

"Kate, Alex, my sincere condolences." David kissed them both lightly on the cheek and took Kate's hand in his. He looked closely at her, as if searching for something familiar in her face. At last he said, "Lilian was a wonderful woman. We'll all miss her."

Kate teared up again. The realization that her family were all gone pressed hard on her heart.

"You were friends with Emma, weren't you?" Alex asked him.

Once Alex got something into her head, it was hard to stop her. Kate wished her daughter would leave it alone. There had been enough talk about Emma today.

David looked down to where his hand still held Kate's. He gently released it. "I was."

People within earshot of their conversation had become quiet.

"We both were." Fiona approached, her voice uncharacteristically loud from the drink.

"Please, Fiona," David pleaded, as if anticipating what was coming.

"You want to know about the suicide, don't you, my dear?" she said to Alex. "She didn't kill herself. I know that for a fact. I know how much she had to live for. And you know that too, David."

Fiona was so tiny with her sloping shoulders and flat chest, yet her blue eyes were sharp with a surprising ferocity.

"Miss Caldicott, let's get you home." Reverend Imogen took Fiona's arm. "The day's obviously been too much for you."

"We trusted the police with their science and fancy ways of getting to the truth, but they let us down. We should have spoken up, all of us, insisted they do more." Fiona voice was shaking. "But we failed her. We failed Emma."

As she manoeuvred Fiona toward the door, Imogen offered Kate an embarrassed look. "I'm so sorry."

Kate looked toward David who was staring into his empty glass. He seemed to be avoiding her gaze. "Mr. Sutherland, you said you were Emma's friend."

David's eyes were watery as if he was remembering something bitterly sad. "And I want to believe she'd have come to me before taking her own life. The suicide note rules out an accident, and if it wasn't suicide..."

Kate couldn't help but finish his thought. *Then it was murder.*

She stared at the familiar faces in the room, the people she considered her family.

And if it was, the killer could be standing in this very room.

CHAPTER 2

"Why didn't anyone tell me?" Hannah Sutherland's voice, shrill with emotion, filled the entrance hall of the Sutherland home. Her words were punctuated by the pounding of the rubber tip of her cane against the black and white checkered floor. "Nobody tells me anything. Jane, why wasn't I told?"

Jane hurried from the drawing room to find her sister standing in the afternoon sun as it filtered through the narrow leaded windows on either side of the heavy oak front door. Dust particles drifted in the twin rectangles of light around Hannah. She couldn't have created a more dramatic effect if she'd planned it, and Jane often thought Hannah planned for just such an effect. "Are you all right?"

But Hannah brushed aside any attempts to help her. "Stop fussing, Jane," she barked, and then suddenly turned and walked into the drawing room.

Physically Hannah was having a good day, but Jane wasn't so sure about her mental state.

"Why am I always the last to know anything? Why do you all conspire to keep things from me? I'm not a child," and she fell back into the armchair by the window.

A badger waddled across the lawn in front of the gravel drive. Jane stood watching until it disappeared beyond the sight of the window, allowing Hannah some time to calm down. "Let me get you a cup of tea."

"I don't want tea," she barked again. "And I wouldn't have thought you, of all people, had bought into the feeble-minded belief that tea is the solution to the world's ills."

Jane settled on the sofa facing Hannah. Her sister was ill, she reminded herself. Hannah didn't know what she was saying. But it was so easy to lose patience with her. In an effort to calm herself, Jane fingered the plain silver cross that lay against her freshly pressed white blouse. She knew what Hannah was like when she got herself worked up. It had been bad enough when she was younger, but now it seemed to happen more often and with greater ferocity. At least today she seemed to be making some sort of sense. She didn't always.

"Don't fidget, Jane. You're not helping matters."

Jane gripped the cross, her nails digging into the palms of her hands. When she was having a bit of a rant, as their younger sister Sophie called it, Hannah's long face seemed to get heavy, her grey-blue eyes dark. Her body, once fit from hours of walking and hiking, had grown stocky as she'd grown older and less active, more reliant on her cane. Her once-muscular legs were now encased in grey support hose, making them look like the thick skin of a rhinoceros. Sophie had once confided her jealousy of Hannah's good looks, but Jane had recognized this as pride and envy. Women only wish to be attractive in order to be found desirable by men. Hence the desire to be attractive was a desire for lust. Humility and modesty were what the Bible taught. Humility and modesty were what Jane strove to practise.

Jane sat quietly and let Hannah talk. It often calmed her if she thought she was in control.

"Now answer me. Why wasn't I told?" Hannah sat back, her blue-veined hands folded on the cane, upright between her knees, her head erect. "The funeral. I missed the funeral."

Jane bit her lower lip. "Well, dear," and she continued to keep hold of her cross, a silent plea for God's acceptance that the motivation for her lie came from love, "we thought it might tire you. You haven't gone out for such a very long time, and it would have been so hard on your poor knees."

"But I should have gone, Jane." Hannah leaned forward, and her tone changed as if she was imploring Jane to understand. "I should have gone."

She was right, of course. One of the sisters should have gone. But Sophie, who usually did that sort of thing, was just getting over a cold, and Jane had to stay to keep an eye on Hannah. They'd sent a card and an expensive floral arrangement from the good florist in Porth Madryn on the mainland. It's not as if they ever saw Kate and her daughter—or Lilian, for that matter. The Sutherlands didn't socialize much with the general population of the island. It wasn't their way. Besides, David had represented the family. People much preferred to see David.

"It's all right," Jane tried to reassure her. "I'm sure everyone understands. They know how much of a burden it is for you to leave the house."

Hannah pulled a white handkerchief out of her sleeve and held it to her face. Jane could see the tears watering her eyes. Now what was wrong? These days Hannah could go from one extreme to the other so quickly. She seemed to be at the mercy of her emotions, as was the rest of the house. "But I'm her teacher."

Jane shook her head. Hannah was getting all muddled up again. "It was Lilian, Emma's mother, who died. We did tell you."

Hannah stared down at the polished oak floor. "No, it was Emma. Emma drowned. They told us yesterday. Don't you remember? It's her funeral. They'll expect me to say something."

With some effort, Jane lowered herself to her knees beside Hannah's chair. She stroked her sister's white hair, so thin Jane could almost count each individual hair. Hannah used to have such thick, dark hair. Jane hated when Hannah got everything jumbled up. It was a reminder that her once sharp mind was becoming lost to them. "No, dear. Emma died a long time ago."

Hannah turned quickly and stared into Jane's face with cold eyes narrowed to slits as she tensed her lips. The cane fell to the floor with a hollow clatter as her fists gripped the arms of the chair. "She tried to hurt our David."

"That was a long time ago. Don't let's talk about it. What about a nice walk in the garden? Get some fresh air," and Jane clasped her sister's hands, hoping to divert Hannah's mind from the accusations which she'd voiced over and over and had finally driven David from the house.

Hannah pushed her with such an unexpected force that Jane fell back onto the floor. "She was a scheming little minx. She tried to break up our family, take away our good name. She wanted to destroy David's life. She deserved to die."

CHAPTER 3

The next morning Kate sat at the dining room table, a mug of cold coffee in front of her. Ever since she'd arrived on the island, she'd managed to distract herself with the arrangements for the funeral. Now that it was over, she was aware of a profound sense of absence. Even though the cottage was filled with overstuffed furniture, knick-knacks, and family photographs on every surface, it had never felt so empty.

Dominating the living room was Lilian's floral easy chair that was positioned so she could watch television but also look out the front window to keep an eye out for anyone walking along the road and on the weather coming in from the sea. She'd fallen asleep in that chair six days ago and never woken up. Would Kate ever be able to bring herself to sit in it?

Kate wasn't the kind of person who was sentimental about places, or who anthropomorphized inanimate objects, but she felt that with Lilian's death, there was no love left in the house. Was that what was upsetting her? Had yesterday's talk about Emma only served to remind her of the extent of her loss?

She'd lain awake most of the night, searching her mind for every scrap of conversation, every mental picture she had of her aunt that might provide a clue to the cause of her death. But they were the memories of a young child—impressions and shadowy images of the two of them running through the meadow at the back of the cottage, looking for shells on the beach, digging for buried treasure. There had been no arguments, no one who might have posed a threat.

Once Alex was awake, she and Kate made a start at clearing out Lilian's things, sorting her life into piles and bin bags. Alex turned from a drawer in the heavy sideboard where she was pulling out embroidered tablecloths. She furrowed her forehead, something she always did when working herself up to broaching an unsettling subject.

"This might not be the best time to ask, but what are you thinking of doing with the cottage? Look, I understand if you're thinking of selling. This is prime island real estate. With the sale of this place, the royalties from your books—"

"Such as they are," Kate interjected in a vain attempt to lighten the mood.

"—and your teacher's pension, you'll be able to live quite comfortably on the mainland."

Kate knew exactly what her daughter was doing. As much as Alex would love to keep the cottage, she was giving her mother permission to sell.

"You're right. It's probably best I sell," Kate said. "Moving back to the island just isn't practical." I haven't lived here for over thirty-five years. This was Lilian and Mum's house. My home is on the mainland. It's probably best I sell it. You aren't disappointed, are you?"

"Do what you have to, Mum. I'm working so much, I barely see my own place these days, so I'm hardly one to offer an opinion."

Alex picked up Emma's photograph that held pride of place on the mantel. She studied it for a moment, no doubt looking into Emma's deep blue eyes, searching for a clue in her expression. "The family never got over her death, did they? That look in the cemetery—I've seen it on all of you."

"Emma was taken before her life had barely begun. When someone dies like that, I don't think anyone ever gets over it. You try to put the pain to one side, but every so often you catch a glimpse of it, and it nudges you with a dagger-like sharpness to let you know it's still there."

Alex settled herself on the sofa beside her mother. "Tell me what else you remember about her," she asked in a soft, almost reverential voice.

"You know she took care of me while Mum was studying on the mainland."

"Gran's bookkeeping courses," Alex said.

"She wanted to improve her chances of getting a good job so we wouldn't be a burden on Lilian and George after my father died. But all I knew was that Mum wasn't here, and Emma was. Emma read me stories, we played games, and she bought me ice-cream and sweets. Sweets were only allowed on special occasions, so it was our secret, and we broke the rules together." Kate smiled at the thought. "One of my earliest memories was being snuggled up in bed, listening to her reading bedtime stories. She did all the sound effects and the characters' voices like I used to do for you. Mum once told me that after hearing Emma's rendition of Humpty Dumpty—complete with screams as he fell from the wall—I'd refused to eat eggs. For some reason, I've always had an image of myself sitting at the table, pushing my breakfast away, in tears at the thought of Humpty being served on my plate. But did it actually happen, or did I imagine it from Mum's story?"

Before Alex could respond, there was a loud knock at the door, and the sound of a woman's voice. "Anyone home?"

"You know, the one island tradition I'll never get used to is people letting themselves into your house," Alex whispered to Kate. "Or them being insulted if you lock them out. I think this might be a good time to check my emails."

Although it had seemed perfectly normal when she was growing up, Kate now had to agree that it impinged on people's privacy, especially if they didn't want to be disturbed. Kate's writing needed long stretches of uninterrupted concentration. She'd not get that on the island.

Alex disappeared up the stairs as the visitor stepped into the hallway. It was her hair Kate first noticed—long, red, cascading waves, reminiscent of a Pre-Raphaelite painting. The woman was in her early forties with flawless white skin. Her loose dungarees, the bib and braces smeared with what looked like paint or clay, hung over a tight yellow tank top. A Celtic knot was tattooed on her right shoulder. She was Siobhan Fitzgerald, one of the island artists.

She held out a jar of red jam and a plate piled with scones. "These aren't mine. I'm quite literally the only person on the island who doesn't bake. The scones are from Winifred—she gave them to me when she saw I was heading your way—and the jam is..." and she hesitated, twisting her mouth while she tried to remember. "Oh, I don't know who made the jam, but it's still good. Nothing in my place lasts past its sell-by date."

The plate made a dull landing in the middle of the dining room table. "I'm sorry I missed the funeral, but I was on the mainland at a craft fair. It was booked four months in advance. But I'd much rather have been here to see Lilian off."

Kate brought the mugs, plates, and knives to the dining room table. "We met briefly at Lilian's one hundredth birthday party at the pub."

"Now that was a great party." Siobhan settled herself at the table, reached for a knife, and covered a scone with a thick layer of jam. "I seem to be off on the mainland every other time you're here. Summer, Christmas, they're my busiest times. But Lilian talked about you all the time, your books and all."

"You're a potter or a sculptor, aren't you?"

"I explore the various aspects and interpretations of the female form, which is an artsy way of saying I sculpt naked women. But I also do bowls, mugs—nothing tatty, but definitely more mainstream. That's the stuff that pays the rent, or the mortgage, in my case."

Kate returned with the tea pot, sat down, and took a scone.

"Are you allowed to eat those?" Siobhan asked.

Kate was confused at first but then realized why Siobhan was curious. "Oh, it's all right. I'm vegetarian, not vegan."

Now it was Siobhan's turn to look confused.

"That means I eat dairy and eggs. I just don't eat meat or fish." Kate poured out the tea.

"Why?" Siobhan asked, adding three heaping spoonfuls of sugar to her cup.

"My ex-husband insisted on meat at every meal. I was convinced it was just a matter of time before one of us had a heart-attack, and it was probably going to be him. I thought if we changed our diet, we'd live longer. He never bought into it. We divorced soon after."

Kate remembered one particularly fierce argument when James had shouted that Kate only had to stand in front of a classroom and chat about Shakespeare, while he had to endure long hours chasing criminals and for that he needed large amounts of protein. It was one of many arguments toward the end of their marriage that escalated to an absurd extreme. Before it was over, he'd declared with a completely straight face that she was trying to emasculate him. It had taken a lot of self-control not to laugh.

Siobhan still looked bewildered, as if the idea of denying herself anything was beyond her comprehension. "But you can still eat scones?"

"I can still eat scones." Now firmly entrenched in middle-age, Kate seemed to have given up sex, the ability to tuck sweaters and blouses into her trousers, and perky breasts, so there had to be some pleasures left in the world. Sadly, aged Lancashire cheese and buttered scones were it.

Apparently satisfied that Kate wasn't some raving dietary lunatic who was going to try to convert her, Siobhan helped herself to another scone. "I heard about what happened at the wake. Fiona's normally quite well-behaved when the occasion calls for it."

"To be honest, I'm glad she said it."

There was a forced cough at the front door, and Winifred's head appeared.

"Oh Siobhan, you're still here, dear. Kate, I wanted to have a word with you about Lilian. If you'd rather it was another time..."

"I can go," Siobhan popped the rest of her scone into her mouth as she stood up.

Kate waved her hand to indicate they both could stay.

Seating herself at the table, Winifred accepted Kate's offer of tea.

She looked like a woman who didn't want to be there. She slowly stirred her tea, put down her teaspoon, and took a slow sip.

As if unable to put if off any longer, she finally said, "Over the last few months, Lilian had been feeling her age, but you knew that."

Kate looked at Winifred but said nothing.

"We were taking turns popping in to see if she needed anything. She wasn't sleeping well toward the end, and she'd begun to talk to me about Emma. She blamed herself for not protecting her daughter. And she kept coming back to the suicide note."

To think that her grandmother had been in so much pain, possibly the whole time Kate had known her. "Lilian never told me what was in the note."

Winifred gripped her hands together. "It was something to the effect that Emma was afraid of bringing shame to the family, but no one could understand what it meant."

Tears began to sting Kate's eyes.

Winifred reached over and took Kate's hand in hers. "Oh, my dear, I didn't mean to upset you, truly I didn't." She took a large brown envelope from her bag and pushed it across the table.

"What's this?"

"Your mother didn't believe the suicide verdict. She started to look into her sister's death herself."

"Gran?" Alex was standing at the bottom of the stairs.

Kate let the contents of the envelope slide out onto the table. There were pages of notes and annotated newspaper clippings from the *Porth Madryn Observer*, with underlining in red pen.

Winifred continued. "She even approached the police with her suspicions, but they said there was nothing they could do. There was no new evidence."

"Mum did all this?" This was not the woman Kate knew, the woman whose telephone conversations were full of island gossip, complaints about the weather, and reviews of the latest television costume drama.

"If the family wasn't satisfied with the verdict, why didn't they hire a lawyer to put pressure on the police?" Alex said.

Winifred shook her head. "George said the people who knew what they were doing had decided it was suicide, and that should be an end to it. He told Miriam to let it go."

"But I would have thought he'd want to learn the truth," Kate insisted.

"Lilian felt he was in a lot of pain, and this was his way of dealing with the grief, but she also suspected he wanted to protect you. A suicide is bad enough, but to grow up distrusting everyone around you—he didn't want that for you."

Kate exchanged looks with Alex. Kate had done for Alex what George had done for her.

"Deep down in her heart, Lilian always hoped new evidence would appear to prove her darling girl hadn't taken her own life," Winifred said. "The fact that she kept Miriam's research all these years must tell you something."

"Poor Lilian," Kate said.

"She made me promise to give you this envelope in case she didn't see you again." Winifred paused before continuing. "She wanted you to convince your James to review the case. She hoped that with new scientific tests, you might finally learn the truth."

"We have to ask Dad," Alex said. "It was Lilian's last request."

"Alex, we shouldn't get our hopes up. The police won't open a fifty-year-old cold case without new evidence."

Alex looked to her mother's face with that determined look Kate had seen so often. "Then we'll find some."

CHAPTER 4

After Winifred and Siobhan had gone, Kate and Alex carefully spread the contents of Miriam's envelope across the dining room table. The papers were held together with black bulldog clips under the headings Suspects & Motives, Suspicious Actions, Newspaper Clippings, and Photos. As a bookkeeper, Miriam's job had been to itemize people's lives into categories to ensure everything added up, balanced out. She'd been attempting to do the same with Emma's death.

Kate turned first to the suspects list. Here were many of the is-landers Kate was closest to, people she considered family. At the top of the list was David Sutherland.

It was too easy to forget that many of these people, whom she now regarded as mellow pensioners, were once hormonal-ly-charged teenagers. They would have been competing for atten-tion, acceptance, and affection. As a teacher, Kate knew that teens could become emotional at the slightest provocation, seeking re-venge with sharp words and worse. Could Emma's death have been the result of a disagreement that got out of hand, the suicide note an afterthought to protect the killer?

Every suspect had their own page where Miriam had outlined her rationale for including them. Alex quickly glanced through the handwritten pages. "I still can't believe Gran did this."

"I can. You knew her as an old lady, but she was only a few years younger than you when Emma died."

Alex gathered the papers up. "There's nothing much here we can use. It's her thoughts rather than any hard evidence."

"It's hopeless," Kate decided. "Besides, I don't have the time to devote to this. I've got a deadline looming, a writer's conference coming up, and I have to prepare the cottage for the estate agent. I can't waste time on a wild goose chase."

Alex took her hand and looked into her eyes. There was that determined look again. "Let's give it a week. If not for Gran and Lilian, then for Emma. What if her murderer is still alive?"

Her daughter must have seen the look of reluctance on Kate's face, but Alex wasn't about to give up. "You're an academic. You think nothing of burying yourself in research for your books. Imagine you're writing a book about Emma's murder. Where would you start?"

But Kate's hesitation was more than being uncertain how to begin. "Lilian called me two weeks ago. She said there was something she needed to ask me, but it had to be face to face. I didn't want to take time away from my work, so I promised to come during the summer holidays. One of the last things she said to me was, 'Don't leave it too long.'"

Kate looked away. "I should have made the effort. She must have known she didn't have much time left..."

Alex took her in her arms. "Oh, Mum. You weren't to know what was going to happen."

Kate reached for a tissue. "All right, then. A week. For Lilian. We can work on it together while we're clearing the cottage."

Alex smiled and went to put her grandmother's notes back into the envelope, but Kate took them from her. "You know, Mum made these within weeks of the murder. She would have known what was going on the island, the chatter, the gossip. This could point us in a direction we might not have thought of going."

A long envelope slipped from Kate's hands. Inside was a black bankbook for a bank on the mainland, with Emma's name and an account number on the inside, written in black ink, when entries were written by tellers with precise penmanship. There were seven entries, each only a month or so apart, for different sums totalling

£783.

Alex did a quick internet search on her phone. "My God, that's £17,000 in today's money."

"Where on earth would she get that?" Kate's voice had become agitated.

"Certainly not by saving her birthday money!"

"And why use a bank in Porth Madryn? Most islanders have a post office account at the island store. Only people with businesses bank on the mainland."

Alex looked at Kate with an expression that warned she was about to say something her mother might not want to hear. "Or people hiding something."

Kate ignored Alex's inference. There had to be a reasonable explanation. "I assume the bank won't be much help."

"There might be archived records going that far back, but they won't tell us where the money came from."

"I hate to say this, but it might be time to get your father involved." Kate felt like she was admitting defeat before she'd even begun.

"Do you want me here for moral support?" Alex asked.

"I think this is something I have to do myself."

Alex touched her mother on the shoulder and went upstairs.

Kate sat for a minute, trying to decide on the best way to begin the conversation with James. No matter what she said or how she phrased it, he would find some excuse to refuse her. And he'd be right. There were just too many questions, too much missing information. The police had declined to reopen the case when Miriam approached them fifty years before. Why would they do it now?

Kate took a breath, grabbed her phone, and dialed James's number.

It rang twice before he picked up. "Kate."

"Hello, James."

"How was the funeral?" She knew from the sound of his voice this was a good time to call. When he was stressed by a case, his baritone voice became hard. Today it was almost silky.

"Typical island funeral—just what she wanted. Thanks for the flowers by the way. They were lovely." The small talk over, she told him of Fiona's outburst at the wake, her conversation with Winifred, and Miriam's investigation. "How can we get the police to re-open the case?"

"We can't."

She imagined the disapproving frown on this face. "Aren't you the one who always says a case isn't closed until it's solved?"

"It was solved. There was a police investigation and an inquest. What did they tell your mother?"

"They weren't prepared to do anything without new evidence," she was forced to admit, knowing how he'd respond.

"Exactly. Nothing has changed."

"James, the suicide note was typed. It seems a little impersonal. Why type, unless you can't forge Emma's handwriting? And it was hidden."

"Is that all?"

Kate could feel herself getting agitated. "She also had the modern-day equivalent of £17,000 hidden away in a Porth Madryn bank."

"I'm surprised at the amount—"

"I thought you would be." Kate felt some measure of satisfaction.

"But I'd hardly call a bank on the mainland 'hidden away'. It's not exactly an offshore account."

"But you have to admit it's suspicious. You know the islanders. No one goes to the trouble of setting up an account on the mainland unless they want to fly under the radar."

"Under the radar?"

Kate had regretted her choice of words as soon as they were out of her mouth. He'd no doubt be smirking. "You know what I mean. And just where did the money come from and did it get her killed?"

"Was this all shown to the police?"

"I assume so."

"So there's nothing new."

"Stop saying that! What about testing the suicide note for DNA?"

He sighed. He always did it when she said something he considered naive. She'd always hated that sigh. Kate felt the tension building in her jaw.

"I'm sure the evidence has been compromised by now, if it even still exists."

"So you're not prepared to do anything!" It came out harsher than she'd intended.

"It's not my decision. It's the jurisdiction of the Porth Madryn police, but you're quite welcome to call them and get the same answer."

"This is my aunt, James. She could have been murdered, and the police are prepared to let the killer get away with it."

"If you're looking for the police to make an arrest, chances are the perpetrator's dead by now. At the risk of sounding patronizing, Kate, you're too emotionally involved." But he did sound patronizing. "Perhaps you need to look at the reason why this is suddenly so important to you. Is this your family's guilt that none of you could stop her from killing herself? Or is it regret that you didn't visit Lilian as often as you thought you should?"

How dare James think he could psychoanalyze her. He might think he understood the minds of criminals, but he didn't know the first thing about what she was feeling. Kate wished she'd called on Lilian's landline. At least she'd have the satisfaction of slamming the receiver down.

"Never mind," she snapped. It was what she always said to shut down conversations when they were at an impasse. Then she'd go off and do what she was planning to in the first place.

"I'm sorry. I know you were hoping for a different outcome."

"I said never mind."

He sighed again. "Kate, if you want to talk about this further—" but she hung up.

Upstairs, Alex's phone rang. No doubt it was James calling to moan about how unreasonable her mother was being.

She'd forgotten how bloody condescending James could be—and how much it infuriated her. This must have been the way her mother had been treated by the police. They would have smiled, metaphorically patted her on the head, and sent her on her way.

Well, her mother might have been willing to accept condescension from men in authority, but she sure as hell wasn't.

CHAPTER 5

People stood outside The Filly with their pints and glasses of whis-key, blowing smoke into the afternoon air, erupting into laughter, and arguing long-held opinions. Kate was greeted with shouts of welcome and offers to buy her drinks. The flag by the community centre was now back at full mast, and that pricked at her heart.

When she stepped inside, heads turned and called out greetings. Siobhan waved from where she sat in a corner with Feebles, Gooley, and Smee. Kate felt guilty leaving Alex on her own, but after her conversation with James, she needed to be with people who had known Emma.

The landlady, Flo, leaned across the bar. "What can I get you, Kate?"

Flo was decked out in her full-on landlady gear—lavender eye shadow, fuchsia lipstick, and low-cut knit top stretched over a black lacy bra. Her thick blonde hair was back-combed into a beehive where a gauzy mauve butterfly looked as if it had just alighted.

"Whiskey please, Flo."

"My pleasure."

Everyone loved Flo. She was always there to offer tea—usually with a shot of something stronger—and sympathy to anyone who needed it. Kate had never heard her lose her temper or say an un-kind word about anyone. Maybe that's why her husband, Julian, had left the priesthood for her.

Julian and Flo had come to the island to run the pub some fif-teen years ago. With his mane of thick, dark hair and good looks,

Julian had fired the romantic imaginations of the island's young women. His decision to leave his vocation for the woman he loved only enhanced his appeal.

Kate had never understood why Julian hadn't just switched denominational teams. As a Protestant minister he would have been encouraged to marry. Flo's sweet nature—and a more conservative wardrobe—would have made her the ideal vicar's wife.

"And whatever Siobhan and the gentlemen in the corner are having," and Kate pointed in the direction of Siobhan's table.

Flo smiled. "I'll bring them over."

Feebles stood up to let Kate slide in between him and Gooley.

"Good to see you out, lass," Feebles said. "Where's Alex?"

"She has some legal notes to review before she goes home." Kate felt guilty lying, but there was probably some truth in there somewhere. Alex never went anywhere without work.

The gentlemen nodded knowingly, but Kate doubted they understood anyone choosing to spend time working over drinking. Feebles looked across the table at Kate. It was the same look David Sutherland had given her at the wake. What was it they all saw?

"Siobhan tells us your mum was looking into what happened to Emma," Feebles said.

Siobhan looked sheepish, as if she felt she might have spoken out of turn.

"She was," Kate said.

"Did she come up with anything the police could use?" Gooley asked.

Kate was still angry from her conversation with James, but she kept her emotions under control. "The police weren't interested. Still aren't."

"Nothing to stop you taking up where your mum left off," Gooley said. It sounded like a request.

"Actually," she replied, "Alex and I have decided to do a bit of digging, ask some questions."

"Good," said Smee. "Good."

Flo delivered the tray of drinks.

Rupert Gooley was the first to reach for a glass. He was a man of such even proportions, short and wide, that he appeared square. Even his hair reinforced the effect—the same length all round, just brushing his collar. He gulped back half of his whiskey with surprising speed, licking his full, fleshy lips to ensure that in his haste he hadn't missed a drop. He had the look of one who was well satisfied with life, a look Kate remembered seeing even as a child. "You're a grand lass, ma darlin'," he purred.

"A fine lass," said Smee with conviction.

Joseph Smee's face was narrow and pinched with a deep crease running down either side of his nose and thin lips. Although his grey hair was yellowed from years of hair cream, Kate remembered it as jet black, so thick and unmanageable that she'd always imagined him at home in the Scottish Highlands or on a mountaintop, not somewhere as tame as Meredith Island.

Kate took a sip. "What do you remember about Emma?"

"Now there," said Gooley, "was the grandest lass of them all. To Emma," and they raised their glasses before realizing they were empty.

Kate signalled another round to Flo.

"We were at school together, although us lads didn't stick at it," Smee said. "We left as soon as we could to work on the boats."

"She was a friend. That was all. She wasn't interested in the likes of us, if you know what I mean. But Feebles had a bit of a go, didn't you, old son?" Gooley's voice crackled.

But Quentin Feebling, known to everyone as Feebles, continued to stare at his empty glass. He had a dignity that clashed with the impertinence of the name. Today, though, his white hair, salt and pepper moustache, and beard were all in need of a trim. Except for the pouches under his eyes, which reminded Kate of an aged basset hound, his face was relatively unlined for a man who'd spent most of his life on the boats being buffeted by wind and sea. His eyes had an intensity, an intelligence she didn't find in the others. If the other two had easily accepted their lot in life, there was something in Feebles' face that told Kate he had never reconciled himself to his.

Growing up without a father, Kate had a special place in her heart for Uncle Quentin. They'd sail around the island while he told her fanciful tales of pirates and shipwrecks. And he always gave her books for her birthday. So while his romantic relationship with Emma had made him one of Miriam's suspects, Kate refused to believe he could have hurt her aunt.

"Then Sutherland took a fancy to our Emma," said Gooley.

"Nobody was very happy about that relationship." Smee reached for another whiskey from Flo's tray. "Not us—"

"And not the Three Weird Sisters," added Gooley. Kate hadn't heard that expression for a long time. It was their name for David's older sisters.

With three daughters and no son, Cecil Sutherland, father of Hannah, Jane, and Sophie, had adopted David when he was seven or eight. When Cecil's wife died two years later, it fell to his daughters to help raise David. All older by ten to fifteen years, they were more like mothers to him than sisters, Hannah especially, being the eldest.

"So what did they have against Emma?" Siobhan wanted to know.

Smee took a long gulp. "Hannah thought Emma'd hold him back. They had plans to send him away to study. They thought he was too good for the island. The Weird Sisters have always thought they're better than us. Look down their noses at everyone just because they have a bit of money and gave their house a fancy name—Sutherland Hall. Hall, my arse!" He slapped the table with the flat of his hand. "Just a big house, and not all that big either. I couldn't repeat with ladies present what my old da used to say when Old Man Sutherland paraded around like he was Artemis Faraday himself. And the sisters are no better, giving themselves airs. Their great-whatever-grandfather might have been Faraday's estate manager, but that means bugger all. The Sutherlands come from servants, the same as the rest of us."

The ghost of Artemis Faraday was a constant presence on the island. Over one hundred and fifty years before, this American industrialist, a man obsessed with British history and the capital to indulge that obsession, bought the island, renaming it in honour of his young English bride, and built his vision of a Gothic manor house. He hired the best servants from across the UK to help him run it. When his wife died in childbirth, he abandoned the island to the servants. Except for incomers, everyone on the island could trace their family back to the Faraday estate.

"Did the sisters try to break Emma and David up?" Siobhan asked.

Smee bent forward and said in a low voice, "There was this one time when Emma and Sutherland were in The Breeze having some tea or like, and Hannah marched right into the place and demanded David come home. He was a young man at the time, but she was still ordering him about like he were a nipper."

"Probably because of his inheritance," added Gooley.

"What do you mean, his inheritance?" Kate asked.

"Well," Gooley continued, "the old man's will said Sutherland would get part of his inheritance when he turned twenty-one if he was free and single. But he'd have to wait 'til he was thirty if he married."

"Well, that doesn't make sense," said Siobhan. "Wouldn't he need the money sooner if he was married?"

Gooley tapped the side of his forehead with his index finger. "The old man wanted to make sure the boy didn't give up on his studies. The money was a bribe so the lad wouldn't get himself weighed down with a wife and kiddies too early. Old Man Sutherland kept a firm hand on all of them, even from the grave."

"So Hannah had a motive to stop Emma and David from getting serious," Siobhan said.

Smee leaned toward Kate. "She'd have done anything to stop Emma interfering with her plans for David. She's a right temper on her, Hannah Sutherland has. If you ask me, I wouldn't put it past her or Sutherland to have done our poor Emma in."

Was that why Hannah Sutherland was on Miriam's suspect list? And what had Smee meant Hannah had a temper? Kate had never seen any evidence of that. She was about to ask for clarification when she noticed David Sutherland standing at the bar. So did Smee.

"Hey, Sutherland," Smee shouted. "It were you, weren't it?"

David to turned to see where the voice was coming from.

"It were one of you Sutherlands done in our Emma. She was an inconvenience, wasn't she? All you care about is yourselves, the whole lot of you. You don't care who gets hurt."

David returned to his drink in an effort to ignore the taunts.

Smee staggered to his feet. "You Sutherlands have blood on your hands, and you know it."

"You're drunk, Joseph," David said wearily.

"Doesn't change what happened, do it?"

Gooley was tugging at Smee's frayed shirt sleeve. "Sit down, lad."

"Let the past rest, Joseph," David said.

Smee pushed Gooley's hand away and stepped forward as if to rush at David. Feebles stood up, prepared to hold him back.

"You're not the one who's dead!" Smee snarled.

At the sound of raised voices, Julian came around from the living quarters behind the bar. "Gentlemen, either resolve this or take it outside."

Smee's eyes were bulging and his hands clenched into fists. "Oh, I've been waiting a long time for this..."

It was getting out of hand. "Uncle Joseph," Kate begged him, "please don't do anything rash."

Smee pointed at David, his eyes bulging. "His family are murderers. He knows what I'm talking about."

"Then let me look into it." She placed her hand on his arm, but he pushed it away.

"This is no business of yours, Kate. It's between him and me," and he grabbed his jacket and left the pub.

CHAPTER 6

Siobhan was sitting in her back garden in a sagging wicker chair, the long grass scratching her ankles, a fried egg sandwich balanced on her knees. Smee's argument with David the previous afternoon had unsettled her. David was her friend. When she'd asked what it was about, all Feebles and Gooley would say was that it was Smee's business and had nothing to do with Emma.

She'd just taken a bite of sandwich when she heard rustling branches and soft treading sounds from the bushes at the bottom of the garden or perhaps from the expanse of open meadow beyond. There were always creatures moving about—sheep, hedgehogs, badgers. A young male peacock made regular visits to the garden, having developed a taste for her lemon balm.

He was the descendant of one of a dozen left behind when Faraday departed. Since then they'd grown to a sizeable party. Siobhan had looked it up. There were at least half a dozen names for a group of peacocks, but her favourite was party. The males were certainly dressed for it, but they had an irritating tendency to help themselves to people's gardens.

"Percival," she called out through a mouthful of egg. Go home," wherever home was.

The morning became quiet again, punctuated only by the whistling and chirping of insects, the squawks of gulls.

Pleased that she'd successfully asserted herself, Siobhan took the remains of her sandwich into the house. There was one more thing to do before she could start to work. On her dining table, beside her laptop, was an unopened letter from a London estate agent, unopened because she knew exactly what was inside it.

The letters had come regular as clockwork for the last eight months with ever increasing offers to buy her cottage, all substantially over the market value. But she wasn't interested, and she'd already emailed the estate agent several times, telling him exactly that in no uncertain terms. However, the letters continued.

She turned on her computer. She'd tried the softly, softly approach. Now it was time to spell things out in terms the agent would understand. She started to type what she hoped was the last email, accusing him of harassment, coercion, and strong-arm tactics, but she needed a big finish, a parting shot across the bow. Everyone knew estate agents were shifty at the best of times, so the last thing he'd want would be to have his business dealings come to the attention of someone who could do him harm. As much as Siobhan had an aversion for authority figures, she finished with a threat to report him to the police. She hit SEND before she had a change of heart, and closed the laptop, confident this would finally put an end to it.

—

Kate needed to get organized about the investigation, so she set up two corkboards in the dining room. On the first board, she pinned her mother's notes and photographs of people in Emma's life. On the second, she started a timeline, not only for the day Emma disappeared, but the months leading up to the event. She wanted to know everything that had happened on the island that summer. Anything out of the ordinary could lead her to both a motive and a suspect for Emma's death.

Alex came into the dining room as Kate stood back to admire her work. "Impressive incident room," Alex grinned.

"And the coffee's better too," Kate said.

"Police coffee has to be the worst. I swear they make it that way on purpose. They promise the accused that if they confess, they won't have to drink it. I've always thought it should count as police brutality."

"Have you shared this with your father?"

"Are you kidding? He actually likes the stuff."

Kate stared at the boards. Now came the hard part—picking up where her mother had left off.

After what she'd witnessed in the pub, it was obvious there was old business between David and Smee, something deeply personal and still raw after all these years. Even though Smee didn't want to share, he'd mentioned murder, and Kate wasn't prepared to let the matter rest. Perhaps David would be more forthcoming.

"I'll see you later. I'm just stepping out for some air." Kate grabbed her cardigan as she opened the door.

Alex had a disappointed look on her face as if she wanted to be asked along, but before Kate could make up an excuse, she spotted a white baking dish sitting on the doorstep. It contained a pie with a golden-brown crust. She brought the warm dish into the house and placed it on the dining room table.

Alex lifted up a corner of the crust with her finger. "Beef, maybe lamb, carrots, peas, and lots of mushrooms. It smells fantastic. Sorry about the meat."

"Not to worry. It's all yours," Kate said. "I'll be back soon."

"If you don't end up in the pub again."

"Cheeky!" Kate walked out the door.

She'd purposely not invited Alex to accompany her because she wanted to make this visit alone. If David Sutherland was like most men, he might lie or withhold something if he thought it would make him look unattractive to a young woman like Alex. But he wouldn't be trying to impress Kate. As an older woman, she was invisible to most men. In fact, on more than one occasion a man had actually walked into her on the street.

It was a brisk walk from the cottage to David's studio, one of the two-storey row houses beyond The Filly on the other side of the harbour. As Kate passed through the warm odour of ale, the greasy smell of fish and chips, and exuberant voices drifting from the open pub door, she fought the urge to nip in for a quick shot of courage.

Why had her mother put David on her suspect list? Did she

know about Smee's accusations? Surely she didn't believe that being someone's boyfriend gave them a motive for murder?

Kate wished her mother was still alive so she could ask her. Miriam had died just twenty-two months ago, after being diagnosed and hospitalized with metastasized lung cancer. In spite of Kate's urgings and the numerous pamphlets and website links she'd sent to encourage her, Miriam had been unable to stop smoking. All her life, Kate had lived with the fear that it was just a matter of time before the habit killed her mother. So when Miriam called to give her the news, Kate's first reaction was anger that her mother let it happen, that she was going to leave them before her time, not be around to see Alex become partner in her firm, get married, have children.

But it had been an infection, not the cancer, that killed her—an infection contracted in the hospital after her first chemotherapy treatment. In spite of all the antibiotics they'd pumped into her, Miriam's heart had simply given out. In the days leading up to Lilian's funeral, Kate had wondered more than once if Lilian's heart had also simply given out, weakened by the deaths of her husband and both daughters.

Kate gently pushed these memories aside as she let the black metal door knocker fall against David's red door.

"Coming," his voice rumbled from deep within the house.

She ran her hand over her hair and reached into her purse for the emergency lipstick she always kept there, sliding it over her lips with practised precision, then slipping it out of sight as David opened the door.

"Kate." He seemed genuinely surprised. She searched his face for signs of disappointment or irritation but saw none. Then he smiled. "Please come in."

In spite of the overcast sky, the interior of the house was surprisingly light with its white walls and open spaces. As with most houses on the island, it was full of dark polished furniture, but taking centre stage was a hunter green leather sofa and two matching side chairs. Kate imagined when you sat down this furniture would hug you, invite you to put your feet up and get comfortable. As she expected, the walls were covered, yet not overcrowded, with pictures—landscapes, cityscapes, abstract splashes of colour. Despite their varying styles, they seemed to belong together, assembled by a perceptive eye.

With his studio at the back of the house, the smell of oil paint and turpentine lingered in the air, a smell to which David had no doubt become so accustomed he barely noticed it.

His outstretched hand invited her to sit down. Her assessment of the chairs had been correct. David crossed to a cabinet delicately accented by a border of marquetry diamonds and opened one of the leaded doors. "Sherry or whiskey?"

"Whiskey, thank you."

On closer inspection, she realized the furniture was of much higher quality than would probably be found in any of the other island homes. His success allowed him to purchase fine pieces.

He poured them each a generous glass and handed one to Kate. "Your health and Alex's."

Easing himself into the other armchair, David crossed his legs and balanced the crystal whiskey glass on the arm. He wore a black shirt under a cream Aran pullover. His shoulders were still broad and his black corduroy trousers didn't hang on him like they did on so many other men his age. He obviously kept himself fit.

He leaned forward. "I want to apologize for what happened with Joseph in the pub yesterday. The last thing you need is two old men reliving ancient grudges."

"Actually, Mr. Sutherland—"

"David, please."

Kate had never visited him before. To have a successful career, he'd spent his adult life on the mainland, rarely returning to the island. "David, did you know my mother carried out her own investigation into Emma's death?" It felt strange to be on first-name basis with such an illustrious artist.

"No, but then I left for Paris right after the inquest."

"Last night, Joseph accused you of having blood on your hands.

What did he mean?"

David returned to the cabinet to refill his glass. Kate got the impression he was playing for time. "You know how he is. He says things that don't make sense when he's had a skinful."

It felt like David was dismissing the incident.

"It didn't sound like he was confused."

"He's never liked the Sutherlands. I'm the first to admit Hannah and Jane can be a bit full-on about family honour and public standing, and all that. I also suspect my success has contributed to his resentment." He finished pouring his drink. "The animosity goes all the way back to our fathers, but why Joseph insists on holding on to it... To be honest after all these years, the whole thing is tiresome. I just wish he'd deal with it and move on."

"Could he have been jealous of your relationship with Emma? How serious were you two?" Kate felt uncomfortable demanding answers to personal questions, but she had to learn all she could if she was going to make sense of Emma's death. Perhaps these were the questions her mother had been unable to ask, or maybe she already knew the answers.

"Emma meant a great deal to me, even though we had an unspoken agreement that we wouldn't get serious. After all, I was coming into my inheritance and leaving the island, and she was off to Cambridge." He turned toward Kate and took a large gulp of the whiskey, cradling the glass in his hand.

"But you dated, didn't you?"

"I wanted to marry her," he said gently.

Kate was surprised.

David walked over to the window and looked out at the sea before continuing. "I should have tried harder. I should have protected her."

"Surely you don't blame yourself for her death?"

"When someone as beautiful and intelligent as Emma, with so much promise, takes her own life... We all look for someone to blame." He drained his glass. "Otherwise we have to blame Emma."

"Or we blame the person who murdered her." Kate paused. "I

read the newspaper reports. You weren't on the island the afternoon she disappeared."

"Convenient, that." He grinned self-consciously. "Some might say too convenient."

"So what happened that day?"

"There was a note in Hannah's handwriting telling me I had an appointment at Lord Enderby's estate, and it was imperative I take the next ferry to the mainland. It was a commission for a series of paintings of his country house. I didn't normally do houses, but the opportunity was too good to pass up. Enderby's circle was composed of some of the richest and most influential people in the country, and I thought if I made a favourable impression, I might pick up some more work. But when I arrived, the housekeeper said the Enderbys were on holiday in France and weren't expected to return for another month. She had no idea who could have contacted me. As I'd missed the last ferry, she offered to let me stay the night, and I returned the next day."

He paused. His eyes looked sad. "It was then I learnt that Emma was missing. It seemed too much of a coincidence. I couldn't help but wonder if someone had sent me off the island to establish an alibi.

"Once I'd reined in my ego, I realized the phone call must have been a hoax." He laughed softly as if reflecting on his own foolishness. "The Enderbys can trace their peerage back eight hundred years. They have an art collection that—well, let's just say I've never seen so many old masters outside a national gallery. So why would Enderby even consider offering a commission to a student? My father had done some—I guess now you'd call it consulting work for Lord Enderby, so he was familiar with our family, but we weren't friends. We exchanged Christmas cards but not much more. When I questioned Hannah about the message, she swore there'd been a telephone call from the estate."

"Who would have wanted to insure suspicion didn't fall on you?"

He was silent as if considering her question. Then he took her hand. "I want to show you something."

He led her out into the studio, an extension on the back of the house, windows on three sides. Two easels stood in the middle of the room, placed to take advantage of the light. A long table was covered with half-squashed tubes of paint, palettes, and jars of brushes. Canvasses were leaning against the fourth wall. Hanging above them was a picture of a young woman, soft heart-shaped face, long hair the colour of polished mahogany.

It was as though Emma was standing in front of them. Kate gasped, drawing David's attention. "I'm sorry. It's just...it looks so much like her."

A green satin dressing gown slipped from her shoulders, one round breast exposed. Her lips were slightly parted, and her eyes had what Kate could only describe as a profound understanding of the world. This was how he remembered her.

"We'd only ever kissed so I certainly wouldn't have let her pose for me like that, but it's how I imagine her."

Kate noted he'd used the present tense.

Standing there with David was like suddenly rounding a corner and finding yourself watching a young couple in an intimate embrace, believing they were safely hidden from the rest of the world. This picture was the only intimacy with Emma that remained for him, and Kate felt she was intruding.

She gently pressed her hand on his shoulder and left him in the studio, staring into Emma's face.

CHAPTER 7

Angelica Lynley had taken advantage of the calm afternoon weather to sail her yacht to the far side of the harbour. She leaned against the railing and took a sip of her vodka martini.

This part of the coastline was quite dismal—a few cottages, the lifeboat station, and the island community centre, an unremarkable oblong building, made of the same ugly red brick, in contrast to the grey stone-cottages that littered the island. Beside the centre was an open field, the location of the school-end celebration, where students came together on the day before summer vacation to run and jump and yell at the top of their lungs. It was an occasion where girls who weren't pretty or popular or smart were forced to compete with girls with beautiful clothes and soft hands, girls who won prizes and flirted with handsome boys who didn't walk away in disgust. While Angelica had thankfully never been such a girl, she'd met plenty in her life who were and knew the shame stayed with them like a bad smell.

Her imagination swept away the ugly buildings, and in their place arose a commanding structure of concrete and glass. It was the kind of design her late husband, architect Anton Lynley, hated. He would have said it stood in jarring contrast to the surrounding landscape. But he was wrong. The island was full of sharp angles and steep rock faces. Besides, this building was going to be her legacy, so she would create it any way she damn well pleased.

It would be the first thing everyone saw upon approaching the island, majestically dominating the landscape. The first two floors, safely protected from the harmful effects of the sun, would house her and Anton's—well, hers now—art collection, on generous loan to the Angelica Lynley Gallery, her name prominently displayed in large chrome letters. The spacious central gallery would be devoted exclusively to the work of David Sutherland. David would naturally have pride of place as the complex was to be named after him.

The first floor would share space with a gastro-pub and a shop, while artists' studios would take up the third floor. The public would be able to watch them labouring over canvases, sculptures, pottery wheels, and looms. Since a regular parade of curious onlookers was excellent self-promotion, she couldn't see them complaining. And anyone who did—well, there was only so much artistic temperament Angelica could stomach.

The second building phase would be the convention centre and multi-storey hotel with an exclusive restaurant run by a Michelin-starred chef. It would be acclaimed the world over for its elegance and innovation. She would have the best suite in the hotel and her own table in the restaurant. The maître d' and chef would fall over themselves in their attempts to please her when she appeared. She'd be treated like royalty.

"Welcome, my dear Mrs. Lynley. You honour us with your presence."

There was a sputtering noise behind her, and she turned, prepared to confront whoever had dared to disturb her. It was that stinking tug belonging to those old fools Feebles, Gooley, and Smee. As it swung closer, she could see two of them on the deck, the little fat one and the tall one with the scruffy hair. They were both standing to attention, saluting her with stupid grins plastered on their faces. Probably drunk out of their minds. She wouldn't be surprised if they dropped their trousers. That was the sort of men they were. They had no respect for anyone with refinement and taste.

"Stupid fools," she said, loud enough for them to hear. She fought the urge to shout. It was unseemly for a woman such as herself to descend to their level.

She gulped down the rest of her martini, grinding the olives between her teeth. She'd be damned if she was going to allow them to spoil her day. She shifted her attention back to the shoreline. But her shimmering building had vanished.

—

Needing some time to reflect on what David had just told her, Kate went for a walk along the thin strip of beach. The tide was at its highest and the water smacked against the wharf, the thick waves rocking the moored boats. The sun shimmered on the sea like burnished metal, while the ever-present gulls screamed overhead.

It was on a day just like this that Emma had chased Kate across the sand, both of them laughing and screaming. Emma had suddenly scooped her up, supporting her arms and hips. "Fly, Katie, fly," Emma shouted over the roar of the air rushing past Kate's ears. As Emma ran, Kate stretched out her arms in the shape of an airplane. They circled round and round, Kate's hair blowing into her eyes. She felt like she was really flying. It was magical.

This was the Emma Kate knew, just as the woman in David's painting was the Emma he knew. He was in love with her. He'd wanted to marry her. Had that somehow contributed to her death? Had she rejected him? Had someone else wanted her? And what had any of it to do with what had happened between David and Smee's fathers?

As she came up the steps from the beach, Kate saw Siobhan leaning against the wall in front of the pub, empty pint glass in hand.

"You want to grab some lunch?" Siobhan asked.

"I'd like that," and they went into the pub.

They found a table in the corner. After minimal consultation, Kate went to the bar and gave Flo their order.

For the lunch trade, Flo set up large tables with red and blue cloths and wildflowers in chunky vases, the same cloths and vases she'd put out for Lilian's wake. The pub and The Sea Breeze, the island's only restaurant, had worked out a mutually beneficial arrangement. During the day, The Breeze functioned as a tea shop while Julian and Flo handled the lunch trade. In the evening, the pub restricted itself to bar snacks, while the restaurant offered a full dinner menu. It was a perfect arrangement—no toes were stepped on, and no punters were poached.

"Was your mum's information any help?" Siobhan asked when Kate returned with their drinks.

It must have been Kate's hesitation that made Siobhan say, "Shouldn't I have asked?"

"It's okay. She compiled a list of suspects with speculations, rather than anything tangible. I'd rather keep it to myself for the moment, at least until I've got something more definite. It's not fair to the people involved."

"I understand," and from the look on her face, she really did. Lilian always spoke very highly of Siobhan. She'd once said that if you ever wanted a completely honest opinion, ask Siobhan.

When their food arrived, Siobhan asked Kate about the day Emma went missing. So as Siobhan took a large bite of her triple-decker club sandwich, Kate began to tell her what she'd pieced together from her mother's notes and newspaper clippings.

"The day before she disappeared, Emma received notice of her admittance to Cambridge. The next day the family was planning to go down to the pub to announce it to the whole island. That was the afternoon Emma didn't come home. This was unusual because she was always responsible about calling if she was going to be late. Everyone, including the police, believed she was still on the island, since Peregrine Tully—"

"Peregrine?"

"Basil's father," Kate said. "The job of ferry pilot is handed down through the Tully family."

Siobhan nodded and took another bite.

"Anyway, Peregrine told the police Emma had been on his midday trip from Porth Madryn. People searched the island from top to bottom, but they couldn't find her." Lilian and George must have been frantic. If it had been Alex, Kate would have been out of her mind with worry. "Two days later, her body was found on rocks on the other side of the island. The initial finding of the police was that it was an accident."

"What was she wearing?" Siobhan asked through a mouthful of chips.

"A pair of navy-blue shorts and a red blouse. Why do you ask?"

"I'm not sure." Siobhan frowned as if struggling with an idea that was eluding her. "I don't know what people who are preparing to drown themselves are thinking, but she wasn't dressed for going into the water. She could have been going about her everyday business and been pushed off the cliffs or a boat or the edge of the dock at high tide, or knocked over the head and disposed of at sea, or any number of things."

Knowing what Emma was wearing when her body was discovered made the image more real. Kate couldn't help but wonder if Emma had felt pain or fear, or indeed if she'd even been conscious as she'd slipped down below the cold, grey water. Kate looked down at her cheese salad sitting untouched on the plate.

"This must be difficult for you," Siobhan said.

"I'm fine." Kate wasn't sure how true that statement was, but it satisfied Siobhan. She would have to get used to talking about it.

She pushed her salad about and continued. "Mum's notes say that Emma had bruises and superficial wounds consistent with being in the water for at least forty-eight hours. There was nothing in her blood to indicate she'd been drugged before she drowned. But we can't rule out that she could have been knocked unconscious. It might have been impossible to distinguish if she fell as a result of being struck or she hit her head as she fell, and as you pointed out she might have been pushed over or out of something. My mum believed the verdict of death by misadventure—was based largely on the suicide note."

Siobhan offered Kate one of her last chips, which she took. "Where was the note found?"

"Under her pillow in what became my room."

"You had Emma's old room?" Siobhan sounded surprised.

As a child, it had made Kate feel closer to her absent aunt. She'd never thought other people might find it morbid.

"What I don't understand about Emma's supposed suicide is why hide the note," Siobhan said. "Isn't the whole point of a suicide note to say goodbye and tell people why you did it? It should have been propped up on her dresser, the mantelpiece, somewhere obvious."

"Mum thought that was suspicious as well. And it wasn't found until three days after Emma died."

"Didn't the police go through her belongings?"

"Maybe if they thought she was still on the island, they didn't bother."

"It seems a little simplistic that the suicide verdict was largely based on the note. It's like they didn't try very hard to look for other explanations," Siobhan insisted.

"You're right. And the note was typed which seems terribly impersonal. Emma had clear handwriting, so there was no reason to type it unless someone else wrote it. The problems with the note were central to my mother's request that the police reopen the investigation. They'd already dusted it for fingerprints and found only Emma's, but then the paper could have come from Emma's room and the murderer could have worn gloves."

"Bloody coppers." Siobhan shook her head in disbelief. She was obviously not a fan of the police. "Other than Peregrine, were there any other witnesses?"

"Sami Sparrow was on the ferry with Emma. She told the police that Emma said she'd just learnt something that was going to change her life but didn't tell Sami what it was."

"There's no one called Sparrow on the island."

Pinned to Kate's corkboard was a picture of a young woman taken in the Galways' back garden. She had cropped dark hair and was wearing dungarees, a man's flannel shirt with heavy work boots. Her face and hands looked dirty. Even though she'd obviously been told to smile, only one corner of her mouth was upturned, so that it looked to Kate as if she was sneering. Maybe she wasn't used to smiling. Maybe she didn't have much to smile about.

Kate closed her eyes and conjured up an image of a man out in the back garden, digging and clipping. "Sami and her father, Clive Sparrow, worked in our garden when I was little. Sami was the same age as Emma, a bit of a tomboy. It was just her and her dad. The mother left when Sami was still young. They lived down the road, close to your place, but I can't remember which house. I think Clive also worked the boats. When I was five or six, he had a stroke or something and was moved to a nursing home on the mainland. I remember my grandfather saying it must have been torture for him to have to leave the island, a man who loved the sea as much as he did. He died maybe a year or so later."

"She could have been one of the last people to see Emma alive. If we could track her down..." The volume and pitch of Siobhan's voice rose with her excitement. "Any idea what happened to her?"

"Probably moved to the mainland to take care of her father. Never heard anything more about her. Fiona might know."

Siobhan signalled to Flo to bring another round of drinks. "Anyone else interviewed by the police?"

"Beatrice Danby, a tourist, made the last known sighting of Emma just before 6 that evening. Emma was standing on the wharf looking out to sea, so she must have disappeared soon after. David Sutherland had already left the island and didn't return until the following day."

"Where did he go?"

"Someone on the mainland wanted to talk to him about an art commission."

Siobhan took a gulp of the fresh pint Flo had just placed in front of her. "Did your mum keep copies of the newspapers? Did they have any theories?"

"Once they learnt about the suicide note, everyone had pretty much made up their minds. And none of the islanders spoke to the press—out of respect, I imagine. All, that is, except Hannah Sutherland."

"Why her?"

"She was Emma's teacher. In fact, she was everyone's teacher. She was the headmistress and one of the senior teachers at the island school for years. But she couldn't give any insight into what happened. She said some nice things about Emma being one of the most intelligent and promising students she'd ever taught, how everyone liked her, and how her desire to achieve and her drive for perfection was an inspiration."

Siobhan snorted softly.

"What?"

"Your aunt was one of those girls."

"What girls?"

"Swots, overachievers."

Kate had been one of those girls. Siobhan obviously had not. "What were you like in school?"

"All right in the classes I was interested in, and a lot of that depended on the teachers. Rubbish at the rest. I just managed to get the results to get accepted into art college, but most of that was probably due to my portfolio, and the short skirt I wore to the interview. Most of the interviewers were men."

Kate stared at her from under raised eyebrows. There was no hint of irony in Siobhan's voice or on her face.

"Emma was ambitious. If that makes her an overachiever..." Kate was aware she was feeling protective of Emma. Did she remind Kate of herself at that age? Is this where Kate had inherited her scholastic drive?

Siobhan downed the rest of her pint and signalled for the bill. "I'm sorry, but I have to get back to work."

Kate looked at her own full pint.

"Drink up," Siobhan said.

Kate took two quick mouthfuls. Siobhan finished the rest.

CHAPTER 8

Kate had said goodbye to Siobhan and was approaching her own cottage when she spotted Winifred standing in her garden, as if waiting for Kate to return home.

"Kate, I'm sorry, but it's Alex. She's been taken sick."

"What happened? Is she all right?"

"Something she ate, but you're not to worry. She's fine. Dr. Marcus has her at the hospital."

The island hospital was a short walk to the other side of the harbour, close to David's studio, and Kate wasted no time in getting there, anxious to see for herself that Alex was suffering no ill effects. Once inside the large square building, she marched quickly down the white hall, peering into rooms, searching for her daughter.

Dr. Marcus Benedict must have heard her footsteps, as he came out to greet her, his white doctor's coat spotless over a crisp white shirt. His face was fleshy with middle-age, making him look kind. He took Kate's arm and gently guided her into Alex's room. "Don't worry. She's perfectly all right."

"Are you sure?"

Kate was acutely aware she had a reputation with both Alex and James of overreacting to every childhood scrape and cut. James, who had seen mutilated bodies and other horrific scenes, could always be counted on to take things in his stride, whereas Kate had a fit every time Alex fell off her bike or tripped in the playground. As she grew older, Alex had taken it upon herself—primarily out of embarrassment, Kate suspected—to reassure her mother there had been no harm done.

Alex lay pale against the white sheets, her short brown hair clumped flat against her face. Her eyes were dully staring off into space.

Kate sat down on the bed and pushed the damp hair from Alex's forehead. "Love, are you really all right?"

Alex smiled up at her. "I'm fine, Mum. No permanent damage, so I understand."

Kate forced a laugh.

Alex struggled to push herself up, as if to embrace her mother, but fell back exhausted. Kate looked over at Marcus, seeking reassurance.

"Everything seems to be out of her stomach, but we're treating her for dehydration," Marcus checked the drip in Alex's arm. "She should be able to go home in the morning."

Kate held her daughter's hand, rubbing her cool damp skin. "What caused it?"

"Mushrooms," Marcus informed her. "They were in the pie."

"The pie we found earlier?" Kate never would have allowed Alex to eat food left on her doorstep on the mainland, but here... This is what she got for being so damn trusting. It only reinforced her decision to return to the mainland. "Oh, love, I'm so sorry."

But Alex shook her head. "It's not your fault, Mum. I'm a big girl."

"What were these mushrooms?" Kate asked Marcus.

"Widow's Teacups."

She stared at him, struggling to fully comprehend the implications. "So it was done on purpose?"

"Widow's Teacups?" Alex's eyes were wide with alarm. "But they're poisonous."

"That's what Lilian told you to make sure you didn't pick them. They're not outright poisonous, but they can be nasty."

"But didn't someone on the island die from them when Faraday was still here?" She asked apprehensively.

"The story goes that one of Mr. Faraday's servants made mushroom broth and gave it to her husband every day. He died, but whether it was from natural causes or the mushrooms, nobody really knows."

"It could have been from the boredom of drinking mushroom broth every day." Alex tried to laugh.

"There are no lasting side effects from eating a lot of them at once. You can't keep them down, as you discovered," Marcus explained.

But Kate wasn't ready to dismiss it so easily. "All the same, I think it's suspicious. We've all been trained since we were children to avoid them. No islander would cook with Widow's Teacups."

She didn't want to believe someone had deliberately tried to hurt them. "There was meat in the pie, so it has to be someone who doesn't know I'm a vegetarian."

Knowing they'd just taken one step closer to solving the mystery brought back some of the sparkle to Alex's eyes. "All this talk about Emma's murder... I think we've rattled someone's cage."

—

That evening, Siobhan was heading home from The Filly. She'd promised herself an early night. Not only was spending every evening in the pub becoming expensive—the Old Gents had a predictable habit of being short of the readies whenever it was their round—but she wasn't as productive in the morning as she used to be. In her twenties and thirties, it had been up with the sun, a greasy fry-up, and then into the studio. She'd keep going until five or six, sometimes later, then off to a bar or club until the early hours. But she could no longer get away with only a few hours sleep.

The story of the mushroom pie had been the topic of choice at the pub. People had shaken their heads and expressed both disbelief and dismay that anything like that could happen to Lilian's family. Siobhan shivered at the thought that the perpetrator had been someone on the island, someone she might have met at Craggy's in line for bread or milk. They'd better not try anything like that with her.

As she came up her front path, she noticed the door was ajar. Maybe the latch hadn't caught when she'd left, and the wind had blown it open. Perhaps someone had come looking for her.

Kicking off her shoes, she padded to the kitchen to pour herself a glass of water. She flicked the studio light switch. Her three figures stood in the light, naked and sturdy with their round bellies and thick thighs. The plastic sheets and damp cloths had been removed, neatly folded in a pile on her worktable. Every time she was away from her work for any length of time, she was fanatically careful about covering any unfired pieces to keep them from drying out. She couldn't afford to forget. She scrutinized the figures for damage and re-covered them.

Then she examined the table, the windows, the back door, searching for clues as to who had done this. If they'd stolen something, she might have been able to understand, but this creeping around, moving things. Siobhan felt uneasy, and it was a horrible feeling. She'd bungee-jumped off bridges and parachuted out of planes with barely a hesitation, but this... Someone had come into her space, touched her things. This was some sort of in-your-face demonstration of power. He—and she decided it was a he—was trying to frighten her, and she was damn well not going to let anyone do that.

She fastened the lock to the studio door. It took only a few seconds for her to cover the length of the cottage and lock the front door, rattling it to make sure it was securely fastened. If this was the only way to keep the bastard out, her doors, windows, everything that could be locked were damn well staying locked from now on.

When the last light had been switched off and the latches on the windows secured, she pounded up the stairs to her bedroom. Having assured herself that she was safe from whatever might be lurking outside, all she wanted to do was to curl up in bed. She flicked on the overhead light and gasped. Sitting in the middle of her duvet was a piece of paper.

The message had been pieced together from letters cut from a magazine. It was like something out of a second-rate suspense film. She wanted to laugh, but the laugh choked her when she read the message.

FILTHY WHORE
GET OUT WHILE YOU CAN

CHAPTER 9

True to his word, Dr. Marcus released Alex the next morning. Once home, Kate insisted her daughter spend the rest of the day in bed, but no sooner had they stepped into the house than Alex received a text that there had been an important development in one of her cases. *Can't someone else handle it?* Kate wanted to ask. But knowing the answer, all she could do was watch her daughter pack for the trip back to her stylish flat in the city.

Alex carefully placed the last neatly folded sweater into her open case. "I'm so sorry, Mum. I promised we'd do this together, and here I am abandoning you."

"I can't say I'm happy either, love, but it can't be helped, can it?" Kate slyly added, hoping Alex's guilt would get the better of her.

Alex plunked herself down on the bed in resignation. "I wish I could stay, but it's a high-profile case."

Kate knew that while her daughter wanted to help with their investigation, this case was even more important to her. It would earn her respect from the senior barristers and get her one step closer to being made the youngest partner in her chambers.

"I suppose I can muddle on without you," Kate said with no small measure of resentment.

"Of course you can. You've done all right so far." Alex zipped up her case. "Look, you and Siobhan seem to be getting along. Why not ask her to help out?"

But Siobhan had neither Alex's knowledge of the justice system nor her connections that enabled her to access information that

Kate couldn't acquire on her own. Besides, she'd been looking forward to spending time with her daughter. Alex was usually so busy they never had time for more than a meal together every month or so. That was another reason why Kate couldn't move back to the island. So many of their meet-ups were a result of a spontaneous phone call from Alex saying she had a spare few hours and could they meet at the Indian restaurant by her office, or offering to come to Kate's as she was on her way home from visiting a client.

It just wouldn't be the same working with Siobhan. But she'd be company, at least.

—

Half an hour later, Alex and Kate stood on the wharf. Kate could tell that her daughter was reluctant to get on the ferry, and Kate was reluctant to let her go.

"Goin' back already, Kate?" Ferry pilot Basil Tully had to raise his voice to be heard over the engine. "I thought you had a murder to solve."

"Just seeing Alex off," Kate said.

"I'll see she gets there safely. I hope we'll be seein' you again soon, Miss Alex."

"I certainly hope so, Basil," and she gave her mother a knowing look. They both understood her return was dependent on Kate's decision about the cottage.

While she had Basil's attention, Kate took the opportunity to ask a few questions. "Your father was one of the last people to see Emma alive before she disappeared, wasn't he? Do you remember him saying anything about the trip back from the mainland?"

Basil scratched his head. "He didn't talk about it much, other than to say it were a real pity she died. He brought her back from Porth Madryn, and she seemed over the moon. Chatted to Sami Sparrow the whole way, and then said she was meetin' your grandmother at The Breeze. Her death was the end to a strange old summer. As if there were somethin' in the air."

"What do you mean?"

"Fights and arguments and such. The young folk couldn't get along. Well, they're not so young now."

"Fights?"

"Aye. There was a big bust-up between David Sutherland and Smee at the school-end celebration. Started over a football game, I think. Then the plants in the flower competition gardens all died. It were a bugger of a time—oh, excuse my French." He reached down to take Alex's suitcase onto the ferry. "Sorry, ladies, but I've got a schedule to keep."

Alex crumpled her forehead. "Do you think any of this had any connection to what happened to Emma? Or was it just a coincidence?"

Kate inclined her head. "What does your father say about coincidences?"

"No such thing!"

Basil's crewman was waiting for Alex to board so he could cast off.

"Look, Mum, I feel awful leaving. If there's anything I can do from my end, just ask."

"Are you're offering the services of your stable of private detectives?"

"Among other things."

"I'll keep that in mind, and I promise to keep you in the loop," Kate pulled Alex to her. "Have a safe trip. And remember, you're still recovering, so don't work too hard."

"How do you expect me to make partner with that attitude?"

"There's plenty of time for that."

Alex kissed Kate on the cheek. "C'mon, Mum. I take after you— never do things by half," and she stepped onto the ferry.

The boat slowly pulled away from the wharf, and they waved to each other until the ferry disappeared around the harbour.

On her way back home, Kate paused in front of Siobhan's cottage. Sitting in the drive was an old blue pickup truck that looked like it was held together by sheer force of will.

After speaking with her yesterday, Kate realized Siobhan had a less conventional way of looking at the world than most people. She not only seemed to think outside the box, Kate doubted she realized the box even existed. Kate was more of a rational thinker, honed from years of academic training. Maybe Siobhan's perspective would help her gain an insight into the events surrounding Emma's death that Kate's traditional way of thinking would miss.

While Basil had given Kate some interesting glimpses into the events of that summer, she knew someone who could fill her in on the details, someone who had been there. It was time to pay a visit to Fiona.

—

Siobhan hadn't been able to get comfortable in her own bed, so she'd spent a sleepless night in the spare room. She'd always been a sound sleeper, joking that she'd probably miss the end of the world because she'd sleep right through it. But not last night. They say people who have their homes broken into feel violated. She understood that now. She wanted to clean everything in the house. She'd got up early to wash her sheets and duvet and hang them on the line outside.

It wasn't that someone had called her a whore. That was laughable. She'd never been especially bashful about her spirited enthusiasm for sex. But she'd restricted her sexual exploits to those times when she was on the mainland, partly because the islanders were such gossips, but also because the selection of island men was limited. Most islanders over the age of eighteen were either pensioners or married, and she drew the line at married men. There was only one man on Meredith Island she'd seduced, and that had finished long before she'd ever moved here. Besides, they'd both been careful to keep it to themselves. So the question was who had sent the letter and, more interestingly, why?

She was working in her studio, secure in the knowledge her figures hadn't suffered any ill effects by being exposed, but her mind kept wandering to the person who had invaded her space, wanting her to feel uneasy in her own home. So when Kate came by to ask if she was up for a visit with Fiona, Siobhan grabbed the keys to the truck and practically dragged her out the door.

—

Hannah Sutherland thrust her hand down into the refuse bin, pushing aside crumpled cling film, tin foil, and a cracked glass. Halfway down was a red tea tin, English Breakfast in white letters. Taking her spoon, she pried off the top. At the bottom of the tin were a few tiny curls of tea leaves. Hannah insisted on loose tea. One had to keep up standards. She'd told the housekeeper, Simmons, time and time again not to throw out the tins. They were necessary to her purpose, but Simmons never listened. The woman should have been dismissed years ago. Incompetence must never be tolerated.

Hannah needed the tins to protect her secrets. It was the only way to keep them from falling into the wrong hands. *Can't trust anyone. Can't risk anyone finding out things they shouldn't.* People were spying on her. They'd been in her bedroom. She could smell them, feel the dirt their hands left on her things.

She placed a folded piece of paper into the tin, replaced the lid, and pounded it shut with the heel of her hand. Almost finished. Just one more thing, and her secrets would be safe.

—

Kate and Siobhan bounced along the road in the truck. It wasn't the most comfortable of vehicles with a large tear in both the driver's and passenger's seats, and it would benefit from new shocks, Kate noted.

"How do your pots and things survive these bumps?" she asked.

"I pack well. Besides, I figure if they can survive the trip down to the harbour, they'll have no problem surviving anything British

Rail can throw at them."

Upon reaching Fiona's cottage, they were greeted by the familiar smell of freshly baked bread. To Kate it was the smell of warm afternoons in Fiona's kitchen, drinking lemon squash and eating slices warm and buttery right out of the oven. At least one cat was always established in a chair, purring like a finely tuned scooter.

Fiona's lawn was scattered with crocuses and snowdrops, while skeletal branches of climbing roses, ready to come alive with the warmer weather, framed the bright yellow front door. Softening the windows were lace curtains, making the cottage look drowsy. To Kate it seemed nothing had changed since she was a girl. She and Siobhan walked around to the back and stepped through the open door.

There was an assembly line in progress in the warm kitchen. A long table was covered with cooling loaves, while the scarred wooden counter held large bowls of dough rising under white tea towels. This was a common sight on the island. Descended as they were from the Faraday servants, the islanders were at their hearts a community of farmers, fishers, and cooks who prided themselves on their ability to be as self-sufficient as possible.

Fiona, her shirt sleeves rolled above the elbows, pushed and pounded dough on a floured board. She wiped a flour-smeared hand across her forehead as she looked up. "Oh, my dears."

Siobhan inhaled deeply and perhaps too obviously.

"Sit down, sit down, and I'll fetch the jam," and Fiona cleaned her hands as best she could on a tea towel and scurried off into the pantry.

When she returned, she placed two jars of jam on the table—strawberry red and gooseberry green. Siobhan broke into what Lilian would have called a Cheshire cat smile. Fiona reached for the bread knife while feeling the brown loaves for one that had sufficiently cooled. She paused, the knife hovering in the air. "Kate, before you say anything, please let me apologize for the other day. I never meant to spoil Lilian's celebration. I wouldn't upset you for the world."

"There's no need. We've all suspected it at some point. In fact, I've just discovered Mum started her own investigation, and I've decided to continue where she left off."

"Oh, my dear," she said with a relieved smile and sat down. Then she reached out and grasped Kate's hand, dried bits of dough still clinging to her own. "Thank you. You don't know how glad I am to hear you say that."

Fiona sawed at the bread until six thick slices were cut and arranged on a large white plate decorated with red poppies. Siobhan immediately helped herself to a slice. She chewed while staring at a framed picture of Emma and Fiona which took pride of place on the kitchen sideboard. She looked back at Kate.

Kate felt uncomfortable under her scrutiny.

"The resemblance is quite strong," Siobhan said at last.

"It would be. We're related."

"No, it's more than that." She continued to stare. "You know how people in a family have the same shaped head or nose or eyes, but that's as far as it goes? It's more than that with you two. If Emma had lived, she'd have looked almost exactly like you."

"I've always thought that," said Fiona, placing the teapot on the table.

Kate examined the picture. She'd never looked for similarities before, but there was something about the way they both held their heads slightly tilted to the left, a similarity of the lips, full and well-shaped, the widening of the eyes as if responding to the photographer with warmth and familiarity. This must have been what people unconsciously recognized.

With the tea poured and Fiona settled, Kate asked, "Do you remember what happened the summer Emma disappeared?"

Fiona looked off into the distance. "We were both so full of plans. We were going to share a flat, and I was going to get a job as a secretary. That was all there was for women. I'd eventually get married, and she'd be my maid of honour, the godmother of my children. We were going to be friends forever. But then I thought I was going to be with my Billy forever." She reached for a handkerchief, tucked up her sleeve, and blew her nose. "The older you get, the more you realize forever isn't very long at all."

Siobhan reached over and stroked Fiona's arm.

Kate gave Fiona a moment and then asked, "Did Emma ever talk to you about money—how she expected to live and pay for her university fees?"

"We never discussed it. People never talked about money back then. It wasn't something you did. I was going to pay for my half of the flat and food and such from my job, but I assumed her parents would cover her part. Or she had a scholarship from the university."

Kate was disappointed but not surprised Emma hadn't shared the existence of the secret bank account with her friend.

"Did you see her the day she disappeared?" She asked.

Fiona sniffed. "No. But I know she went to the Porth Madryn Medical Centre to pick up a prescription for your grandfather. And she was anxious for the letter—it was supposed to come any day—about her place at Cambridge. Then we'd be off, she said, off to England. It was going to be an adventure, and we couldn't wait."

She sat for a moment as if thinking of the life that might have been—hers and Emma's.

"Is that what made you suspicious of the suicide?" Kate asked.

"Emma had such ambition. She had everything planned out in detail."

"But what about her relationship with David?" Siobhan asked.

"Oh, she liked David. He was good fun. Any of us would have been flattered by the attention of such a charming young man, but she didn't take it seriously. Nothing and nobody were going to stand in her way, and that included David Sutherland. Although he was clearly besotted with her. He was like a dog following at her heels. I've never seen a man so devoted. He could have had any one of us, you know," she said with a lascivious upturn to her thin lips. "You must see what an attractive man he was—still is. He can park his easel in my parlour any time." Her declaration produced a self-conscious giggle.

But when she heard the approving cackle from Siobhan, it deepened into a sensuous laugh, born out of what Kate could only imagine was their mutual admiration for David Sutherland's more tangible attributes.

Fiona paused to catch her breath before continuing. "We were so different, she and I. I barely got through my O-levels, while Emma sailed through her A-levels, top marks in everything. She spent most nights at home with her books. And when she wasn't working, she was looking after you, Kate. She loved the time she spent with you. Do you remember?"

Kate wished she could remember more of those times.

"I'm afraid I neglected my studies. I was too interested in having fun. There seemed to be a lot going on back then, especially for young people. The Reverend Thomas brought films over from the mainland every week, and we had dances once a month. I did so like dancing with all the young men. Emma could have had her choice of partners, but she never came. I asked her, but the answer was always the same. The only way for us to leave the island was for her to...how did she put it?...'do what was necessary.'"

"And what was necessary?" Kate asked.

Fiona placed what was left of her slice on the plate. "Study, revise—she worked her socks off."

"Fiona, Basil told me his father said strange things happened that summer. What do you think he meant?"

She stared off into the distance again as if trying to mentally transport herself back. "At the school-end celebration, during the football game, there was a lot of shouting and yelling, pushing and shoving. David and Smee were in the middle of it all, before the others joined in. Mr. Probert, the senior science and maths teacher was the referee, and some of the boys took exception to his calls. Well, you're a teacher. You know how seriously young men can take a silly game."

"Was there anything else you remember?"

"Sami Sparrow."

"What about her?"

"Well, she usually dressed in her dad's old clothes. Miss Sutherland didn't approve—she liked her girls to dress as young women—but there was nothing she could do about it. She'd tried talking to Sami's dad, but he insisted Sami had to be ready to get to work right after school. In fact, sometimes, she was gone for the whole day, helping him with a job.

"But the day of the celebration she turned up in a lovely flowered frock. We were all shocked. No one had ever seen her in a frock before. It looked like something her mother might have worn from the end of the war. I'm afraid she didn't quite fill out the top, but all the same she looked almost pretty. She might even have been wearing a bit of lipstick, and a necklace of imitation pearls. The boys didn't quite know what to make of her and stayed away, but Emma did what she could to make her feel included, and during the party that afternoon, we girls all danced together. Sami looked happier than I'd ever seen her.

"But then her father came and demanded she come home. No one wanted her happiness to stop, so Emma told him we'd make sure she got home safely if he'd let her stay until the end. But he was having none of it. He acted as though it was a personal insult that she'd come, or perhaps it was because she'd dressed in her mother's clothes. His wife had run off with a mainlander when Sami was only four."

"So did she go home?"

"She did, but not before her father shouted at Emma that he knew what we girls got up to when our parents weren't looking, and he wouldn't trust his daughter with the likes of us, and then he dragged her home. I felt so sorry for her. When my dad found out what he'd said to us, he was ready to go over and give him a piece of his mind."

Kate was pleased Emma had stood up for Sami. Clive Sparrow sounded like a thoroughly nasty man.

"Do you remember where you were the afternoon Emma disappeared?"

Kate expected indignation that the woman who considered herself Emma's best friend was being asked to provide an alibi, but in-

stead Fiona hid her face in her hands as if about to cry. "I was breaking my parents' hearts by telling them I was leaving the island." She
looked up. "Islanders, especially in the sixties when young people
wanted to experience the outside world, simply couldn't understand
why anyone would want to leave. My mother was afraid I'd never
come home again, and my father was convinced I was going to be
led astray by rebellious girls and immoral boys. They were so insistent I wasn't to go that—God help me—when Emma went missing,
it crossed my mind ever so briefly my father had done something to
make her leave me behind. He was so upset, I think he would have
done anything to stop me leaving the island."

CHAPTER 10

Siobhan's house was empty. The man walked around to the back and pressed his face up against the window of the studio. On the worktable, he could make out three sculptures, around two feet tall and covered with cloths and sheets of clear plastic. With the coverings, it was hard to make out any details, but they must be women because two bumps jutted out where their breasts would be.

He'd seen her ladies before. They reminded him of those old paintings of fleshy women reclining on sofas with fat little angels hovering around them. What he couldn't understand was who bought her ladies? Certainly not rich dirty old men. Why pay a lot of money to own something that looked like what they had at home?

He tried the door to the studio. It was locked. Siobhan was learning. Stepping back, he knocked over a red glazed pot which held a large basil plant. "Bugger," he barked at himself, and then "bugger" again for speaking the first one aloud. He righted the pot, noticing he'd put a crack down the side. This merited a third "bugger," as he turned the pot, so that the crack faced the back wall of the studio. Maybe she'll think some clumsy lumbering animal had done it. She wouldn't be wrong. He looked about to make sure no one had seen him. He'd be back.

—

Kate and Siobhan bumped home in the truck as the light started to fade from the sky. Kate looked over at Siobhan's profile. Her thick red hair was swept up into a bunch haphazardly held together by a black plastic hair clip. There was a look of tenacity to her face, due in a part to her strong bones and determined jawline. Kate suspected Siobhan could be either a fierce opponent or a steadfast friend. It depended on which side of her you fell.

They travelled in silence for a few minutes. Eventually Kate realized Siobhan was waiting for her to comment on what Fiona had said.

"I got the impression Fiona believes her father was capable of harming Emma," Kate said at last.

"'He would have done anything to stop me leaving the island,'" Siobhan quoted.

"I don't think it means anything. I really can't believe he would have murdered Emma to keep Fiona at home. People just don't do that. What is significant, though, is that this is the second time someone has brought up the school-end celebration and David and Smee's altercation. How well do you know David?"

Siobhan didn't respond, and Kate wondered if she'd thought Kate was prying.

"I just thought as you're both artists, you might be friends. It would help to know your impression of him."

Siobhan kept her eyes on the road. With the constant danger of an animal darting out in front of them, islanders had to be vigilant. "I met him about eleven, twelve years ago, through a mutual friend." She fell silent again. Kate wondered if she was trying to decide how much to reveal to someone she didn't know all that well.

"You don't have to tell me anything personal."

"No, it's all right. It's just I've never given it much thought, why we became friends. I'd been trying to get my work known, build a reputation, but I was a snob. I was only interested in producing and selling 'art.'" She took her hands off the steering wheel long enough to indicate quotation marks. "I thought anything else was selling out, prostituting myself. David told me there's nothing noble or virtuous in being poor. I didn't want to listen."

Kate waited for her to continue.

"It took a while to convince me, but he kept drilling the message home. I'd always thought since he was a big deal in the art world, had more money than God, that he had to have sold out. For that reason, I'd never taken much notice of his work. But then I looked at it, looked hard, and I liked what I saw. He said when he was first starting out, he took every commission he could. He's even done portraits of pets. Anything to get noticed and get his name out there. So I eventually started doing some commercial stuff. I even took a commission for some mugs as corporate Christmas presents. I still can't believe how much I made for that job.

"If I hadn't followed his advice, I don't think I'd have my studio or the cottage. My commercial stuff allows me to work on my sculptures. Hell, money is money as long as it doesn't come from doing anything illegal or unethical. Not everyone is able to buy a £500 sculpture, but a lot of people can afford a £15 mug. I owe a lot to David."

"He sounds like a good friend."

"He is. When we first met, we were both living in London. He raved about the island, and it sounded like the ideal place to live and work. He must think so too because he seems to be here all the time. It wouldn't surprise me if he sold his London flat."

"I went to see him yesterday," Kate said, "to ask him about what was going on between him and Smee."

"And?"

"He didn't give me any details, but apparently it goes back to their fathers."

"So nothing to do with Emma?"

"David says no."

"Is he a suspect?"

"He was on my mother's list."

Kate didn't want to reveal too much. She suspected David had been able to share his feelings because of her connection to Emma, and she couldn't betray that trust.

"But yesterday you said he had an alibi," Siobhan insisted.

"He went to the mainland on the ferry, but it wouldn't be that difficult to rent a boat and come back. Just because he wasn't seen on the island, doesn't mean he wasn't here. But he cared very much for Emma. He still does. I think deep down he believes she committed suicide, and it haunts him that he couldn't stop it."

"You can see it in his work."

"Don't tell me you subscribe to that tortured artist cliché?" Kate said rather too dismissively.

"Not as a cliché, no. But the reviews of his work all mention a shadow, a darkness at the heart of his paintings."

Kate remembered him standing silently in front of Emma's portrait in the studio. "I don't want it to be him."

"Me neither."

—

The truck squealed to a stop in front of Lilian's cottage, and Kate climbed out. Waving good-bye, she rubbed her lower back. Siobhan made a mental note to get island mechanic Evan Cragwell to look at the shocks—and the brakes.

Passing the six cottages that separated her house from Kate's, she noticed most people's lights were on. The hollow sound of televisions drifted into the night. Too tired to manoeuvre the truck into the garage, Siobhan parked in her drive and walked through her front garden. She wanted to get inside and make sure everything was safe.

Unlocking the door, she strode the length of the cottage and flicked the studio light switch. Her figures were still covered. She examined the plastic to make sure they were secure.

Relieved that everything was as she'd left it, she checked the lock to the studio door. In the light that spilled out onto the patio, she saw a scattering of soil beside her potted basil. The pot had a crack in it. Had it been knocked over by a wandering animal? But then it would be tipped onto its side. Someone had definitely been here.

The fact that the locked door seemed to have kept them out gave her only a small measure of comfort.

She leaned with her back against the door, her arms crossed. Someone was messing with her head. And no one did that to Siobhan Fitzgerald and lived to tell the tale.

CHAPTER 11

Kate stood on the road in front of the cottage, a cup of coffee in hand, watching the early morning light spread out over the sky. It was going to be a clear day, not a cloud in sight, just a never-ending expanse of sky slowly turning blue as far as she could see.

She pulled her fleecy dressing gown closer to her body. Here on the island, anyone passing would say hello, comment on the weather, and never bat an eyelash at her attire. That wasn't something she could get away with in the city. People there would think she'd lost her sanity and cross the road to avoid her.

Thoughts of the school-end celebration had been rattling about in her brain since she'd left Fiona's the previous afternoon. Whenever Kate thought about her own school-end celebrations, it was always a day like this. During the welcoming speech, the Reverend Dawkins, the island's minister who tended toward the theatrical and was renowned for his spectacular Christmas pageants, would throw his hands up to heaven and proclaim that the good Lord was smiling down on the island, rewarding the hard work of the children by sending them a beautiful day. "The island is truly blessed," he'd declare. If Kate had been inclined toward spiritual belief, she might have agreed with him, but the pragmatist in her had simply observed they'd been extremely lucky with the weather once again.

Nothing out of the ordinary had happened at the celebrations she'd attended. Granted, there was always a group of youngsters who became frustrated with the egg and spoon race and headed down to the beach for some unsupervised paddling, but that hardly constituted anything of consequence. But if 1965's celebration had been the catalyst for a series of events which had culminated in Emma's death, Kate needed to know exactly what had happened.

Changing out of her pajamas, she headed down to Craggy's Store by the harbour to buy milk and coffee, and maybe a jar of her favourite thick-cut marmalade.

She wasn't expecting to run into anyone. After all, today was Sunday, and everyone was either curled up in bed with a good book or taking their time over a full English breakfast. Those who were so inclined would soon start making their way up the road toward the church.

The last person she expected to see was Rupert Gooley standing in front of the pub.

"Hello, lass," he said, smiling. "What gets you up this early?"

"I could say the same about you."

"Fancied some fresh air." He leant in as if telling her a secret. "When you get to be my age, ma darling, sleep doesn't come so easy. It's the rheumatism, and the like."

"You're still a young man, Uncle Gooley."

"And you're still able to warm an old man's heart, Kate Galway," and he planted a sloppy kiss on her cheek.

"I think this is my favourite time of day on the island."

"Aye. People are just starting to rouse themselves before they start to go about their business."

Kate became aware of the smell of frying bacon filling the air. Gooley sniffed hard.

"People have been talking about the school-end celebration the summer Emma died. Do you remember it?" she asked.

His eyes grew round. "It was a funny old summer, and it all seemed to start at the celebration."

"You're the second person who's told me that. Do you remember who was there?"

"Well, Fiona, who'd left the year before. And Sami Sparrow. She was a year younger than us, but she was leaving to help her da with the gardening business. Sutherland, of course. There were us three lads. We'd left school when we turned fifteen to work on our dads' boats, but we wanted to be there for Emma, and it promised to be a good do. Two of the teachers were leaving so it was a bit of a farewell."

"Who was leaving?"

"The primary teacher, Miss Lambert. Felicia—no, Felicity her name was. Lovely lass. She was off to teach French at some posh school up in Scotland. And Alun Probert, the science and maths teacher. Oh, and Gwynie Morgan was there as well. She was friends with Emma—on and off. She moved away, married some rich lad. She's a lady now, title and everything."

"I hear there was a fight between Smee and David."

"There was always some ruckus or other between those two. I paid no mind." He stopped to think. "Now I do remember something. We lads had brought a few bottles and stashed them in the bins behind the community centre. We thought we were all grown up 'cos we were working and had some brass in our pockets." He shared a self-conscious grin that told her he was fully aware that, upon reflection, they weren't as mature as they'd thought. "Anyway, I went to get a bottle and heard Hannah Sutherland giving our Emma a right rollicking."

"Shouting at her?"

"Saying terrible things."

"Like what?"

"Like it was Emma's fault everyone on the island was gossiping about Hannah. She called her a horrible, ungrateful girl, said it was her fault the school was losing a good teacher, and the sooner she was away from the island, the better. Emma said the gossip had nothing to do with her, but Hannah wasn't having none of it."

"What gossip?"

"That Hannah was having an affair with Mr. Probert."

Kate couldn't believe it. Hannah would never do anything to jeopardize her reputation. Besides, gossip spread like wildfire on the island, and Hannah would have known there was no way she could keep something like that a secret. "Was Emma responsible for the rumour?"

"You'll have to ask your Uncle Smee about that."

"Smee?"

"I think the real reason Hannah was so upset was because of Emma's relationship with David." Gooley was obviously trying to change the subject. "She'd told him to end it with her, but they were still seeing each other, defying her. Liked to be in control, did Hannah Sutherland. Put her in a right strop, people not doing what she wanted them to." He paused as if visualizing the scene. "The look on Emma's face, like Hannah'd slapped her. But Emma must have thought enough was enough, 'cos she left Hannah hollering at her. *Don't you dare walk away from me!* But Emma just kept on going. Got to give the lass credit. She never backed down, that one."

Good for Emma! However Gooley was the second person who'd said Hannah Sutherland couldn't control her temper. Could Emma have pushed Hannah over the edge by refusing to give up David? But according to Fiona, Emma wasn't interested in David. So why all the fuss? And if Hannah was so angry that she was prepared to kill Emma, why wait until she was about to leave?

"Do you remember anything else that happened that day?"

"Old Clive Sparrow was a right misery guts about Sami being at the dance. He hated that she was enjoying herself. I don't think that poor lass ever had a good time in her whole life. And he accused Probert of taking liberties with her."

"What made him think that?"

"Old Clive figured since Probert was doing the business with Hannah, there'd be nothing stopping him having a go with his students."

"Do you think he did?"

"With Sami? No. The way Old Clive dressed her, it was hard to tell if she was even a girl. If Probert was going to go after anyone, it would've been Emma."

—

Miss Hannah was burying things again. Miss Hannah liked to bury things in the garden. Toby balanced his crossed arms on the top of the rake handle and tried to remember everything Miss Jane had told him. He was to look closely when he weeded the flower beds for anything that shouldn't be there, especially a tea tin. He was to dig it up and bring it directly to Miss Jane. And don't open it. She repeated that, and then asked him if he was sure he understood. Miss Jane said it was their special secret. If he found something, he was to bring it to Miss Jane right away and not tell anyone, not even Miss Sophie. Toby liked secrets.

Miss Hannah didn't know anything about gardening. Everybody knows you can't grow tea by planting a tea tin. He didn't know an awful lot about most stuff, but he knew about making things grow. That's why Miss Jane and Miss Sophie let him take care of the plants. They even let him live in the little cottage at the bottom of the garden, and Miss Simmons let him eat his breakfast and lunch in the kitchen of the big house and brought him his supper on a tray. He got to eat what the ladies ate. He always told his grandmother what he had for supper and what Miss Hannah and Miss Jane and Miss Sophie were doing, and she gave him bars of chocolate. He liked chocolate, especially with raisins. But he never told his grandmother about Miss Hannah burying things in the garden. That was a special secret between him and Miss Jane.

—

Gwynie Charlton stared down at Emma Galway's grave. A cluster of dead irises lay against the headstone. Emma had loved irises. There was that one cold autumn day—when Gwynie and Emma were thirteen or fourteen—they'd spent all afternoon on their hands and knees, planting hundreds of bulbs on the promise that Lilian's garden would be full of purple the following spring. They'd all came up, and the garden had been so rich with colour that anyone walking along the road stopped and stared. But that was before Emma started seeing David. That was when Gwynie and Emma had still been friends.

David and Emma had been the dream couple, at least in other people's eyes. Emma was smart, seemingly unconscious of her own beauty, ambitious, living out the hopes of so many young islanders who dreamt of some excitement. David was the Lord Byron of his generation, handsome, sensuous, and escaping to a bohemian life in Paris.

But Gwynie knew Emma never saw herself and David as a couple. Emma had always wanted something more, even though for most of her friends, there was nothing better than to be David's wife.

Gwynie turned at the sound of a twig snapping behind her. David was coming up the rise from the road, growing taller with each step. Gwynie waited for him to recognize her.

At first, he stared blankly. Now that he was close, she could see the fine lines around his soft green eyes. His thick blonde hair was a bit thinner, but he still had those high cheek bones.

His eyes widened as if it had just dawned on him who she was. "Gwynie?" He stood taking her in, perhaps looking for the teenager he'd once known in the matronly woman standing before him.

"Good to know I haven't been forgotten." She extended her hand, and he took it.

"Where are you staying?"

"At the pub. I'm keeping a low profile. There are things I need to get done while I'm here, and I don't want my time taken up with visitors and endless cups of tea."

"You moved to Cardiff, or was it London?"

"Both—and more. Aberystwyth in '69 where I married Hugh, a pharmacist. Wonderful man—we're still married, with two sons, Bryn and Owen. Then it was Swansea, and later London where he took over his father's business. But the city wasn't for us. We found a place within commuting distance that was a better environment for the boys. They've families of their own now and are running the company, so Hugh and I packed up and moved to the Gower

Peninsula."

"I heard some talk about a title."

"Hugh was given a knighthood several years ago, and now I'm cursed with Lady Charlton."

David laughed, but not at her, Gwynie felt. David knew her well enough to understand how she must hate the fuss and silliness that came with a title, even an honorary one.

His laugh felt intimate, like they were old friends. He was looking down at Emma's headstone.

"What are you doing here?" he asked.

"All the talk about her death made me think of her again."

"Kate's determined to uncover the truth. I hope you've got an alibi for the day she disappeared."

Even though she was fairly certain David was teasing her, Gwynie tensed, but she forced her voice to remain calm. "I had no reason to murder Emma. She was one of my best friends."

David's eyes narrowed as if puzzled by her response.

It was time to change the subject. "Emma was a long time ago. I hope you're not still holding onto the past." She put her hand on his arm. "We all have to move on. I found my Hugh."

For all their disagreements over when the boys were old enough for bicycles, or what colour to paint the lounge, or even what brand of coffee to buy, she could honestly say there hadn't been one day when she hadn't thought herself lucky to have a man like Hugh Charlton.

"And you went on to marry, twice, wasn't it?" she asked, knowing full well the answer. It gave her a perverse pleasure knowing David's marriages had failed, while she and Hugh had just celebrated their forty-sixth wedding anniversary.

"And twice divorced," he added, as if she didn't already know. "You're lucky, Gwynie, to have found someone you could stick it out with."

Stick it out! Gwynie fought to keep her mouth shut. If David saw marriage as an exercise in endurance, it's no wonder he was divorced.

Gwynie let go of his arm. "And what happened to you, David? Oh, I know all about the professional success, but what about the rest of it?"

"The rest of it?" he said. "There is no rest of it. My professional success, as you call it, is everything. I'm invited to gallery openings, film premieres, charity dos because of what I do, not who I am. The only one who never knew the legend was Emma."

It was obvious David still had feelings for Emma. Love or nostalgia, Gwynie didn't know which, but he was still attached to her, an emotional tether reaching across the years. And for a reason she couldn't articulate, it annoyed her. "She knew about us, you know."

David looked confused.

"Don't play the innocent."

"There was no us." He said it angrily.

Gwynie wasn't sure which of them he was trying harder to convince. "She cornered me one day after school and told me she knew what we'd done. I stood there, feeling embarrassed and guilty. And then she laughed and said she didn't care."

David shook his head as if he didn't believe her.

Gwynie continued. "She said everyone feels guilt about something they've done. I thought she was talking about life in general, but she was talking about herself. I believe she had a secret, a secret she kept even from you."

Gwynie didn't know where all this resentment was coming from. She hadn't meant to hurt David, but being here, talking about the past, was making her feel uncomfortable, and she was taking it out on him.

She'd done her worst. There was nothing more to say. She turned and walked away. She half expected him to call after her, ask her to stop and explain what she'd meant. But all she heard was the scream of a gull.

CHAPTER 12

Once she was back home, Kate sent off two emails. The first was to Alex, asking her to track down Alun Probert and Felicity Lambert. The second asked James for a copy of Emma's police and post mortem reports.

The phone rang. It was James.

"I just got your email."

"Well, that was quick. Nothing to do?" she teased.

He ignored it. "You shouldn't count on me to get the information you want. The chances of a police file being available on a closed case after all this time is slim."

"I was afraid of that."

"What is it you're hoping to find?" There was some suspicion in his voice. Once again, he was the professional who knew better.

"Mum took notes at the inquest, but there might be something that wasn't brought up. I don't want to miss anything important."

"I don't know whether you know this, but as next of kin, you might be able to request a copy of the post mortem report."

"Really?"

"If it's available, and it might take a while, but that's your best bet. Don't say I never help."

She imagined him sitting at his desk, smiling to himself.

"I'll do that. Thanks, James."

Her next call was to Siobhan. "Are you in the middle of anything?"

"Nothing that can't wait. Why?"

"We're going to Sutherland Hall."

"You're more likely to get an audience with the bloody Queen." There was shock in Siobhan's voice. "Nobody goes there unless they're summoned."

"I need to talk to Hannah."

—

Angelica Lynley picked at her fish. It wasn't that it was badly cooked. In fact, it would have been quite pleasant under different circumstances. It just wasn't what she expected.

Latching onto Sophie as they'd walked out of the church at the end of Sunday service, Angelica had managed to finagle an invitation to dine at Sutherland Hall. Sophie had been more than happy to invite her, but judging by the thunderous look on Jane's face and the ferocity with which she'd clutched her prayer book, Angelica would have to make her excuses right after dessert so as not to outstay what little welcome Jane was according her. Angelica had been looking forward to a traditional Sunday dinner—thick slabs of slightly underdone beef covered in rich gravy with Yorkshire pudding. What she got was a thin piece of fish.

There were just three of them sitting at the large polished table which could easily seat eight or ten. Hannah was missing. Jane had explained Hannah wasn't feeling well and had sent her apologies. Angelica had made sympathetic clucking sounds, but she knew the truth. Hannah was slowly losing her grip on reality.

Sophie sat across the table in a loosely belted dress, one of those intolerable old lady prints—all green and blue muddled swirls that were supposed to represent something with petals. Yet in spite of her poor dress sense, there was something spontaneous and open about Sophie, a sparkle in those blue eyes that matched the hues in her dress. She would often make observations or ask questions that straight-laced Jane must have found inappropriate. Despite— or perhaps because of—these social faux pas, Sophie was Angelica's favourite. Besides, Angelica enjoyed how Sophie's spontaneity irritated the hell out of Jane.

Sitting erect in her chair, Jane looked like the head girl at some snooty school, the girl who always followed the rules and the teachers had nothing but praise for. But people like that were painfully boring. You quickly ran out of things to talk about. Jane ate slowly, chewing each mouthful the requisite thirty times. She drank water rather than wine, still rather than sparkling. There was nothing sparkling about Jane. Her dresses were much the same shape as Sophie's, but in drab solid colours. Angelica would see her as a matron in a women's prison. Jane could strike terror into even the most hardened of criminals.

Angelica sighed. So far, the meal had been a dismal disappointment. But it wasn't just for the possibility of a few slices of roast beef that she'd invited herself. She'd been hoping to get an endorsement for the art institute. Having the Sutherlands as her allies would definitely strengthen the project's appeal to potential investors. Surely with the Sutherland name prominently displayed on the side of such an imposing building, the sisters couldn't help but enthusiastically embrace the project as a legacy to their family, even though in reality no one cared a damn about any Sutherland except David.

But with everyone eating in silence, there'd been no opportune moment to raise the topic, and she was enough of a businesswoman to recognize that timing was everything in these matters. She should probably wait until Hannah was present. Hannah had always been the decision-maker of the family. Even with her mind precariously balanced on the knife-edge of sanity, the others would agree for no other reason than to keep peace in the house.

However Hannah was nowhere to be seen.

Angelica reluctantly turned her attention back to her food. She tipped back the rest of her insipid Chardonnay and waited for someone to offer her more.

Jane raised her head. "Did you hear a car?"

"I didn't hear anything," Angelica said.

Jane settled back, apparently trusting Angelica's hearing. "Probably not."

—

Kate was being dragged by Siobhan toward the back of the Sutherland house. "We should go to the front door," Kate whispered in protest. "The Sutherlands aren't like other islanders. They stand on doing things properly, and I don't want to get on the bad side of Hannah before we've even spoken with her."

But Siobhan kept pulling on her arm. "How are they going to know we're here? They're busy eating Sunday dinner."

"I'd really feel more comfortable waiting in the car," Kate pleaded.

"I want to see the garden. It might give me some ideas for mine."

"Really? I thought you were just snooping."

Kate reluctantly followed Siobhan past the Sutherland garage. If they kept quiet and out of sight, they just might get away with it. "What if they catch us?"

"I'll think of something. I always do."

"What do you mean always?"

They'd reached the garden, with neat grass and colour-coordinated beds, with stone rabbits and birds keeping guard. In front of the French doors was a grey slate terrace and steps down to a broad expanse of lawn. It was quite impressive, but then they had a full-time gardener, that young lad, Toby. Her lawn would look this good if she had a full-time gardener.

"Who's that?" Siobhan nudged Kate, forcing her to look where she was pointing. From around a bush, Kate could see what looked like a woman's bottom. The rest of her was bent over a bed of pink and white Sweet Williams.

"It's hard to tell from this angle."

"I guess one Sutherland bottom was very much like another, except for David's, of course," Siobhan snorted.

There was the flick of a trowel.

"What's she doing?" Siobhan asked.

Kate stepped to one side to get a better angle. Beside a freshly dug hole was a clean red tin. Kate returned to the safety of the bush. "I think she's burying a tea tin."

"She's burying a tea tin?" Siobhan repeated as if not quite sure if she'd heard right.

"That's what it looks like."

"Well, that's got to be Hannah. Several sandwiches short of a picnic. What's in the tin?"

"What did your last psychic die of?" Kate was getting nervous. She always got a bit snippy when she was nervous. "Can we go around to the front now?"

They'd just turned to go back when Hannah called out. "Emma Galway! What are you doing in my garden?"

Hannah was standing upright in heavy orthopaedic shoes, leaning against her cane, and gesturing at them with the dirty trowel. The tea tin had disappeared.

Kate stepped forward. "Miss Sutherland, it's Kate Galway."

Hannah pointed the trowel at Siobhan. "And who's that red-haired hussy?"

There was a look on Siobhan's face that Kate couldn't quite read. She was either about to give Hannah a piece of her mind or burst out laughing.

But before Siobhan could respond, Hannah drew herself up as tall as she could without losing her balance. "I don't appreciate you sniffing around my David. Not you and certainly not that peculiar bird-girl. So don't get it into your head that he'll marry you if you get yourself pregnant. That trick won't work. My boy has a great talent, and no little tart is going to ruin his life. I'll see to that."

Jane opened the doors and came out onto the terrace. "Hannah, is everything all right?" Behind her, Sophie and Angelica Lynley were watching through the French doors.

Jane moved surprisingly fast for a woman in her eighties. Firmly taking her sister's arm, Jane guided her back toward the house like a naughty child who'd been up past her bedtime.

"We're sorry, Miss Sutherland," Kate said. "We were just admiring your garden. We didn't mean to upset Han—Miss Sutherland.

Is she all right?"

Sophie came down the stone steps and took Hannah the rest of the way into the house. Jane turned abruptly toward Siobhan and Kate as if to berate them. "She's not feeling herself, Miss Hewitt," she calmly explained.

Kate noted that while Jane hadn't foregone the island traditional use of Miss for all women. She'd made a point of using her married name, a name no one, not even Kate, had ever used. Probably a dig at her being divorced, a state Jane would not have been able to reconcile with her religious beliefs.

"You will excuse us. We are in the middle of Sunday dinner. Please find your own way back to your vehicle," and she closed the doors.

Angelica stood watching Kate and Siobhan, with a look Kate of self-satisfied superiority.

"Bloody hell," Siobhan huffed, "who tied her panties in a bunch!"

Kate laughed out loud, grabbed Siobhan's arm, and together they walked back to the road.

———

The blue truck was rattling back from Sutherland Hall when Siobhan announced, "I bet you a week's worth of biscuits Hannah killed Emma."

"Why would you say that? Hannah's suffering from dementia. The poor soul obviously didn't know who we were or what she was saying."

It had been a shock for Kate to see Hannah so fragile. The Hannah Sutherland she remembered had always been strong, athletic even, believing in fresh air and daily exercise. Hannah, in her early forties and sturdy shoes, would lead Kate's class on long marches across the island, regardless of the weather. "Robust in body and mind," was her mantra for all her students but especially her girls.

Siobhan gripped the wheel. "But you know what they say about Alzheimer's. People can't remember what they had for breakfast, but they can remember every minute of their distant past. Hannah was remembering the time she knew Emma and what she really thought of her. You heard her. She was obviously afraid Emma was going to get pregnant to trap David. What if Hannah killed her to make sure David could leave the island?"

"David said he'd never even seen Emma in the nude, and I believe him. He worshipped her. Strange as it sounds, I think he would have seen it as some sort of desecration to have had sex with her. Besides, Fiona told us Emma wasn't interested in David."

"Yes, but Hannah obviously still saw Emma as a threat. 'No little tart is going to ruin his life. I'll see to that.' You do remember her saying that."

"I also remember her saying something about a peculiar bird-girl. Who was that?"

Siobhan slammed on the brakes. Kate's body jerked against the seat belt. Siobhan's face was bright with self-satisfaction. "It's in the tea tin."

"What is?"

"The evidence. She was burying the evidence." Siobhan stared at Kate. "Are you rolling your eyes?"

Kate was prepared to swear on the complete works of Jane Austen she had never rolled her eyes in her life, and she certainly hadn't just rolled them now. All the same, she did think it was a ridiculous theory.

Siobhan continued. "Just listen for a minute. She was obviously thinking about Emma otherwise she wouldn't have gone off at us like that. And she was thinking about Emma because there was something in the tea tin that had to do with Emma. And why was she burying it? Because of what happened with Fiona at the wake. Guilty conscience."

"But Hannah wasn't at the wake."

Siobhan folded her arms across her chest. "Well, I think we should go back tonight and dig up the tin."

Kate threw up her hands. "Trespassing isn't enough for you. Now you want to add theft as well."

"What if there's evidence in that tin? What if it'll solve the whole mystery?" Siobhan wasn't prepared to let it go.

Oh, if it were only so simple, Kate thought. "That's a whole lot of 'what if's.'"

"Look, tell me if it's none of my business—I mean, Emma wasn't my aunt—but I really want to help. And more importantly, I don't trust the Weird Sisters. Well, not Jane and Hannah at any rate." Siobhan pursed her lips together. "Yes, all right, I've probably heard one too many stories from the Old Gents, but you have to admit Hannah was hiding something in the garden. Aren't you the slightest bit curious to know what it is? And if it can help us—you—figure out what happened to your aunt, so much the better."

Regardless of Siobhan's motives, there was no way Kate would agree to sneaking about Sutherland Hall. She prided herself on her keen sense of morality, a respect for the law. It would have been impossible to have lived with James for so long without it. But trespassing, the invasion of Hannah's property wasn't the most disturbing thing.

If Siobhan's suspicions about the tin were correct, Kate would be intruding on Hannah's privacy, and that would violate the covenant of trust the whole island community was built on. People never locked their doors. If a passerby saw an open window during a rainstorm, they came in and closed it, but then they walked right back out again. It felt wrong to betray that trust.

Hannah Sutherland had been devoted to her students, and Kate didn't want to believe for one minute she could have killed Emma. Hannah had been fully aware Emma was leaving the island and therefore posed no threat. The Hannah Sutherland Kate knew and respected wasn't a murderer.

"Look, they're old ladies. They're probably tucked up in bed with a cup of cocoa by eight o'clock. Black clothes, a torch, and a trowel. We'll be in and out in ten minutes." Siobhan had it all figured out.

"What about the Oonagh Simmons, the housekeeper?"

"She'll be asleep too. She has to be up early to cook breakfast and light the fires."

"You make it sound like something out of *Downton Abbey*. What Toby?"

"He lives in a cottage on the edge of the garden down among the trees. He won't hear us. He'll be playing music or computer games." Siobhan cocked her head, as if she was trying to convince her mother to let her keep a puppy.

"I'm sorry, I can't do it."

Siobhan screwed her mouth into a determined pout.

Kate was suddenly reminded of conversations she used to have with teenaged Alex about attending concerts of particularly disreputable bands. "Siobhan, I really don't think it's a good idea."

"What if she knows something?"

"Then we'll talk with her."

"How are we going to do that? She doesn't even know who we are." Siobhan sounded frustrated.

"I can't do this," Kate repeated. "I respect her too much."

Siobhan sighed, a little too loudly for it not to be for dramatic effect. "Fine, then I'll just have to go by myself."

CHAPTER 13

Gwynie was waiting for Gooley to arrive at the pub. She was feeling uneasy. She'd basically turned her back on most of the people she'd grown up with. Now she had to cozy up to someone she hadn't spoken to in over forty years, ask a favour he might not be willing to grant her.

"Gwynie, lass, is that you?" Gooley bellowed as he approached. Feebles and Smee stood beside him, just like in school—the Three Musketeers. "You're looking good."

Smee sneered, "I hear you've been made royalty."

"Tea and cucumber sandwiches every Sunday with the Queen, eh, Gwynie?" Gooley teased.

She forced a laugh. "Rupert, could I have a word," and she looked at the other two, "in private."

Gooley grinned. "I'm getting quite popular with the lasses. They can't stay away. Must be me aftershave."

"You don't wear aftershave." Smee sniffed. "Must be the fish!"

"Go on, lads. Get a round in."

"Don't take too long," Feebles warned him. "You've only time for the one."

After the other two had gone inside, Gwynie tugged at Gooley's arm and steered him toward the stone steps leading to the beach.

"Did Kate Galway speak to you?" she asked in a quiet voice, afraid of being overheard.

"Aye." He had a look on his face, as if he wasn't sure where she was going with this conversation.

"Did she ask you where you were on the afternoon Emma disappeared?"

"No, lass. Just what happened at the school-end celebration." His expression had become serious. "Why do you ask?"

Gwynie swallowed to get rid of the constriction in her throat. "Rupert, if Kate asks, could you say you were with me by the community centre."

"But I was on the mainland with my da and brother, taking in a film."

"This is really important."

He stepped back from her.

"I don't like to lie, lass, not to Kate. What if someone catches me out?"

Damn it, why couldn't he just say yes and be done with it? "But they won't. Your da and your brother are both dead, aren't they?" That was cruel. But at this moment, her own preservation outweighed his feelings.

"Gwynie!"

"I'm sorry, Rupert, but I'm desperate." Maybe she should tell him the truth, but to avoid having to tell the truth was the whole point of this conversation. "Do it for old time's sake, for what we meant to each other."

He looked at her, his eyebrows knit in confusion.

She ran her hand up his arm. "I know you used to like me. And I was quite fond of you. If I hadn't left the island, maybe things would have turned out differently." She smiled. It was a smile she usually only reserved for her husband, and that made her uncomfortable.

"If this has anything to do with Emma's death..."

"It doesn't. I swear on my grandchildren's lives. But there's something I can't have people knowing."

He stared out over the sea as if he couldn't bear to look at her.

"Rupert, please." She forced herself to lean in as if to kiss him on the cheek.

He shook her off like she was an irritating insect and went into the pub. Would he give her away? And what would she do if he did?

No one must ever know she was down by the harbour when Emma disappeared. No one must ever know who she was waiting for. And no one must ever know that only a few hours later, she would take a life.

—

Kate walked up the uneven stone path toward Siobhan's cottage, determined to talk her friend out of invading the Sutherlands' garden. She paused at the door and turned the knob. It was locked. It seemed ironic that given what Siobhan was planning to do that night, she'd secured her own home. Kate knocked.

Siobhan opened the door, a purple towel stained grey with clay thrown over her shoulder, and invited her inside.

With Siobhan's ability to embrace life in its many facets, Kate expected her place to be stuffed with furniture rescued from charity shops, and treasures picked up at car boot sales. Instead, the interior of her house was surprisingly sparse. The living room was dominated by an overstuffed sofa and chairs in red velvet paisley fabric, along with two circular side tables with claw feet. Under the window was another sofa with green and cream striped upholstery, looking like it had been lifted from a Regency salon. Two gothic style bookshelves stood against the far wall. None of it matched, yet it was all Siobhan.

About the room were scattered vases and bowls and, like David's place, a selection of framed artwork hung on the walls. A small oil painting of a woman's hand cradling a Chinese teacup, with David's signature in the lower right-hand corner.

Siobhan was wiping the last of the clay from her hands. "Not what you were expecting?" She must have seen the surprised look on Kate's face.

Kate said nothing. She was embarrassed about her presumptions.

"If I had the space and the money, it might look quite different, but the truth is I hate clutter, especially where I work. As much as

I keep seeing things I like, I'm forced to be selective. One of these days I'll get around to getting everything upholstered so at least the colours go together." Siobhan paused. "Do you want to see my women?"

"Yes, please."

She led Kate to the back of the cottage. Under the bright illumination of the studio lights were an oversized kiln and a pottery wheel. On the large worktable, three female figures, approximately two feet tall in unfired grey clay, took centre stage.

Each had a thick waist, ample breasts and thighs, and a round belly. One had a Celtic knot etched onto her stomach, the same knot tattooed on Siobhan's shoulder. On another was a muscular tree, its branches embracing the woman's breasts, the roots reaching deep into her pubic hair. The last had wings emerging from her back. They all had curling tendrils of hair, reminiscent of Siobhan's. Kate could see a connectedness with the earth, a spirituality, in each figure.

Siobhan was watching Kate's face, as if trying to gauge her reaction, but Kate feared any words she could come up with would sound trite compared to these exquisite creatures. "They're so powerful." Frankly, she was surprised that Siobhan, with her offhand attitude towards life, had created these women. Yet she realized in order to do so, there had to be some part of their creator in each one.

Siobhan walked around the table, touching an arm or a shoulder, as if they were precious children.

"How can you bear to part with them?" Kate finally asked.

"I keep a photographic record, but I need to sell them to live." She sighed. "That's the trouble with being an artist. There can only ever be one true original, and when it's gone, it's gone. I sometimes wish I were a writer like you. Then there would be thousands of copies of my creations in the world."

Kate laughed. "But you'll never have to suffer the indignity of finding your latest creation marked down to 99p for a quick sale."

Siobhan covered the figures with damp squares of material and sheets of translucent plastic, tucking the ends close to the base of each sculpture. "You didn't just pop by to check out my work, did you?"

"No. I came to try to talk you out of going tonight, but then you already know that, don't you?"

Siobhan walked to the back door and flipped the lock shut. "Is this what happens when you're married to a copper?"

She was dismissing Kate's sense of ethics as something she'd adopted as James's wife, rather than a belief system that was an innate part of her. "No, it's what happens when you grow up on the island. People respect each other, take care of each other."

Siobhan looked out over the meadow that lay beyond the studio, before turning back to face Kate. "I understand that. But maybe finding the truth is more important than people's privacy. Look, it'll take ten minutes tops. I'll do the digging, the trespassing, breaking all the rules of decent, civilized behaviour. Just come and keep lookout. I'd rather not do this on my own."

While she still didn't feel right about going, Kate recognized that Siobhan wasn't the most practical or cautious of people, and she didn't want her getting into trouble. "All right, but just as lookout, mind."

A big broad grin spread over Siobhan's face. "Thanks, you're a mate."

"Not much of a mate. I should have tried harder to talk you out of it."

"My mates know they can't talk me out of anything."

—

He watched Siobhan and Kate in the studio. Siobhan had been showing off her ladies. In the time he'd been watching her cottage, he'd grown quite attached to the ladies with their round stomachs, breasts, and bottoms. These were women you could grab hold of, not like the young things today who were all bones. His generation was one of solidity—big men, big women, and big babies. Big meant healthy.

He headed toward the bottom of the garden, just behind the bushes. In his black pants and sweater, he blended easily into the oncoming darkness, and the sweater protected him from the evening chill. Unfolding his canvas chair and opening his flask of tea—generously laced with whiskey—he settled in for the night.

CHAPTER 14

The sun had disappeared below the horizon, making the Sutherland back garden feel much larger than it had earlier in the day. It seemed to Kate as if she and Siobhan were trying to feel their way across a dark football pitch. With Siobhan's torch lighting up the ground in front of them, they moved as quickly as they could, all the while Kate praying Siobhan's estimate of ten minutes was accurate. It was a fair dash to the car parked down the road if something went wrong.

"Do you remember where Hannah was digging?" Kate whispered.

"A little further over here," Siobhan replied. "Pink flowers. Pink flowers in front of a large tree."

"I remember now. Find the edge of the flower bed and follow it until you find the Sweet Williams under an elm tree." With no ambient noise—no crashing waves, no screaming peacocks, no blaring television—Kate worried that their voices would carry all the way to the house. Every step, every rub of fabric seemed amplified in the silent night.

The light from Siobhan's torch rose up a deeply furrowed trunk. "Is that an elm?"

Kate took the torch and revealed the flowers among its roots. Pink Sweet Williams. "They're the right flowers. Just dig so we can get out of here."

"It would go faster if you helped."

"That wasn't the deal, remember?"

Siobhan handed Kate the torch and fell to her knees. "Are you sure we're in the right place? These damn flowers go on forever."

"She didn't bury it too deep. Feel around. You should be able to hit it with your trowel."

Siobhan began throwing dirt about, some of it landing on Kate's feet.

"Steady on."

"You want fast or tidy? You can't have both."

"Just be careful," warned Kate. "We don't want anyone to know we've been here."

"Won't the old—Hannah—know when she finds the tin gone?"

"I doubt anyone will believe her. But it's not her I'm worried about. And don't step on any loose soil. It leaves footprints that can be traced."

"All right, all right," and Siobhan trowelled the disturbed earth back into place. "You're not having a good time, are you?"

Kate didn't answer. The sooner they found the damn thing, the sooner they could leave.

Siobhan was moving further and further away, feeling among the continuous mass of flowers, but it seemed like she'd gone too far. Just as Kate was about to tell her to come back, Siobhan's trowel made contact with a dull metallic clunk. "Got it. Bring the light closer."

Without warning, there was a quick shuffle of feet on the grass, some heavy breathing, and then a thud. The torch went out, and they were in darkness. Something hard hit Kate across her upper arm, and she dropped to the ground, crying out in pain. Another swing glanced off her shoulder, and she swung her arms wildly in an attempt to protect herself.

Whoever it was seemed to have moved on to Siobhan. Grunts and dull thumps came from where she'd been digging.

"Stop it, damn you," Siobhan cried out more in anger than in pain. "Get away from me, you crazy bastard. I have a black belt in karate."

Kate heard another blow and then nothing. She crawled toward where she'd heard Siobhan's voice. "Are you all right?" and she reached out to find her.

"Who the hell was that?" Siobhan barked. "Are you hurt?"

"A blow to the shoulder, but he missed my head." Kate touched her hair. There was a stickiness on her hand. "No, he didn't. I'm bleeding."

Siobhan began to yell for help and didn't stop until the lights went on inside the house.

—

David hadn't set foot inside Sutherland Hall in more years than he cared to remember, but when Sophie called to say Kate and Siobhan had been found injured in the garden, he didn't hesitate.

His feet crunched the gravel as he walked toward the polished oak door. Should he knock? It was his house, yet it hadn't been his home for many years. He'd inherited the property when his father died, held in trust by Hannah until he turned twenty-five. The will stipulated the sisters could live here until they married. None of them ever had.

The door was slightly ajar, and his footsteps summoned Oonagh Simmons. She was wearing the traditional uniform of the Sutherland housekeeper—a long-sleeved black dress that reached midcalf, shapeless except for a loose belt at the waist, and accented only by plain white cuffs and collar. How depressing it must have been for a woman to have spent her best years in an outfit so unflattering.

"Mr. David, come in. They're in the drawing room." She added in a low whisper, "Good to have you back, sir."

He followed her into the drawing room. David couldn't help being curious about the room, to see what had changed since he'd last been here. But his attention was immediately drawn to Kate, sitting in one of the easy chairs, her face streaked with dirt and her head wrapped in a striped tea towel.

"Kate, are you all right?"

"I'm fine. It's worse than it looks."

He brushed some dirt from her cheek. "It's still a head injury. Marcus is on his way."

Siobhan was slumped in the other chair, also looking somewhat worse for wear.

Within minutes, Marcus arrived and examined Kate's head, then cleaned and temporarily dressed the wound. Thankfully he didn't think it was concussion, but he wanted her to accompany him to the hospital to properly treat the cut and to observe her overnight.

At first Kate refused, but David insisted. "It's for the best. Let Marcus take care of you. Please," and he looked into her eyes, willing her to listen to reason.

She nodded her agreement.

Marcus was examining the marks on Siobhan's arm and back, predicting a painful shade of purple by tomorrow. Luckily nothing was broken.

"Well, now that's over with, may we ask what you were doing in our garden at this time of night?" Jane demanded, trying to project authority in a navy plaid dressing gown.

She continued to stare at Siobhan, while Sophie tugged at her sister's sleeve to get her to sit down. "They're all right, Janey. Let it go."

David noticed Hannah wasn't in the room.

"I will not let it go. They were trespassing in our garden for the second time today."

"The second time?" Knowing Siobhan as he did, David was fairly confident the whole thing had probably been her idea.

"So I ask you again, why were you sneaking about in our garden?"

"We saw Hannah burying a tea tin this afternoon and came back to dig it up," Kate said.

"A tea tin? Why in heaven's name would you want to do that?" Jane said, with an incredulous edge to her voice. Jane had a way of belittling anything she didn't approve of. As a boy, David had been the recipient of that tone on more than one occasion.

"It was my idea," Siobhan said in an uncharacteristically sheepish voice. It looked like she wasn't going to let Kate take all the blame. "I thought it might contain some evidence about the death of Kate's Aunt Emma."

But Jane didn't berate or scoff. She laughed. Everyone turned to observe this rare occurrence.

"Evidence of your aunt's death? Do you have any idea what my sister hides in those tins of hers? Teaspoons, nails and screws, bits of soap, in fact whatever she can get her hands on. She's especially fond of burying the car keys. Will that help in your investigation? I'm afraid that on her bad days, Hannah is prone to delusions and what she's decided these things are, we really don't know."

Jane wearily ran her hands over her eyes. The many lines about her eyes and mouth reminded David of how hard it must be to have to deal with Hannah in her present condition.

"We no longer know how her mind works," Jane continued. "Some days it doesn't work very well at all. Today was one of those days. Hannah's condition is a family matter, and we'd appreciate it if you kept this to yourself. I'm sorry you were hurt, but that's what you get for prowling about in other people's gardens in the dark."

"But that doesn't explain who attacked us," Siobhan said. "Where's Hannah?"

"She's in bed with a sleeping tablet," Sophie said. "She always has a sleeping tablet and her heart medication at nine o'clock, and the door to her room is locked in case she wanders during the night. You can check if you wish."

"Don't be ridiculous, Sophie," Jane snapped at her. "They're not the police. We don't have to provide our sister with an alibi." She stood up. "Now, if you don't mind, there has been entirely too much excitement for one night. We'd be grateful if you would all take yourselves off so we can get back to our beds."

David looked over at Siobhan's bruises and then wiped a fleck of dried blood from Kate's forehead. They looked like they'd been through the wars. "Are you sure you're both all right?"

"Speaking for myself, more embarrassed than anything else," Kate said, looking over at Siobhan.

"Let's get you to the hospital," Marcus said. "Siobhan, can I drop you at your cottage?"

Siobhan insisted she was well enough to drive.

David made sure Kate was comfortable in the doctor's car, tucking a blanket about her to keep her safe from the damp evening air. He waved as the car drove off and stood watching until the red tail lights disappeared into the darkness. He gave Siobhan a quick hug and a spare torch so she could find her way to the truck.

Once they'd left, David went around to the garden to survey the damage. Siobhan's torch lay on the ground half-buried among some loose earth. Bending to scoop it up, he spotted a trowel. With the light from his torch, he swept across the earth looking for the tin Kate and Siobhan were so anxious to find. But all he saw was a hole among the Sweet Williams.

—

The bruises on Siobhan's arms and back were tender. Having declined Marcus's painkillers, she was now cursing her stoicism. She attempted to sleep on the unbruised arm and then her stomach, but however she positioned herself, she couldn't get comfortable. Marcus would be keeping an eye on Kate at the hospital, and Siobhan was considering walking over and begging for something to help her sleep. Then she heard the sound of shattering glass.

She ran downstairs, eager to confront whoever had invaded her home, but all she could hear were the soft sounds of her bare feet on the stairs.

When she flicked on the light in the studio, she found a large jagged hole in the middle of the window. The Green Woman—from the oak tree engraved on her body—was lying in pieces on the floor. Her head, her left arm, bits of her hair lay dismembered about her. Siobhan bent down and touched them as she would a beloved dead pet. In spite of her anger, she thought how ironic that it had been the oak tree that had succumbed.

Then she saw the rock, a piece of brown parcel paper wrapped around it and tied with string. She tore the string away and the note floated to the floor. GET OUT WHILE YOU CAN, HARLOT was printed with cut-out magazine letters.

Taking the rock in her left hand, she gripped it hard, feeling its weight. It would feel so good to fling it through one of the intact windowpanes, but she stopped herself. A wanton act of self-destruction wasn't what she needed now. It was revenge, burning hot. She wanted to get whoever had done this and hurt him very badly.

CHAPTER 15

The next morning Sophie watched through the French doors as Toby marched back and forth, steering the sputtering lawn mower over the grass. Sophie was amazed that the ancient machine had hung on this long. Any day now there would be one final gasp, and that would be the end of it. It was temperamental at best, but Toby probably felt it wasn't his place to ask for a new one. Besides, Jane held a firm belief that replacing things still able to fulfill their function, however ineffectually, was a waste of money.

Perspiration plastered the lad's thin dark hair to his round red face. His shirt tail bounced over his thick denim pants. Even though he was what people used to call sturdy—a much kinder word than overweight—he had a flat rear end. Poor boy. Women valued a good rear end on a man. So said the women's magazines Simmons bought for her, and Sophie hid under her bed, away from Jane's critical eyes.

Jane stood beside Sophie, her hands clasped together at her waist and smelling of mint toothpaste. Once for her birthday, Sophie had treated her to some lavender water. But she'd never used it. It was probably pushed to the back of her wardrobe, unopened. Sophie liked a splash of lavender water, a touch of face powder. It made her feel like she'd made an effort to face the day. Her sister, on the other hand, had more than once asserted that anything beyond basic hygiene was vanity.

"Do you think it was Hannah who attacked Kate and Siobhan?"

Jane asked.

Sophie wasn't surprised at Jane's suspicion. Jane was simply the one with the courage to say it.

"She's slipped out before," Jane added.

Toby and the lawn mower gradually descended toward the lower part of the lawn.

"She must have a key hidden somewhere," Sophie said and sighed. "We'll have to look for it."

"We can't go prying into her things. It's not right."

"But if she's going to attack people..." Sophie couldn't complete her thought. If it was true, it meant Hannah was getting worse. Eventually they would have to do the unthinkable—put her into a nursing home on the mainland. They'd never been separated. No one and nothing had ever come between them.

"We'll just have to be more careful. Keep a closer watch," Jane said with determination.

"Should we postpone tomorrow's dinner?" *It might be for the best,* Sophie thought. It wouldn't do to get Hannah excited, and strangers in the house always did that.

"No. Simmons has already bought the food. It would be a terrible waste. Besides, if we cancel, there'll be gossip. And we can't have that."

"No, Jane."

—

Kate was back home. Refreshed by a good night's sleep courtesy of Marcus's sleeping tablets, she realized she'd been sidetracked by the whole tea tin incident. It was time to refocus. She stared out the kitchen window at a robin hopping across the back lawn, and she suddenly remembered Hannah's reference to the bird-girl. Had it been something thrown up from Hannah's fractured mind, or was she a real person? Was it someone who liked birds or possibly looked like a bird, all thin and spindly? Birds...types of birds...gulls, choughs, magpies, robins, sparrows. Sami Sparrow! Had Sami been interested in David? She'd been at the celebration, dressed up possibly for the first time in her life. Did Hannah think she'd done it to attract David's attention?

Kate's speculations were interrupted by a knock at the door, faint, as if the visitor lacked conviction they should be there. She was surprised to see Joseph Smee. She stepped aside to let him come in. "Can I get you a drink?"

He nodded.

As she poured the whiskey, she noticed he was examining the corkboard.

"So these are your suspects, are they?" No doubt he recognized a picture of his younger self among them.

Kate handed him his drink. "Just people who were involved in Emma's life."

He stared intently at the photographs of the unlined faces. "We were so young," he observed wistfully.

Kate offered him a place to sit. "Do you have something to tell me, Joseph?"

He threw back his whiskey as if he needed the courage. "Where do you want me to start?"

She reached for her notepad, causing Smee to look startled that his words would be taken down.

"I've heard there were some disagreements the summer Emma died," she prompted him. "Gooley told me he overheard Hannah having a go at Emma at the school-end celebration, accused her of spreading rumours, said it was her fault Mr. Probert was leaving. Do you know any more about that?"

"Just that Hannah was practically foaming at the mouth. Now, there's someone who could have murdered our Emma." Smee pointed with his crooked finger to emphasize his accusation.

"Feeling hard done by surely isn't much of a motive."

Smee helped himself to another drink. "You know the Sutherlands and their pride. You don't humiliate Hannah Sutherland and get away with it. Although, it weren't Emma that started it all."

Kate looked up from her notepad, staring into his face. "It was you, wasn't it? You started the rumours."

"Aye," he admitted reluctantly. "I saw Hannah and Probert all chummy in The Breeze, smiling and laughing. Hannah Sutherland don't smile and laugh without a good reason, and I figured a decent-looking, educated bloke like Probert must have been it."

"Why did you do it?"

Smee shrugged as if he now realized it had been a pointless thing to do. "Just wanted to make trouble. Get the island laughing about high and mighty Hannah Sutherland making a fool of herself over a man."

He really did hate the Sutherlands.

"You had a fight with David during the football game," Kate reminded him.

"He cheated. Couldn't win fair so he cheated. Sutherlands always have to get what they want, and they don't care who they hurt. He had the most beautiful girl on the island, and he was still sniffing around Gwynie Morgan."

"What makes you think that?"

"At the celebration, Emma was off having a good time with the girls. David was feeling left out. So when Gwynie tried to get friendly-like, he let her. When Emma went to find him, they were both gone."

"That doesn't mean they were together."

Smee fell silent. At last he said, "It didn't matter how many plans Emma made. He was never going to let her go to that university."

"Are you saying David might have killed Emma because she rejected him?"

"I'm saying Sutherlands always put Sutherlands first, and God help anybody who gets in their way."

—

Siobhan stayed in her studio all day. The glass had been swept up and the pane replaced. It looked as if nothing had happened, except for the destruction of the Green Woman. The figure lay on the worktable like a stillborn child, a soul that had never had the chance to live. Siobhan had created her and therefore had a responsibility to mend her, so she was determined to work as long as it took.

It wasn't until the middle of the afternoon that she was satisfied with the progress of the repairs. Only then did she rest, and the full implication of what had happened during the night come over her. Somebody was trying to frighten her away. Someone hated her so much they were prepared to do the one thing no islander would ever think of doing—destroy her art. All islanders, artists or not, understood art was both livelihood and an expression of the creator's being. It was a sacrilege to butcher someone's creation, and yet some bastard had done just that. But who? And why her? Siobhan poured herself the first of many whiskeys.

The more she thought about it, the more she realized she couldn't face another night in the house. The cold bile of fear continued to rise from her stomach. She now understood why they called it the fight or flight syndrome. At various times during the day she'd wanted to run down to the ferry and leave this place. Any of the faces she would meet in Craggy's or The Breeze or The Filly could be the person who wanted to hurt her, and that meant she couldn't trust anyone on the island, except Kate, and of course David. And the Old Gents. She couldn't believe it could be one of them. Or Fiona or Winifred or Julian or Flo. As she added more names to her "safe" list, the fear began to lift. But in its place was anger, a searing, burning rage.

People say when you're angry, you see red, but it's not true. You don't see anything out of the ordinary, but you feel, you feel waves of adrenaline pounding against your brain, and it's so strong you lose all sense of restraint and the ability to care about what's socially acceptable or what people will think or say about you. All you know is you're compelled to act, and act now.

—

In spite of her drunken state, Siobhan noticed a hush fall on the crowd when she staggered into the pub. She didn't care that her hair was bushy and tangled, her face flushed from both the whiskey and the speed at which she'd propelled herself down to the harbour. Her chest rose and fell with an effort that frightened even her, but it didn't matter. Nothing mattered except what she'd come here to do.

She swallowed hard. "I know one of you is trying to drive me away, trying to frighten me out of my home. I've seen your pathetic handiwork and stupid notes. I'm here to tell you it won't work. I don't care how many rocks you throw through my windows or how much of my art you destroy, I'm not leaving. I know what a coward you are, sneaking around in the night, and you won't get away with it."

The steam was going out of her under the scrutiny of so many eyes, these people she couldn't bear to imagine ever harming her. A sob rose in her throat. "I'm not afraid of you. You can't hurt me."

The sob choked her, and the tears started to flow. "I've taken on better than you. I won't let you beat me, I won't let you..." and she felt Flo catch her as she collapsed against the bar. Flo hooked Siobhan's arm around her neck.

"Call Kate," she heard Flo tell Julian as she was helped into their sitting room behind the bar. "Then put the kettle on."

—

Kate arrived at the pub to find Siobhan crumpled in an armchair with a blanket around her, a cup of what was probably sweet tea in her hands. Kate carefully dropped to her knees and looked up into Siobhan's face, pale with patches of red on her cheeks and around her eyes. "What happened?"

The tears were streaming down Siobhan's swollen face. "Whore letter, rock, Green Woman..." and the rest of her words disappeared into her teacup.

Kate looked up at Flo. "What's been going on?"

"As far as I can make out, someone's been terrorizing her. But you know Siobhan." Flo was seated on the arm of Siobhan's chair, stroking her hair. "She'd never ask for help. She needs to appear indestructible."

Kate took Siobhan's tear-stained face in her hands. "Let us help you. Tell me what happened."

So Siobhan told her about the note on her bed, the cracked flowerpot, and the rock though the window.

Her empty teacup was traded for a mug of sweet black coffee. Now that she was getting over the shock, the coffee would start to counteract the whiskey.

"Do you have any idea who's been doing this or why?" Kate asked.

Siobhan's red hair shook. "I've been trying to think if I've insulted anyone or not paid for my round... I just don't know," and the tears started to flow again.

Kate took Siobhan's head and held it against her own shoulder, rubbing her back, careful to avoid where she thought last night's bruises might be.

Feebles, Gooley, and Smee were standing in the doorway.

"I'm sorry, lass. We couldn't catch him," Smee said.

Siobhan looked up. "What?"

"A while ago it was, we saw someone hanging about your house in the dark, so we decided to keep an eye on the place," Feebles said.

"Taking it in turns, like. It was me who broke your pot." Gooley stared dejectedly at his feet. "I'll get you a new one, m'dear. Smee was on duty yesterday, but by the time he heard the glass break, the person'd run away."

"We're not as fast as we once were," Smee reluctantly admitted.

"You knew this was going on, and you didn't say anything?" Kate's voice was sharp with anger.

Gooley was staring at the carpet. "We didn't want Siobhan frightened. We thought if we could scare him off or catch whoever was doing this, it'd stop. Sorry, lass, but you should've had someone a bit younger."

To Kate's astonishment, Siobhan looked delighted. "I couldn't have wished for three better guardian angels."

The Gents shuffled about in the discomfort of Siobhan's unexpected praise.

"Well, you're coming home with me," Kate told her.

They helped Siobhan to her feet, and together they walked up the road to Kate's house.

CHAPTER 16

Siobhan was lying on Kate's sofa, trying to find something on morning television to occupy her mind. She'd quickly discovered if you didn't want to renovate your house, appraise an antique, or get advice on what to do when your partner went off for a dirty weekend with your best friend, there wasn't much of interest.

Daytime television was a new experience for Siobhan as she was usually in her studio. It had only been twelve hours since her outburst in the pub, and she was sure people thought she was a sad, old drunk. Well, maybe not so much of the old, but definitely sad. She felt like she was hiding out in disgrace. Kate had made endless cups of tea, numerous rounds of toast, and concerned noises. Siobhan felt guilty because she wasn't ill, just too embarrassed to face everyone.

Now Kate was flapping about in the kitchen, scrubbing and wiping things with great enthusiasm. Siobhan never knew whether to admire or feel sorry for people who took so much obvious delight in cleaning.

Siobhan turned off the television and sat up. "You know, we've never talked about that night at the Sutherlands."

Kate threw the dishtowel onto the counter, as if glad of the excuse to take a break.

"When we were up at Sutherland Hall and you were explaining to spooky Jane why we were in the garden, I noticed you said 'we' as if we were in it together," said Siobhan. "You could have just pointed to me and said, 'that daft cow over there made me do it.'"

"But we were in it together."

"I know, but you didn't want to come." Siobhan paused. The next bit was going to be hard. "And it turned out you were right. So I just wanted to say thank you."

"You're welcome."

That went well, Siobhan thought. Better change the subject while she was ahead. "I guess we'll never know who attacked us."

"Any ideas?"

"Well, the crazy lady for one."

"And her motive?"

"She's crazy!"

Kate looked like she needed further explanation.

"She was protecting whatever secrets were in her tin," Siobhan said. "You really didn't buy that buried keys bollocks Jane gave us, did you?"

When Kate didn't reply, Siobhan continued. "So if it wasn't Hannah, what about Jane? Maybe she's trying to protect her sister. Besides, she looks like she'd enjoy giving someone a good smack."

From the look on Kate's face, she was going to need a lot more convincing.

"What are these secrets you keep talking about?" Kate asked.

"That Hannah killed Emma."

"If Jane knew Hannah killed Emma and there was some sort of evidence in the tin, why didn't Jane just get rid of it?"

"That's exactly what she was doing, but then we got in the way."

Kate was looking at her sceptically out of the corner of her eye. "You're making this up as you go along, aren't you?"

"Thinking out loud. Doesn't mean it's wrong."

"I have another idea. You and I have both been under attack since this whole business started. What if—"

Siobhan pointed her finger at Kate. "You don't like 'what if's'!"

Kate sighed at the interruption. "I don't like a lot of 'what if's'. It's possible what happened in the garden is an escalation of what's been happening over the past week. That means we're on the right track, and we're getting closer."

Siobhan had to reluctantly agree it was probably just as reasonable an explanation as Jane attacking them. "So we were assaulted by Emma's murderer?"

The thought that they might have been close to the person who'd killed Emma was more than a bit unsettling to Siobhan, but probably more so to Kate.

"I'm going to search through the island archive," Kate said. "It might shed some light on that last summer."

"We have an archive?"

"In the community centre. Why don't you come with me?"

But Siobhan wasn't prepared to be seen in public quite yet. "There's a show coming up I want to watch—something about hedgehogs."

Kate didn't look like she was buying it.

"I like hedgehogs." Siobhan wished she could have said it with more conviction.

Kate didn't press the matter but smiled and went on her way.

—

The community centre was a late addition to the island, and its red brick exterior made it stand out from the rest of the grey stone buildings. But what it lacked in aesthetic appeal, it more than made up for in function.

Kate stepped into the first room of the cool building, a large open space, with room enough for chairs to be set out for meetings. Large windows offered a panoramic view of the sea, while posters for past island celebrations and sketches of island landscapes and residents covered the walls. Tucked at the back was a small kitchen, because no island get-together was complete without tea and cake.

The third room housed the island lending library and archive. If the pub was the heart of the island, the archive was its collective memory. People donated pictures, letters, and documents to be available for present and future generations which librarian Winifred organized and catalogued. This room was lined with row upon row of shelving, each holding boxes labelled by year, dating all the way back to Artemis Faraday's arrival in 1866. It was quite tempting for the historian in Kate to dip into the older boxes with their pictures of men with bristling mustaches and sideburns, and ladies with corseted waists, but she was after the one marked 1965.

Inside the appropriate box were a number of large brown envelopes subdividing the material. The first was marked Emma Catherine Galway, and her date of death. Inside were newspaper clippings from the *Porth Madryn Observer*, the same clippings Miriam had collected. In another envelope was a collection of pictures taken at the Queen Victoria Celebration held every May on the beach. The third, marked Pride of Meredith Garden Competition, contained application forms from people who had entered their gardens, accompanied by photographs of neatly cut lawns and clusters of flowers. But there were also pictures of dead plants, attached to several articles from the *Observer* about the mysterious blight to attack the gardens in the competition. "Pride of Meredith Sabotaged" read the headline.

At the bottom of the box underneath some miscellaneous documents were three reels of movie film. Islanders were not normally known for being high-tech, but someone had managed to get their hands on a movie camera. Hopefully it wasn't some slick tourist propaganda staged with lots of sun-lit scenery. Kate would learn much more from footage of islanders going about their daily business, so she began to throw open cupboard doors hoping against hope there was a projector hidden away.

After several minutes of searching, she found it, safely packed in its dusty grey metal case. It must have sat here untouched for three or four decades. Kate shoved the films reels into a carrier bag, grabbed the projector, and stepped out of the building. She narrowly missed bumping into a woman passing by the door.

The woman took a step backward. "Kate."

She obviously wasn't an islander, not from the way she was dressed. Her sweater and trousers were casual, but the material looked expensive, possibly cashmere. Her neatly curled grey hair probably saw a stylist every fortnight.

When Kate didn't immediately respond, the woman held out her hand. "Gwynie Charlton—Morgan, that was. My condolences on your grandmother's passing."

Kate put down the projector and shook her hand. "Thank you."

"I'm sorry I wasn't able to pay my respects earlier. I have pressing business on the island. My husband and I own a summer home, right over there," and she pointed to the cottages beyond the field. "We've never really used it, and the lease for the current renters is almost up. I have to decide whether to renovate or sell."

"That sounds familiar."

Gwynie looked over the harbour at the cliffside road. "Your grandparents' place."

Kate nodded.

"I'm sorry. I'd love to stay and chat, but I've got to be going," Gwynie said rather quickly, as if anxious to get away.

But Kate couldn't let this chance to speak with Gwynie slip by. "Can I ask you a few questions about the summer Emma died?"

A look of what Kate recognized as apprehension passed over her face. "Not now. I'm expecting a call from my husband, and I'm afraid I left my phone back at the pub." Without waiting for Kate to respond, she walked away.

"Maybe later?" Kate called after her.

Gwynie gave a quick wave of acknowledgment but did not turn around.

———

The only clue that Siobhan had moved off the sofa was a fresh cup of coffee on the side table.

"How were the hedgehogs?" Kate asked.

Siobhan paused. "Prickly." She pointed to Kate's carrier bags. "What's all that?"

"Hopefully something that will help us. Kate started to unpack the projector. "I found some film."

Siobhan rubbed her hands together. "Is there popcorn?"

"I have biscuits, unless you've eaten them all."

"There might be one or two left," and Siobhan scurried off to fetch the biscuit tin.

It didn't take much to set up the projector and clear a spot on the wall. Kate hoped the bulb was still working. She and Siobhan settled on the coach, she flipped the switch, and the grainy colour film started to run.

The first film showed a group of young men playing football on the beach. Many of them had their shirts off. The men who worked the fishing boats and the island farms were tanned with defined muscles.

"Where's the sound?" Siobhan asked between bites of biscuit.

"Cameras didn't record sound back then," Kate told her.

"Why would you want films without sound?" she grumbled. Then she pointed to the flickering image on the wall. "Stop there!"

Kate paused the film.

Siobhan went up close to the picture and examined two men in the frame, one with a shock of thick, dark hair, both with well-developed muscles, their tanned skin glistening under a sheen of sweat. "Now, they're hot!"

"Siobhan, you realize that's Feebles and Smee."

Siobhan looked like she was processing the information, comparing the toned young men in front of her with her pensioner drinking buddies. At last she said, "Still hot!"

Kate restarted the film, but there was nothing of note.

The second reel was the Pride of Meredith Garden Competition. A close-up of the competition poster introduced the subject. The camera panned through people's gardens with the owners proudly standing by. Kate recognized Fiona's parents and the cottages along the cliffside road. There was a shot of Lilian and Emma surrounded by pink and white roses, purple foxgloves, and other flowers Kate couldn't name. There was a close-up of a small blonde girl in a red striped tee-shirt and red shorts, holding Emma's hand and grinning.

"Who's that?" Siobhan asked.

"That's me," Kate said softly. Emma bent down and tickled young Kate, and she giggled and hid her face against Emma's thighs. She couldn't remember the film being taken, but she loved that there was a film record of her and Emma together.

The next shot was a much younger Sophie and Jane standing in their back garden, Sophie smiling and Jane grimly standing in her characteristic stance, hands clasped in front of her. Then there was the Porth Madryn Observer page with the headline Kate had seen in the archives—"Pride of Meredith Sabotaged"—and the poster again with "CANCELLED" written in thick red pen. The camera documented the gardens that had been destroyed, flowers limp and discoloured in their beds. There were no smiling faces here.

Before the film ran out, a red-faced man, his dirty hands crunched into fists, was threatening whoever was behind the camera.

"He didn't seem too chuffed about being filmed," Siobhan said.

"I think that was Clive Sparrow."

"Did he have something to do with the dead plants?"

"I don't see how. It would have destroyed his business if he had."

The last reel was a party in the pub. People were drinking and singing along with the piano and a fiddle player. Feebles, Gooley, and Smee were clog dancing, each trying to outdo the other with quick, intricate steps. They were surprisingly nimble.

The laughter, the drinking, and the camaraderie, even the work clothes of the farmers and fisherfolk hadn't changed. This could have been filmed today. The only clue that this was the mid-sixties was that some of the young women were dressed in A-line dresses with rising hemlines over textured tights and plastic boots. Then there was the smoke from everyone's cigarettes.

"I don't see Fiona and Winifred," said Siobhan.

"Maybe Fiona was filming. And Winifred is an incomer. She's only been on the island for forty years or so."

Siobhan snorted and shook her head. She must have been aware that even if she spent the rest of her life on Meredith, she'd never be considered a true islander.

Kate felt bad. "I'm only saying she wasn't at school with these people."

The camera caught Emma sitting with David, their heads together, with what was probably lemonade in front of them. David wore a polo-necked sweater, his thick fair hair brushing his collar. While Emma was looking about the room, waving to people, calling out to them, David only had eyes for her.

"That looks like Gwynie Morgan, one of Emma's school friends. I ran into her coming out of the community centre. She has some business on the island."

Gwynie appeared to be scowling at David and Emma.

"What's her problem?" Siobhan asked.

Every so often the camera would make a broad sweep of the room as if the filmmaker suddenly remembered they were there to record the whole party, but it was obvious from the time spent on David and Emma that they were the main attraction.

The camera cut away to the fiddler and piano player and then back to David and Emma. David took Emma's hand and led her to an area cleared for dancing. It was crowded with young people, twisting and jumping about.

Gwynie attempted to cut in on Emma, but instead of getting upset, Emma smiled and gestured her acceptance. Gwynie and David danced for a minute, but when she bent forward to say something in his ear, he shook his head, and walked away.

"What was that all about?" Siobhan asked.

Kate definitely had to speak with Gwynie.

Miriam, Kate's mother, was standing at the bar. She looked so carefree and happy. With her dark hair and deep-set eyes, she had a look of Alex about her. Kate had forgotten how attractive she'd been as a young woman.

Fiona was grinning at Feebles, her dress clinging to her hourglass figure. Emma danced with Gooley who was spinning her around, her head thrown back and laughing.

David walked up and said a few words to Emma. He looked annoyed, but Emma shook her head and laughed. He kept at her, gesturing towards the door, obviously trying to get her to leave. Feebles stepped in their way. David glared at him, as if considering his next move, but then threw up his hands in frustration and walked out. Emma took Feebles' hand, and they returned to the dance floor.

The film ended and flapped against the reel.

Kate shut off the machine and opened the curtains.

"David was acting like a bit of a knob," Siobhan observed.

David had said he'd loved Emma to the point of wanting to marry her, but he'd gone off in a huff when she refused to leave the pub. It looked like he wasn't prepared to respect what she'd wanted, and he'd fought with Smee at the school-end celebration. How would he have reacted if Emma had rejected him? "Smee said he thought David was never going to let Emma go to university. It would be too humiliating to his Sutherland pride to be rejected."

"If I can't have her, no one can?"

"I think that's what he was insinuating."

Siobhan was vehemently shaking her head. "No, I can't believe it."

But Kate wasn't so sure anymore.

CHAPTER 17

Gwynie Charlton had been dreading this evening. In particular, she wanted to avoid spending time with Hannah Sutherland. She'd heard that her former teacher was ill and, God forgive her, she was hoping that would prevent Hannah from making an appearance. But Gwynie hadn't been that lucky. Hannah was sitting quietly at the head of the table, moving the vegetables and the sliced lamb about on her plate. If Gwynie avoided making eye contact, she thought, maybe Hannah wouldn't recognize her.

It felt strange to be a guest of the Sutherland sisters, but then ever since Hugh's knighthood, Lady Charlton and Sir Hugh seemed to get more invitations than plain old Mr. and Mrs. Charlton ever did.

She'd barely eaten a mouthful of food, as Sophie couldn't stop asking her questions. Judging by the subject of her inquiries, it was obvious Sophie deeply regretted never having had a husband and children.

She had to admit it was good to get away from the pub. There was quite a din when the place filled up, voices getting progressively louder as the night and the drinking wore on. Then there was a tirade by some drunk woman last night. Thank God, just a few more days, and her business would be completed. She couldn't wait to get home to her family.

Angelica Lynley—who in the privacy of her own thoughts Gwynie had dubbed 'the mad cow'—was silent on the subject. No doubt she'd insisted there be no squalling brats spilling sticky drinks on her imported furniture, no runny noses and stomach aches interfering with social engagements, and definitely no heirs to claim a share of their father's wealth. If the jewellery she was flashing about was anything to go by, there was no doubt Angelica had wanted Anton Lynley and his sizable fortune all to herself.

"Do you find the island very different from when you lived here?" Jane asked. Up until now she'd been quiet, but perhaps she felt it was time to introduce a new topic.

"Yes, you must find us quite provincial after London," Angelica said, running her fingers over her pearl choker.

"We don't live in London. We moved about twenty years ago. Too much traffic and crime," Gwynie replied.

A smirk plant itself on Angelica's face, the look of someone who thinks she knows everything, and everyone else is blatantly stupid for not knowing it too.

"I've lived in London my whole life. Anton and I never considered living anywhere else. How could you leave the opera and the ballet?"

"Culture isn't restricted to the city limits." Gwynie could feel herself losing her temper. The Lynley woman was bearable as long as she kept her mouth shut, but now the mad cow was making grandiose statements in an obvious attempt to draw attention to herself. How was Gwynie going to endure a whole evening of this woman?

"You know, I believe we've met somewhere Where was it?" Angelica's eyes widened as if trying to take in Gwynie's every detail.

"I remember now," she announced with a smug smile. "It was at a fundraiser for the children's wing of some hospital. I can't remember the name, but my husband, renowned architect Anton Lynley, made a very generous donation on our behalf. So generous I wouldn't have been surprised it they'd offered to name a wing after us."

Gwynie and her husband had attended numerous hospital fundraisers over the years, and she'd hated them all. She'd never felt comfortable around people flaunting their wealth. She couldn't swear she'd ever met Angelica, although here was something definitely familiar about the woman.

"Surely Sir Hugh must find it quite inconvenient to live so far from the heart of the business community." Angelica had returned to her previous topic.

"Mrs. Lynley, my husband is a pharmacist." Hugh hated these types as much as she did. Whenever he was forced into a corner, he'd say he was a simple pharmacist, doling out antibiotics and hemorrhoid cream.

"You're much too modest, Lady Charlton. Your husband owns one of the largest pharmaceutical distribution companies in the country."

"But not through choice. Hugh was forced to take over the company when his father suffered a fatal heart attack." *And I wish to God he'd never agreed to run the business and never accepted the damned knighthood because we've been set upon by people like you ever since,* Gwynie wanted to add. *And for your information, not that it is any of your business, Hugh is the kind of man who would have been just as happy working behind the pharmacy counter at Boots, and I would have been just as proud of him.*

"The one thing I do miss are the art galleries." Angelica laid down her knife and fork. "There are so many creative people living on the island, and they deserve a proper gallery and up-to-date studios instead of having to work out of pokey little rooms stuck onto the back of their cottages. You know, that spot on the other side of the harbour is the perfect location for an art complex. It will provide a significant boost to the island's economy. We'll be able to expand the school, build a state-of-the-art library, improve the roads."

This was definitely a sales pitch, Gwynie decided. The only things missing were the audio-visual aids. But that part of the island was where the community centre and lifeboat station were located, and cottages, her cottage. What did the mad cow plan to do with them?

"I'm certain it'll be enthusiastically supported by the island's creative community," Angelica continued. "And of course once word gets out, artists will be begging to be allowed to establish themselves on Meredith. Why, it will be—"

Jane glared across the table at Angelica. "But we don't want a monstrosity like that on the island."

Angelica's mouth had fallen open. Perhaps no one had ever dared to interrupt her before. Gwynie could come to admire Jane.

But it didn't take Angelica long to recover. "I was going to suggest we name it in honour of David—The David Sutherland Art Institute."

"I don't know what gave you the idea that placing one's name on an ugly piece of concrete will in any way compensate for the destruction of the landscape and the ruination of our community. There will be no art institutes here. Now, let that be an end to it so we can finish our dinner in peace."

Yes, Jane had definitely scored points with Gwynie. Just the idea of—as Jane had so eloquently put it—a "monstrosity" blotting the landscape would never be accepted by the islanders. That Angelica thought it was a good idea and that she could get it accepted showed just how out of touch with Meredith she was. However, from the look on her face, she didn't look like she was prepared to abandon her fight.

Before the conversation could return to a safe topic, Hannah looked at Gwynie, pointing with her fork. "Are you one of my students?"

Gwynie was startled. At last she said, "Yes, Miss Sutherland."

Hannah continued to stare, but there was no spark of recognition. That was a good thing.

"This is Gwyneth Morgan, Hannah," Jane said. "Surely you remember Gwyneth Morgan." Gwynie really wished Jane had kept quiet.

"You're not Gwynie Morgan. Gwynie Morgan was a pudgy, round-faced little thing, wore her hair in a flip," and she gestured vaguely to the side and back of her own head as if trying to reproduce the image in her mind. "Not very bright. Could never have gone to university." Hannah's eyes were like hard marbles. "Whatever happened to her? Married some man and produced a houseful of children, I suppose."

Jane gasped, and Sophie's hand flew to cover her mouth.

A deep flush spread across Jane's cheeks. "Oh, Lady Charlton, do accept our apology. I don't know what's gotten into her this evening."

But an awkward social situation was the least of Gwynie's problems. Although Hannah hadn't connected her former student with the woman sitting in front of her, she'd remembered Gwynie, what she'd looked like, how she'd performed in school. What else would she remember?

Gwynie folded her napkin and was about to announce she had a migraine starting, when Hannah said, "Someone ought to do something about those boats."

"Yes, Hannah," Jane tried to humour her. "The boats in the harbour. They can be dangerous."

Sophie stood up and tried to take Hannah's arm. "Come along, dear. Let's get you upstairs, and you can tell me all about it. I'll have Simmons bring you a piece of cake up on a tray, and you can have it in bed. There's Victoria sponge. You like sponge."

But as much as Sophie tugged at Hannah's arm, she wouldn't be moved. "That girl—Emma."

Jane shook her head. "Not now, dear."

"She was on a boat, and she drowned."

"Yes, dear. She was on the ferry."

"After."

"After what, Hannah?" Jane's voice betrayed her impatience.

"After the ferry. She was on another boat. And then she drowned."

"Don't be silly, dear. How could you know that?" Sophie had stopped pulling at her. "You spent the whole day at the school preparing for the autumn term. You didn't come home until late. We had to wait dinner for you. Don't you remember?"

"But I saw her," and Hannah turned and looked up at Sophie. Her eyes were focussed now.

"When did you see her?" Angelica asked.

Hannah turned and looked directly at Angelica. "The day she died, of course."

"That's impossible," Jane said, her voice harsh with irritation. "Emma didn't know how to drive a boat. It came out at the inquest."

"Someone else was driving."

"Who?" Angelica asked. "Who was driving?"

What's it to you, Gwynie wanted to say. The Lynley woman was an incomer. This was no business of hers. Why couldn't they just all stop talking about it?

But Hannah wouldn't be silenced. "It was the boat. The boat killed her. We have to do something about those boats." She let Sophie pull her to her feet. She clasped Sophie's hand. "You will speak to someone, won't you? Tell Reverend Thomas. Such young, young things—their whole lives in front of them. It's not right. Tell him so no more young women have to die."

Sophie stared at each face around the table and then came back to Hannah. "Yes, dear."

Hannah allowed herself to be led out of the silent room.

—

Toby sat under the big tree and looked at the grass he'd cut the day before. It was in straight lines just like Miss Jane liked. He dug the last piece of chocolate out of the silver paper, put it in his mouth, and licked his fingers. It was his favourite, the kind with raisins. His grandmother had said he deserved a treat. He liked it when she said that. Miss Simmons had brought his dinner to his cottage where it was keeping warm in the oven. If Miss Simmons knew he was eating chocolate so close to dinner, she'd scold him and tell him he'd spoil his appetite. But he couldn't help himself. And since he was an extra special good boy, his grandmother had given him two chocolate bars this time. The second one was in the cupboard in his bedroom where he kept his secret things. He'd eat it after dinner.

He told his grandmother about Miss Kate and Miss Siobhan getting attacked in the garden. His grandmother had laughed, and he'd told her it wasn't nice to laugh at people when they get hurt. The kids at school used to laugh at him, and he didn't like it. She'd told him he was right, and he was a good boy to care so much. Then his grandmother kissed him on the forehead and told him she loved him. He never knew he had a grandmother before he met her, but he'd always wanted one. Now he was just like everyone else.

—

Quentin Feebling was in the pub listening to Gooley go on about their plans for the next day, not that there was ever much to plan. One day was much the same as the next at their time of life. Fish, drink, fish, drink. It was both a comforting and boring routine. Just once he'd like something interesting to happen, an adventure.

He looked up from his glass to find Fiona Caldicott standing before him. It was the first time she'd been in the Filly since the wake. It was good to see her.

"Would you like a drink, lass?"

She ignored his offer. She stared down at him, a bit of a tremble in her hands. "Quentin, I must speak with you."

Gooley nudged Feebles in the ribs. "You're in there, lad."

"Don't be an arse, Gooley," Feebles snapped.

"Can we go somewhere private?" she asked.

When he didn't respond, she added, "Please. This is important."

Feebles followed Fiona outside and down the harbour road, away from the islanders smoking and drinking outside. Two young women walked passed, giggling into their mobiles.

"What is it, Fi?" Feebles asked.

She was quiet as if waiting until she was sure they wouldn't be overheard. Then she said, "I don't quite know how to say this. I've kept silent for so long. You see, it was none of my business. Still isn't. My Billy always said other people's business is other people's business, and if we all stuck to that, there'd be a lot less grief in the world."

"He were a wise man, your Billy." Feebles stared down at her. Her white hair seemed to glow in the fading light.

"But I know what I heard isn't just other people's business. I think it might be Kate's business as well."

"What are you talking about, lass?" Fiona always did go round the houses before she came out with it.

"It was at the school-end celebration. At the end of the dance, I came upon you and Emma."

Feebles looked down at his feet. He had a terrible feeling he knew what was coming.

"You were talking, talk that sounded very serious, about things that were secret."

"You must be mistaken, lass. It was a long time ago, a very long time ago." He spoke quickly, not wanting to linger too long, hoping that if it was said in a rush, she would accept his words and not find fault.

"I know what I heard, Quentin. I remember the words quite distinctly. Emma said it didn't matter that David had behaved badly, because she was up to something much worse. And you told her to be careful and not to do anything that could come back and hurt her, that would stop her getting into university. But the university was why she was doing it, she said, and the less you knew the better."

Feebles looked out over the dark harbour, lit only by the reflection of a sliver of a moon and the lights from the cottages along the cliffside road. He'd never imagined anyone had overheard their conversation. *Damn, why did it have to be Fiona!*

"What were you telling her about David, and what was Emma doing?" Fiona spoke to his profile.

He kept staring out over the water. He could feel her warm beside him. "I can't remember." It came out as one word.

She took a step back. "Fine, don't tell me. But I want you to seriously think about telling Kate."

He wished he could find the courage to look into Fiona's face, to read her expression. Was she angry at him? Disappointed? He didn't want that. They'd been friends forever, her and her Billy, when he was alive. He didn't want to fall out over this.

"Do you think I should? Tell Kate, I mean?"

"It's your secret, so it's your decision." Her voice was hard. He'd never heard her sound so hurt, and he felt guilty it was because of him.

"But you think it could have something to do with Emma's death?" It was something he'd thought about over and over, wondered if he'd done things differently, Emma might still be alive.

Fiona shrugged. "Only you can decide, since you don't want to share the details."

"Don't be like that, Fi." He placed his hand on hers as it lay on the harbour wall. He was surprised at how soft her little hand was. "We've been friends since we were both nippers."

"But not long enough to trust me, it seems."

He removed his hand. "Don't carry on like that. That's a game young lasses play. You haven't been a young lass for a good long while."

"And you haven't been Emma Galway's beau for a good long while, so you have no obligation to protect her." Fiona paused. "Although I'd hate for anything to come out that would reflect badly on Emma. We both thought the world of her."

Neither of them said anything for a while. Then Fiona broke the silence. "If you decide to tell Kate, go carefully. I don't want her to think badly of her aunt."

"Neither do I."

"So you'll do it?"

"I'll give it some serious thought, if you think it best, Fi."

Fiona rubbed his hand in encouragement. He wished his hands weren't so rough.

"Thank you. My Billy always said you were a good man."

She walked on up the harbour road, leaving Feebles in the dark night, wandering what would happen once Kate learnt the truth.

CHAPTER 18

The next morning, Kate managed to convince Siobhan to go for a walk across the meadow behind the cottage by assuring her she wouldn't run into anyone. Kate took advantage of the peace and quiet to work on her manuscript.

But she couldn't stop thinking of David and Emma at the pub party. Why had David been so insistent she leave the party? Only he could answer that. She telephoned, leaving a message asking to meet, perhaps over a drink, and returned to her editing.

It was while she was struggling with a particularly uninspired description of a Cotswold village that the telephone rang.

"Hi, Mum." It was Alex. It was good to hear her voice.

"How are you feeling?"

Kate could hear Alex's exasperated sigh through the phone. "Mum, I'm totally fine. You don't have to keep asking me. Are you still on the island?"

"Why do you ask?"

"Your one-week deadline is up today."

It couldn't have been a week already. Kate did a quick calculation. Alex was right.

"How's the house clearing going?"

"It's not."

"So does that mean you're thinking of moving to the island?"

"It means I've been so focussed on the investigation I've forgotten everything else. This is the first day I've even done any writing."

"Do you still want the information on those two teachers you wanted me to track down?"

"Do you have something?"

"It appears they're both model citizens with uneventful careers. Alun Probert, the maths and science teacher, is no longer with us. He retired from teaching in 1997, settled in a village in Anglesey, and died four years ago from complications of Parkinson's. He left a wife—his second—two children from his first marriage, and a step-child from the second wife's first marriage. Felicity Lambert retired to one of the Orkney Islands. She married her partner of thirty-eight years in 2014 when same-sex marriage became legal. They have two children. I have addresses for the widow Probert and Felicity, if you're interested."

It was doubtful that Felicity Lambert would be able to provide any insight. After all, as the primary teacher, she had little to no contact with the senior students. The person Kate really wanted to ask was Alun Probert, and he was dead. But she asked for the email addresses anyway.

"Will do. So how's the investigation going?"

"Lots of possibilities. Too many possibilities, in fact. I can't come up with a motive that would drive someone to commit murder unless they were a psychopathic killer."

"Do I detect frustration?"

"Is it that obvious?"

"Look, Mum, why don't you come visit for a couple of days. There's a new Thai place just opened close to my flat. I'm sure they'd hold the fish sauce if we asked them."

Lunch with Alex sounded wonderful. Maybe a shopping trip. Kate would love nothing better than to spend the afternoon with her daughter trying on overpriced clothes and complaining about how nothing looked good on her aging body anymore.

"I want to give it a couple more days. We'll make a date to get together when I get back. Talk to you soon."

Kate managed to get an hour of work done on her novel before David called.

"I got your message," he said. "Why don't we meet for dinner?

The Breeze?"

"Sounds good."

"Great. I'll pick you up at seven."

"What sounds good?" It was Siobhan returning through the back door.

"I'm meeting David. The sabotaged gardening competition, the fight at the school-end celebration, the argument in the pub—none of that is a reason for someone to commit murder. I'm missing something. I need to go deeper into what happened that summer."

Siobhan grinned. "Oh, is that what they're calling it now—in-depth questioning?"

Kate glared at her but said nothing.

Before Siobhan had a chance to fire off another sexual innuendo, there was a loud knock, and three grey and white heads appeared around the front door.

"Anyone home?" Gooley called out.

The Gents stepped into the hallway. Gooley held Siobhan's basil plant in a new pot.

With a large dose of flirtatious arm-twisting, they managed to convince Siobhan that people were more concerned than insulted at her outburst and were anxious to see her return to the pub. Although Kate suspected she was still nervous about facing everyone, Siobhan left arm in arm with Gooley.

—

It had just turned six o'clock when Kate started to get ready for David. Siobhan hadn't returned from the pub which Kate saw as a good sign.

Perhaps it was because David was calling on her or they were meeting for dinner rather than a casual drink, but the whole enterprise had taken on an air of formality, and she felt she had to prepare accordingly. Unfortunately, she'd brought a limited selection of clothing, but then it was only The Sea Breeze. It was a step up from The Filly, but that didn't mean much in a place where people thought nothing of dining in the clothes they'd worn all day on the boats or in their studios. On the other hand, she was going to be in the company of a man who probably hadn't bought anything off the rack for as long as she'd been alive.

She was retouching her lipstick when she heard the purr of David's car. From the bedroom window, she watched him pull up in a 1960s convertible MG, British racing green. This was the car that had figured predominantly in many of her teenage fantasies.

David walked up the front path, both elegant and artistic in charcoal grey pants, red pullover, and a grey print scarf wrapped about his neck. A man who made an effort with his appearance always got Kate's attention. James never got dressed up outside of work. His rationale was that anything resembling a suit represented work, and he refused to be on duty twenty-four hours a day, even though he and Kate both knew he was.

David greeted her with a smile and a bouquet of white tulips. Propping the flowers up in the sink in a few inches of water, she returned to the door with her wrap.

"Hungry?" he asked.

"Ravenous."

"Then you must be feeling better," and he pulled the door shut behind them.

He made a point of reaching the car first so he could open her door. When she'd discovered feminism at university, she'd resented men who opened doors. She interpreted this action as symbolic of their belief that women were happy to trade equality for a few social conventions. But it was clear David's action was one of gentlemanly courtesy rather than condescension. It was hard to believe this was the same man who'd insisted Emma leave the pub all those years ago.

Sinking down into the car's soft leather seats, Kate leaned her head back against the headrest, and stretched her legs out as far as they could go under the dash. Out of the corner of her eye, she saw David look over and smile. The engine revved, and they took off down the road toward the harbour. In her fantasies, the top was always down, her hair was flowing out behind her, and her slender legs held the driver's rapt attention. Oh well, at least the top was down.

They were greeted at the door of the restaurant by owner Gabriel Hopkirk in a stiff white shirt. David was addressed as Mr. Sutherland, and they were escorted to a table by the window, one of Kate's favourites. When she was a little girl, Lilian used to bring her here for tea and cakes, and they always sat where they could watch the boats come and go in the harbour.

The decor had been updated with framed seascapes by what were probably local artists, stems of pink and purple columbine in slender glass vases on the tables, and linen napkins, but it was to Gabriel's credit that the place didn't seem ostentatious. That would have been the kiss of death on the island.

Kate scanned the menu. It was a comfortably eclectic assortment of steaks, chops, things over rice, and an extensive selection of pasta dishes.

David leaned forward, suggesting the fettuccine alfredo. Kate agreed, hoping that the addition of a green side salad might convince her she was doing something healthy for herself. She announced her choices to Gabriel as he hovered at the table.

"Go for the Caesar, Kate. It's excellent," David said.

"I'm a vegetarian. No anchovies, I'm afraid."

"Oh, I'm sorry," he said as if offering his condolences for yet another death.

"You weren't to know."

In spite of his recommendation of the fettuccine, David ordered pasta with clams and the Caesar salad.

"And the wine, Mr. Sutherland?"

"This one, Gabriel," and he pointed to the wine list.

"Of course, sir."

Kate didn't want to launch into an immediate cross-examination, so she let him lead the conversation as they ate their salads. He asked what she'd done since she'd left the island, and as they sipped their wine, she talked about university, her teaching career, and James and Alex. Over their entrees, David told her he'd been married twice, first to Olivia, an assistant at a London art gallery, and then Rachel, a cellist with the London Symphony. David had realized too late that his wives' physical similarity to Emma had been a large part of their attraction.

At last he became quiet, staring at the pool of butter sauce on his plate. Then without looking up he said, "You know this may sound strange to you, but I don't know how many times I've wished I'd never met Emma."

"But you loved Emma."

He took Kate's hand where it lay on the table. "But then she never would have died."

CHAPTER 19

A dark car pulled up on the road opposite the restaurant. The driver dimmed the lights and turned the engine off. David and Kate Galway were sitting together, all cozy with their wine and candle on the table, holding hands for all to see. The damn Galway woman had been on the island less than a fortnight, and David couldn't wait to get his claws into her. Probably sizing her up at the funeral. Randy bastard! He was obviously sleeping his way through the island women. Couldn't he see what a fool he was making of himself? Old goat! Two wives who wouldn't put up with it and a string of women from here to London. Even at his own art openings, he charmed, flattered, ingratiated until he found yet another woman weak enough to succumb to the desire to touch greatness by worshipping the phallus of David Sutherland.

He was an old tomcat that should have been castrated a long time ago.

Yet put a woman in front of him who can truly love him, support him, be a real asset to him—a woman like that he ignores.

So many times you've been warned, David Sutherland, so many times. And we both know what happens when you ignore me.

—

The sound of a car engine momentarily took Kate's attention away from David's disclosure. She pulled her hand from under his and took a sip of water. "Did this have something to do with your arguments with Emma?"

"What arguments?" He sounded impatient, as if he shouldn't have to defend himself. "This is Smee, isn't it? He just can't leave well enough alone. What's he been saying?"

Kate didn't want to escalate things between the two of them. "Several people have told me about disagreements between you and Emma, Hannah and Emma, at the school-end celebration, and other places. There's a film that was taken at a pub party that shows you getting angry because Emma refused to leave with you."

He dismissed her comments with a flick of his hand. "Everyone has disagreements."

But Kate insisted on an answer. "Why did you want to leave?"

"I was probably tired."

"Did you always treat her like that?"

"No!" David was getting angry.

"Then why were you insisting she leave with you?"

His mouth tightened. "Because a gentleman always makes sure his companion gets home safely."

"No, it was more than that."

David covered his face with his hands. "Everyone wanted Emma. And why wouldn't they? The truth is I was afraid that once I left, she'd find herself enjoying someone else's company more than mine."

He slowly lowered his hands. He looked so forlorn. "I was afraid of losing her."

Now she understood. David Sutherland, good-looking, talented, wealthy, one of his generation's most celebrated artists, had been an insecure teenager. She'd never anticipated how difficult it would be for him to talk about this period of his life or his relationship with Emma. She was forcing him to reveal feelings he'd rather have kept hidden. "David, I'm sorry. Perhaps we can leave this for another time."

But his reaction surprised her.

"No. I want to find Emma's killer as much as you do. Ask your questions." He drank the last of his wine.

"I ran into Gwynie Morgan yesterday."

He didn't seem surprised.

"How well did you know her? I got the impression that she was quite taken with you."

"What did she say?"

"Nothing."

He leaned forward. He looked relieved. "I suppose quite a few young women found me appealing. Back then most of the island men made their living as fishermen. If you didn't want to marry someone who smelt of fish, your choices were limited. Based on my lack of fish smell alone, I was a prime catch, if you'll excuse the pun. It didn't hurt that I was about to come into quite a bit of money. So were Gwynie and any other number of island girls interested in me? Possibly. But I was only interested in Emma."

"Can we talk about Hannah?"

He sat back and crossed his arms. "If we must."

"Apparently Hannah believed Emma was responsible for spreading a rumour about her alleged relationship with Alun Probert. A witness overheard Hannah shouting at her about it. Hannah was also worried about Emma's relationship with you, something she repeated to me when she confronted Siobhan and me in the garden. She told you to break off your relationship and was angry you were still seeing each other. She was afraid Emma was planning to get pregnant so you'd be forced to marry her, something that would ruin your life. She said she'd see to it that it didn't happen."

"Marrying Emma wouldn't have ruined my life. Hannah did tell me to break off our relationship, but Emma and I decided we were adults and could do what we wanted."

David tipped the wine bottle over his glass. It was empty. He ordered a double brandy.

"Hannah was always possessive of me, jealous of my relationships with women, all women. It got to the point where I couldn't even bring my wives to the island. Oh, Hannah put on a show of being polite and gracious, but behind their backs she was a vicious cow. She was convinced Olivia had married me to further her own career in the art community, and Rachel was too focussed on her music to be the supportive wife I needed. It was as if she was jealous of them, of their importance in my life."

Like an overbearing mother, Kate thought.

David's brandy arrived, and he drank half of it before continuing. "Then one night, it all came to a head. We'd had an argument that had started at dinner—over something trivial. They always started that way. But there was really only one argument, one argument that replayed every time we were together and had been going on since before I went to France—Hannah knew what was best for me. But this time, she was ranting. I don't know why—perhaps she'd been drinking—but something set her off, and she started in on Emma. Emma would have held me back. Emma would have dragged me down. That was the phrase she used, and once she got started, there was no stopping her. In the end, she said it was probably a good thing Emma had died. And that was it. I couldn't take any more. I walked out and never went back." He waved his hand as if dismissing Hannah from his life once again.

"I'm sorry that happened," Kate said.

"Since that conversation, I can't rid myself of the suspicion that Hannah could have played some role in Emma's death."

"What makes you think that?"

David looked away as if suddenly ashamed of having spoken, that by saying it aloud, he'd given it more weight than it deserved.

"There was no reason for Hannah to kill Emma," Kate tried to reassure him. "All she had to do was to wait a few more weeks and you'd be living in different countries. So maybe it wasn't about your relationship. Maybe someone was jealous of her going to university. Maybe it was simply a random act of violence."

David sat in silence, cradling his empty brandy glass. If they sat here any longer, he'd order another.

Kate took the glass from his hand. "Let's get you home."

David dropped two twenty-pound notes on the table and told Gabriel to put the meal on his tab.

Kate offered to drive, but David insisted. He was more melancholy than drunk. All the same, he drove slowly, while Kate kept a sharp eye out for wandering animals.

Bright lights were reflected in the wing mirror of the MG. There were so few cars on the island, it was unusual to come across another on the road, and this one was coming up fast. Kate strained to recognize it. It looked black or dark blue.

"Someone's in a hurry," she observed.

But David didn't respond. No doubt, his mind was elsewhere.

Kate felt it was best he to go right home, but he insisted on walking her to the door. There was an uncomfortable pause as she wondered what to say. "David, I'm sorry if our conversation brought up painful memories."

He pulled her against him, his breath brushing her ear, her neck. For a brief instant, she was afraid he might try to kiss her, and she'd have to push him away. But he just held her, and then without a word pulled back, looked into her eyes for a moment, and turned and walked down the path. Kate stood at the door and watched as he got into the car, started the engine, and drove away. A minute later the same dark car passed the house, following David in the direction of the harbour.

Siobhan was curled up on the sofa. In her grey fleece jogging pants rolled to mid-calf and a white tank top, she looked like a teenager come for a sleepover.

"So how did your date go?"

"It wasn't a date. It was only dinner." Kate saw Siobhan's teasing grin. She folded her wrap and dropped it on an armchair.

"The flowers were a nice touch," Siobhan said. David's tulips were arranged in a glass vase on the small table beside the sofa.

"I'm going to bed," Kate said. "Are you staying?"

"If it's okay." Siobhan held out her hand, and her voice softened. "You do look really awful. What did he say?"

Kate balanced herself on the arm of the sofa. "It seems he agrees with you. He suspects Hannah might have killed Emma."

"Seriously?"

Kate gave Siobhan a summary of their conversation. "But I still don't believe it was Hannah."

"Or David?"

"Or David."

"Good."

"I'm definitely going to bed this time."

"Try not to think about it."

"If only I could." She left Siobhan to her black and white film with weepy violins.

—

The driver of the dark car watched David sway as he emerged from the MG and walked into his house. The lights were switched on and off first in the living room, then in his bedroom. Well, well, well... so he'd struck out with the Galway woman. Good for her. Brushed him off with a quick hug, the kind of thing you'd give an old uncle.

But he wasn't an old uncle, smelling of stale cigarettes and sweat. He was David Sutherland with the lingering aroma of shaving cream, fresh cotton shirts, and pipe tobacco. Kate Galway wouldn't be able to resist him for long, and who could blame her. He was a snake that fixed its prey in its hypnotic gaze and then went in for the kill.

He needed to be taught another lesson. The streets were empty. People were either at home or dug in at the pub until last call. There was no better time.

The driver stepped quickly out of the dark car, car keys in hand, and crossed the street to where David's car stood, the engine still warm. The key made a metallic squeal as it began to bite the letters into the green paint.

CHAPTER 20

Unable to sleep, Kate had risen early, made a pot of coffee, and reorganized the material on the boards. Beside the picture of each suspect, she'd written their possible motive and alibi. There was missing information, but she'd tried to fill in the gaps as best she could.

On the second board, she'd attempted to set up a timeline leading up to the murder, but there were more empty spaces than dates and times.

"Any closer to figuring it out?" Siobhan asked, dropping her toast crumbs on the carpet.

"No." Kate took a sip of her coffee. "It seems like nobody was getting along that summer, but was it just regular teenage stuff, or was it serious enough to fill for? And what had Emma to do with any of it? Then there are things I've learnt that I know are significant, but I don't know how they fit into the whole picture."

Siobhan seated herself at the table. "Like what?"

"When she died, Emma had the equivalent of £17,000 in an account on the mainland."

Siobhan whistled. Kate wasn't sure if it was an expression of admiration or surprise.

"How does a teenager save that in nine months?" Kate posed it as a rhetorical question. "Try as I might, I haven't been able to come up with a reasonable explanation, and that bothers me."

Siobhan looked hesitantly at her. "Maybe she was blackmailing Hannah about the affair with Probert, and the argument Gooley heard was Hannah saying enough is enough."

"Siobhan, my aunt wasn't blackmailing anyone. Besides, the deposits were all different amounts. If you're going to blackmail someone, you ask for the same amount every time."

Siobhan was scrunching up her face in thought. She finally said, "What if we're looking at this the wrong way? Why kill someone who was leaving anyway?"

"That's the big money question!"

"Why couldn't the murderer wait just a few more weeks for her to go? Why did she need to die at the exact moment she did? What if the motive for the murder was timing?"

Maybe there was something to Siobhan's theory. "You know, that actually makes sense."

"Don't look so surprised. I have my moments." Siobhan looked quite proud of herself. "Hannah was afraid Emma would get pregnant. The longer Emma was with David, the greater the chance he could knock her up."

"But David and Emma weren't having sex."

"Forget about the actual truth. This is about what someone believed was the truth," Siobhan insisted. "Hannah got it into her head that David and Emma were having sex. Even if Emma left and later found out she was pregnant, David would insist on marrying her. From Hannah's point of view, she had to get rid of her as quickly as possible. If she was pregnant, the baby would die with her."

Siobhan stopped and looked at what must have been a disturbed look on Kate's face. "Sorry. I keep forgetting we're talking about your aunt."

Kate stared at the smooth, fresh faces looking back at her from the photographs tacked to the corkboard. Somebody killed Emma, and as much as she didn't want to believe it, it could have been one of these people. *So what was so important that somebody couldn't wait?*

—

David had decided to treat himself to a lie-in with a pot of freshly brewed coffee, one—oh, what the hell—two hot buttered croissants, and a couple of chapters of that thriller sitting on the bedside table. No calls, no emails, just some time with no interruptions to try to forget about his conversation with Kate the prior evening. He wasn't sure if it had been the wine or the company, but he hadn't intended to reveal his suspicions about Hannah. Upon reflection, he wasn't even certain how much he actually believed what last night had seemed to be a very real, albeit dramatic, presumption of Hannah's guilt.

"David!"

God damn it, some blasted idiot was shouting and hammering on his front door. Pulling on his woollen dressing gown, David walked down the stairs.

"David!" Julian was shouting through his front window.

What could be so damn important at half past eight in the morning?

He slipped the door off the latch. "Yes, Julian," he said impatiently as he ran both hands through his hair. Then as casually as possible, he pressed his hand against his mouth to wipe away any drool. He was always careful not to look too dishevelled. On more than one occasion an unflattering photograph had found its way into a newspaper or magazine.

"Sorry to disturb you, but have you seen your car?"

David looked over Julian's shoulder at his beloved MG, still sitting on the road. "Yes, there it is." Surely Julian wasn't here to complain about him leaving it on the road. That wasn't Julian's style. David had a parking spot around the back, but he'd been too tired last night. Besides what could happen to it on the island?

But Julian took his arm and led him around to the opposite side of the car.

Scratched into the paint was the word BASTARD.

A cold wave passed over David, and he lowered his head, running his hands over his eyes in an attempt to blank it out. "No, not again."

And if things couldn't get any worse, he looked up to find Kate beside him, her eyes wide with surprise. "Oh God, David. Who did that?"

"An art critic!" he barked at her. He'd recovered from the initial shock, and unfortunately anger was now taking over.

She ignored his bad temper. "David, this is serious."

"I thought this nonsense was over."

"It's happened before?" Julian asked.

Since it had been a while, David had come to believe, perhaps somewhat naively, that it had stopped. "That and more. In London, on and off for years. The same word—it looks like the same writing. It's why I moved the car onto the island. It was costing me a fortune in paint jobs, and as you can imagine, my wives found it quite disturbing."

He felt small in his bulky dressing gown. In spite of his furtive attempts at grooming, his hair was probably still untidy, and he was in need of a shave. His white stubble made him look like an old man, and here was Kate studying him with tender concern.

David felt unattractive and vulnerable. He just wanted everyone to go away and leave him alone.

"It must have happened after you came home from the restaurant. Remember the dark car that was following us? We should be able to figure out who it is."

"Just leave it, Kate." He'd meant it to be a request, but in his frustration, it sounded as if he was telling her to mind her own business.

He turned and walked back toward his front door.

"Where are you going?" Kate called after him.

"Back to bed," and he slammed the door behind him.

—

The rocking of Smee's boat usually lulled Feebles to sleep, as it seemed to have done to Gooley and Smee. They sat on opposite sides of the boat, their fishing lines disappearing into the water, staring at the shimmering surface without a word. But for Feebles, today the sea was a mirror for his worry and guilt.

He'd always wanted a son to help him with the nets and a wife to laugh with and warm the long cold winter nights when the wind blew across the island. He'd hoped it would've been Emma. Feebles and Emma had stepped out for three and a half months, and even though Emma had always said she didn't want anything serious because she'd be leaving the island once she wrote her A-levels, he'd hoped in time she'd change her mind. But deep down he'd always known she was too beautiful, too smart to be satisfied with him.

Then she told him she'd be keeping company with David Sutherland. Not only couldn't Feebles compete with Sutherland's money, but while Feebles wasn't standing at the very back of the line when they were handing out looks, he clearly hadn't been as close to the front as Sutherland.

He blamed Sutherland for taking Emma from him, and that's why Feebles had told her what he had, what he shouldn't have. He'd only ever wanted to show her how easily Sutherland had betrayed her trust. Part of Feebles had hoped she'd see how loyal he was and consider coming back to him.

But he'd seen a side of Emma that frightened and worried him, and he'd told her so. That was the conversation Fiona had stumbled upon.

He should have talked Emma out of whatever dangerous thing she was involved in. But he hadn't. What had happened to her was his fault. He had to do something to redeem himself. He had to tell Kate what he knew.

—

Over mid-morning coffee, Siobhan announced she felt well enough to do some work in her studio. When Kate reminded her there was a spare room in the cottage anytime she wanted it, Siobhan agreed perhaps it might be best if she continued to bunk in with Kate if only to keep her friend company while she sorted out what had happened to her aunt. It was obvious Siobhan was putting a brave face on it. Kate casually suggested she report the harassment to the Porth Madryn police, but all Siobhan said was that she'd think about it. It was ridiculous to be afraid in your own home, Kate wanted to add but didn't.

Kate now had the rest of the day to herself. It was the perfect opportunity to do some work on the cottage, but all she could think about was the investigation. Her pursuit of Emma's killer had ground to a halt. She needed a new lead. But where to look? There was a whole attic full of family possessions to comb through. Maybe if she made a start on those, she'd find there was something which could offer up a new insight.

She pulled the foldaway ladder down from the hatch in the ceiling and climbed up. One tug of the chain attached to the overhead light illuminated the attic.

She manoeuvred around a jumble of possessions—old dressers, broken chairs, a child's dollhouse—no doubt stockpiled by several generations in the belief they could be fixed, reused, or simply dealt with later. The room had a musty paper smell, punctuated with the sharp and almost medicinal tang of mothballs. At some point, the whole attic was going to have to be cleared before she could put the house on the market.

She'd come to Meredith convinced that selling was the right thing to do, but being back here, surrounded by familiar things, sleeping in her old room, she wondered if she could bear to be parted from it all. There was a memory attached to each piece of furniture, each photograph on the mantelpiece. This house had been the home of four generations of Galways. It was her childhood home, and in a way, it was Alex's childhood home as well. She felt she was betraying the family just thinking about selling.

If she came for a visit, she'd have to rent a room in the pub like a tourist. Winifred would probably let her stay next door, but that would be even worse. To see strangers coming in and out of Lilian's front door, making changes to the garden, putting up new curtains—that would be too painful.

Six boxes with Emma's name printed in capital letters in blue pen made a neat pyramid under the sloping roof. Kate pulled the top box down and sat on the dusty floor with it.

Everything was tumbled together, like someone had simply

dumped the contents of a drawer into the box. It contained the minutiae of Emma's life—exercise books, birthday cards, even postcards from friends who'd vacationed in such exotic places as the Lake District and Bath. The senders each expressed the idea that these places, so full of history, would have appealed to their friend Emma. Kate's love of the past was just one of many similarities between her and her aunt.

There was layer upon layer of papers, mostly school reports and essays and notes. Here was a letter, still in the original envelope bearing the name Cambridge University and addressed to Miss Emma C. Galway. The envelope had been roughly torn, as if someone had been in a hurry for the news inside. It was her acceptance to Cambridge.

Stuffed between the pages of a notebook were sketches, black pen on pages torn from lined exercise books, sketches so expertly executed they could only have been the work of a young David Sutherland—peacocks and seascapes, disembodied hands and feet, possibly done in class when he was bored with his lessons. While executed with skill, they looked hurried and unpolished.

Hidden under all the papers was a small box, possibly silver or silver-plated, the top and sides engraved with an elegant scrolling. The bottom was stamped with the lion hallmark, so definitely silver. A snuffbox perhaps? No, inside was an intricately pierced gilded grill. It was a vinaigrette, a small box which had held a piece of sponge or gauze soaked in vinegar or perfume. Essential for the late eighteenth and nineteenth century upper classes, it was wafted under the nose to keep at bay the odour of the stinking masses and the cities' open sewers or to revive women on the verge of swooning.

Several characters in Kate's books had owned and used them. Kate had only ever seen them in museums or in photographs, so it was a treat to actually hold one. She ran it under her nose, hoping to smell the piercing, acid odour of vinegar or the floral musk of perfume, but the pungency had long faded. There was only a faint whiff of silver polish.

It had certainly not belonged to the Galways. Kate had never seen this anywhere in the cottage, and it was too valuable an item to be thrown into a box and forgotten. So how had it come into Emma's possession?

Damn, it was the phone again. She just wanted to be left alone. By the time she made it to the living room, the ringing had stopped. Kate hit the message playback button.

"I know you're there, Kate. Pick up. Please pick up." It was Siobhan. "You need to come to the pub right away." Kate could hear the frantic excitement in her voice.

While the thought of spending the rest of the afternoon in the pub was certainly appealing, she really needed to get on with her work.

"Trust me. It's important." There was a pleading tone in Siobhan's voice. "We might have new evidence about Emma's murder. And she won't talk to anyone but you."

What new evidence? Who was she talking about?

"Come now."

Kate brushed the dust from her pants, grabbed her purse, and closed the door behind her.

CHAPTER 21

The Gents and Siobhan were crowded around their usual table with Oonagh Simmons, of all people. Siobhan was waving at Kate, not that there was a chance she was going to miss them. She wanted a slimline bitter lemon to clear the attic dust from her throat, but Flo was being harassed by an agitated Angelica Lynley, impeccable dressed in an uncreased white linen suit.

Kate made a point never to wear linen. Five minutes after putting it on, it always looked like she'd slept in it, let it sit in the bottom of the laundry basket for a week, and then put it back on. The trick with linen was not to move in it. Now that Kate looked closely, Angelica did look like she had a pole rammed up her—well, her spine. Kate decided to give the bitter lemon a miss. Flo obviously had her hands full.

"Kate, you know Oonagh Simmons," Siobhan said when Kate reached their table.

Only a few years younger than Kate, Oonagh had the potential to be attractive, but it was as if she did everything she could to appear dowdy. Her salt and pepper hair was coiled in a tight bun at the back of her neck, and her dark high-collared uniform made her look severe, and not unlike Mrs. Danvers in *Rebecca*. Oonagh would definitely not look out of place in Manderley.

Kate extended her hand. "How are you, Oonagh?" It was tradition to call servants by their last name, and the sisters were sticklers for tradition. But Kate couldn't bring herself to call her Simmons.

"Fine, Miss Kate." Oonagh had lived at Sutherland Hall since she'd left school, and it seemed the many years of being treated as if everyone was her better had left its mark. She obviously felt more comfortable treating Kate with the formality with which she treated the sisters.

"She has information," Siobhan said.

From the look on Oonagh's face and her hesitation, Kate could only assume she felt guilty being here, as if she was betraying a confidence. After all, there was a bond of trust between servant and mistress, and to have served the sisters for so long, she must really care about them, although it must be a struggle in the case of Jane.

At last Oonagh spoke. "I'm supposed to be picking up the mail and the church newsletter for Miss Jane, and here I am gossiping in a public house."

She looked straight at Kate with a determined look. "But you know me, Miss Kate. I'm a God-fearing woman who believes in justice. If there's a killer on this island, well, it's just not right he gets away with the murder of a young woman who, as far as I can tell, never did no harm to anyone."

She paused before continuing. "There was a dinner party two nights ago, and Miss Jane and Miss Sophie decided Miss Hannah was well enough to eat with the guests."

"Who else was there?" Kate asked.

"Lady Charlton and Miss Lynley. Much of what little I heard seemed to be about what Lady Charlton had been up to since she left the island. Suddenly Miss Hannah starts talking about the boats in the harbour, saying as how someone should do something about them." She was silent again as if gathering her resolve.

"Go on." Siobhan pushed a glass of sherry toward her, but Oonagh declined to drink. No doubt she feared returning to the sisters with liquor on her breath.

"Anyway," she continued, "when she was asked why she was worried about the boats, Miss Hannah said they were dangerous, and people could get hurt. She also said she'd seen Miss Emma on a boat the day she died, after she got off the ferry. And since Miss Jane said Miss Emma didn't know how to drive a boat, then there must have been someone on board with her."

"There was nothing in the newspapers about this. It wasn't brought up at the coroner's inquest, was it?" Kate looked at the Gents. "Were any of you at the inquest?"

"We all were," Smee said. "But we were told the last person to see her alive was some tourist."

Kate turned back to Oonagh. "Did the sisters say why Hannah didn't say anything at the time?"

Oonagh looked longingly at the sherry but continued to resist. "That's the other thing. When Miss Hannah said she'd seen Miss Emma, Miss Sophie told her she couldn't have because she was at the school all day and didn't get home until late."

She paused. "I don't like to say anything against Miss Sophie or Miss Jane, but I'm not sure Miss Sophie told the truth. It was the way she said it. It didn't sound natural. It was like she was trying to convince herself it was the truth, if that makes any sense."

It made perfect sense to Kate.

"I think she was trying to protect Miss Hannah."

Everyone at the table was uncharacteristically quiet, as if considering what Sophie could be hiding. They waited for Kate to speak first.

"I know how difficult it must have been for you to tell us," she said at last.

A painful look passed over Oonagh's face. "I feel very uneasy about this. Miss Sophie's very good to me, and Miss Jane is a Christian woman. It was a conversation I shouldn't have heard—and surely shouldn't be repeating. But there you are."

Kate smiled and put her hand on Oonagh's. "Thank you."

She broke down and took a sip of sherry.

—

Angelica watched the six of them at the table, their heads close together. What was Simmons up to? Something she shouldn't, no doubt. Angelica had experienced nothing but trouble with domestic help in her London townhouse. What they didn't steal, they broke. It was definitely true that you couldn't get good staff these days.

Speaking of staff, here was that tarted-up landlady telling her she couldn't see Gwynie Charlton. Angelica could understand Gwynie had left instructions she was not to be disturbed, but that surely didn't apply to her. After all, they'd dined together only two days earlier. Angelica stared at Flo's teased hair and black eyeliner. This woman was desperately in need of a makeover. If Flo would only put herself in Angelica's hands, with a bit of work she might even begin to look somewhat attractive. How she ended up married to that dishy priest looking like she did was anyone's guess.

As Simmons walked toward the door, Angelica raised her glass in her direction, and Simmons acknowledged her with a small bob of her head. Oh yes, Angelica decided, she'd definitely been speaking out of turn.

Angelica wanted to invite Gwynie to go for a sail on her yacht. She didn't really care for the woman, but then this wasn't a social engagement. Once she'd got her alone, she'd reveal the artist's sketches for the art institute. Gwynie couldn't help but be impressed by its shining glass and concrete exterior. Besides, Gwynie had fancied David, so surely she'd want to do what she could to honour an old flame.

Once the wife of Sir Hugh Charlton got behind the project, it would be the endorsement Angelica needed to convince other investors—eager to upgrade their public image by being seen to be supporting the arts—to make substantial contributions. It would be, as the Americans were so fond of saying, a done deal.

Flo was wiping down the bar with a damp dishcloth, coming perilously close to Angelica's elbow. If the stupid woman stained her jacket, Angelica would see that she bloody well paid for it.

"Miss Lynley," Flo said. "Wouldn't you be more comfortable sitting down?"

The blasted woman was trying to get rid of her. "I'm quite comfortable here. Besides, I want to be able to see if Lady Charlton comes down. And it's Mrs. Lynley, if you don't mind."

Flo slapped the wet dishcloth on the bar. "Perhaps you'd find it a bit more in keeping with your position within the community, Mrs. Lynley, to sit discreetly at a table rather than to display yourself by propping up the bar."

Angelica's head jerked around, and she stared hard at Flo. Angelica wanted to say something biting to put her in her place, but she wasn't going to give the woman the satisfaction of watching her lose her temper. This trollop of a barmaid might not be a lady, but that didn't mean Angelica had to stoop to her level. She calmly placed her martini glass on the bar, took her gold pen from her Louie Vuitton bag, and tore a piece of paper from her notepad. She would leave Gwynie a note.

—

After Oonagh had left, Siobhan sat back and crossed her arms. "So what do we think?"

Smee tapped his finger on the table. "My bet's on that Hannah Sutherland murdering our poor Emma."

"Then why would she draw attention to herself by saying she saw something?" Kate asked.

"I want to know why Sophie lied about where Hannah was," said Feebles.

"That's if she really did lie," Kate added. They only had Oonagh's suspicion Sophie wasn't telling the truth. But then if anyone had an insight into the sisters, it was Oonagh.

"That Hannah Sutherland's a few fish short of a full catch these days," Gooley said. "Maybe she did the murder, then cooked up a story to protect herself. And now she's all muddled up."

"No, I don't believe that," Kate said with conviction. "I know you're all convinced Hannah is our prime suspect, but let's be honest. It's mostly because you don't like her."

She made eye contact with each of them.

All but Feebles looked away embarrassed. "And maybe the opposite is true with you, Kate. You've always said Hannah Sutherland was the reason you became a teacher. Maybe you don't want to believe she could have hurt Emma."

While Kate had said that on more than one occasion, she didn't like it being thrown back in her face. But damn it, they had a point. "All right, I'll agree Sophie was giving Hannah an alibi for the day Emma disappeared. But what she was covering up could be something quite innocent. We have no evidence that Hannah did anything wrong. We have no evidence that anyone did anything wrong."

"There's always David Sutherland." Smee was replaying an old record.

Kate was losing patience. "Again, because you don't like him..." she said directly to Smee.

"What next?" Feebles asked.

Kate searched in her bag for her mobile and dialed the number for Sutherland Hall. "If what Oonagh heard is right, Hannah could have seen the murderer. I just hope she can remember who it was."

The telephone was picked up on the fifth ring. Obviously, the sisters weren't used to answering their own phone. "Sutherland Hall, Miss Sophie Sutherland speaking."

"Miss Sutherland, it's Kate Galway."

"Oh, my dear, are you feeling any better?" Sophie sounded genuinely concerned.

"I'm on the mend, Miss Sutherland, thank you."

"What a terrible thing to have happened. I would never forgive myself if any permanent damage had been done to you or Miss Fitzgerald."

"Don't worry yourself. Miss Sutherland, would it be possible to come up and speak with Miss Hannah? As Emma's teacher, I thought perhaps she could shed some light on something we may have overlooked."

Sophie hesitated. Kate wondered if she was trying to come up with an excuse to deny her request. "Nothing pleases Hannah more than to talk about her students. But as you know my sister has good and bad days. When she's feeling up to it, I'll give you a call. Is that all right?"

"That will be fine, Miss Sutherland. Thank you." Kate hung up and slipped the phone back into her bag.

But she suspected the conversation would probably never happen. From what Oonagh had just told them, the Sutherlands couldn't take the chance.

CHAPTER 22

Before Siobhan left for her studio the next morning, she'd finished off the last of the bread, cereal, and milk, so Kate nipped out to Craggy's for a quick shop. As she walked toward the harbour, a gull swooped over the beach, keeping a watchful eye out for discarded chips and sandwiches. She strongly suspected this bird had eaten better than she had that morning.

After her conversation with Oonagh, Kate was convinced Hannah knew the identity of Emma's murderer. What would happen if she showed up at Sutherland Hall asking to see her? Jane didn't seem like she was especially receptive to people dropping by. No doubt Kate would be promptly dismissed with some fabricated excuse as to why Hannah wasn't available to speak with her.

"Kate, hold up." Quentin Feebling was coming up behind her. He sounded out of breath. "I wondered if I might have a word."

He looked uncharacteristically anxious.

"Of course."

"Perhaps somewhere a bit more private," and he indicated the path that led down to the beach where a handful of elderly day trippers were wandering close to the water's edge.

Once they were down on the sand, Kate waited for him to speak. Instead he played with the change in the pockets of his green waxed coat.

"What is it, Quentin?" she finally asked.

He cleared his throat several times before he spoke. "Would you want to know something about Emma, even if it wasn't very nice?"

Kate's stomach started to tighten. Did she really want to hear this? "It's not the nice things that get you killed, is it?" she finally said.

Feebles was silent.

She turned to face him. "What do you want to tell me?"

He cleared his throat yet again. "Not want. Should."

They started walking, making well-defined tracks in the wet sand below the tide line.

"Emma might have been involved in something illegal."

"No, I don't believe you."

"I'm afraid it's true. Trouble is, I don't know what, exactly."

"So what do you know?"

He dug his hands even deeper into his pockets. "I was jealous, jealous of her and Sutherland. I wanted to make her angry, so she'd finish with him. When I told her what Sutherland had done, she spouted off what sounded like poetry, something like 'a man kills what he loves.'"

Yet each man kills the thing he loves. Kate wanted to tell him it was Oscar Wilde, but she doubted he would know or care who Wilde was.

"What had David done, and what had this to do with Emma doing something illegal?" She wished he'd get to the point.

"I'm getting there." He paused. He obviously wanted to do this his own way. "After I told her about Sutherland, she laughed. I thought at first, she was hysterical-like, but then I realized she thought what I told her was funny. She called me a good friend and said what David got up to didn't concern her, and he wasn't the only one who was acting badly. I asked what she meant, but she said the less I knew the better. No point both of us getting into trouble if it all went wrong. I told her she wasn't to risk getting not into that fancy university of hers. But she said she had no choice and that university was why she had to do it."

"But what did David do?"

"I can't tell you. It involves another person, and that person's still alive."

Kate didn't need him to spell it out for her. If what Smee had told her was true, it didn't take much to imagine what David's indiscretion had been. "Is she still on the island?"

He was silent.

"You have a frustratingly keen sense of morality, Quentin."

"That's not true. I should have stopped Emma. If I had, she might still be alive."

"Why does everyone keep telling me that."

She wanted to hug him to make them both feel better. but he looked like he'd pull away, that he wasn't deserving of her compassion.

"I don't completely understand what this is about, but whatever my aunt did, it was her decision," she said, as much for her benefit as his.

From the pained look on his face, Kate could see he didn't believe her. He'd carried this guilt too long to let it go easily.

"Are you sure I can't convince you to tell me who else was involved? Your loyalty could be standing in the way of us punishing Emma's killer."

"Then there'll be two injustices—Emma's murder and her killer's escape. I won't betray someone who can still be hurt. If Emma's killer continues to go free, it'll be on my conscience."

She put her arm through his. "Quentin, I don't believe for a moment that Emma's murder had anything to do with you."

He attempted a weak smile. And while he didn't look like he felt any better, she doubted he could feel any worse.

But she had one more thing to ask, a question it seemed no one was prepared to answer. "Quentin, why does Joseph hate the Sutherlands so much?"

"I shouldn't say."

"It could be important."

"Smee never did nothing to our Emma."

"I know that. But he's running around saying David could be responsible for her death. If he has evidence, I need to know. Please."

Feebles stopped and looked down at the sand. Kate could tell this was really hard for him. "He thinks Old Man Sutherland killed his da."

Kate hadn't been expecting that. "What? How?"

"It was just before the school-end celebration. It was a bad season for the fish and like most of us, Smee's da had only enough money to feed his family and no more. Then his boat needed a new engine, but he had no savings. Few fishing families did, especially that year. He were a proud man, Mr. Smee was, but he swallowed his pride for the sake of his family and went to Old Man Sutherland to ask for a loan."

"Why Sutherland?"

"He was the richest man on the island. And Smee's da was hoping he'd see it as helping out a fellow islander."

"I take it he wasn't successful."

Feebles shook his head. "Smee overheard his parents talking about it. Sutherland had told Smee's da not to come around begging, that he wasn't no bank. When Smee's da told him banks don't loan to working men, Sutherland said he had no money for the likes of him as he had to send his boy to art school. Smee's da said, 'And I've got to feed mine.' In the end, he had no choice but to sell the boat."

Poor Mr. Smee. "Then what happened?"

"He took to the drink. It was the feeling he'd let down his son that done him in. All of us look forward to working the boats with our das. And when the time comes, the boats get passed on to the next generation. But that stopped with Smee's da. His brother offered to take on his nephew. Mr. Smee was grateful, but he always saw it as charity."

"I'd heard Mr. Smee had lost his boat, but I never knew the whole story. Joseph inherited his uncle's boat, didn't he?" Kate asked.

"Aye, when his uncle retired. He had three girls, so he was glad that someone in the family wanted to keep on with the fishing. But Smee's da never forgave himself—or the Sutherlands. And Smee's convinced his da died because Sutherland was such a tight bastard.

He's never forgiven any of them."

"The fight between David and Smee at the celebration wasn't about Emma, was it?"

"No, lass."

—

"You were up early," Kate said, following Siobhan into her studio

Siobhan seated herself at her sculptor's table and began to refine the nose of one of her figures. "I'm getting behind in my work."

Kate looked out at the meadow, aware this was where the brick had come flying through the window. "Do you have any idea why someone's trying to drive you away?"

After a minute, Siobhan put down her sculpting tool. "You think it might have something to do with the investigation?"

"I don't know. Tell me everything that happened leading up to it."

"I'd better put the kettle on. Did you bring biscuits?"

Kate rummaged in her carrier bags by the front door and brought a package of chocolate digestives into the kitchen. Siobhan's clay-streaked hands tore open the package.

"What do you want to know?" Siobhan asked.

"Did anything strange happen before that letter appeared on your bed?"

"Nothing," she said through a mouthful of crumbs. "It just came out of the blue."

"Are you sure?"

"Unless you count being badgered by an estate agent wanting to buy the cottage."

"Badgered how?"

"Letters, for months, way over the market value and each one increasing the offer. Do you remember Old Alred? He bought this cottage in the late sixties. When he went to live with his kids on the mainland, he turned it into a summer rental, hoping his children would eventually want to move back. But when he died, they listed it. They wanted a quick sale, and I was prepared to take it as was. It was in rough shape, but it's the only way I could afford it. It took years of hard graft to scrape together the money for the renovations, most of which I ended up doing myself. I'd just finished the studio extension and moved in the new kiln when I got the first letter. I could have taken the money, but I didn't want to move. It's the perfect location. Close enough to the harbour that I can walk to the pub, but not so close people drop by all the time when I'm trying to work. I've got the sea in the front and the meadow in the back. So I told the agency I wasn't interested."

She pushed her hair out of her face and poured out the tea. "But they wouldn't take no for an answer. Two months later an agent shows up at my door telling me to name my own price. The letters all say the agency is acting on behalf of a numbered corporation, and that really ticked me off." She jerked open the drawer and clanged the cutlery about until she found a spoon. "I was afraid some development company wanted to buy up all the cottages and turn the island into some sleazy tourist trap full of caravan parks and fast food restaurants."

"Has anyone else had one of these offers?" Kate asked.

"Not that I know of."

"So why you?"

"No idea." Siobhan took a deep breath. "Last week I'd finally had enough and sent an email telling them to back off or I was going to report them to the police. The next day someone left a note in the middle of my bed."

"What exactly did it say?"

Siobhan pulled the letters out of the kitchen drawer and handed them to Kate. "Something about me being a whore. The second one was wrapped around the brick."

With their mismatched letters, the notes would have been comical if they hadn't frightened Siobhan so much.

"You know, when I was growing up, nothing ever happened here," Kate said. "If you'd asked most islanders about their worst experience during the past ten years, most of them would say it was when the pub ran out of their favourite ale, and they had to drink something else for a couple of nights. Now something strange is happening almost every day. It's too much to write this all off as coincidence. I mean, I've been here less than two weeks and Alex has been poisoned, we've been physically attacked, someone has tried to drive you from your home, and David's car has been vandalized."

Siobhan looked puzzled. "But they've been after me to sell my place for almost a year. The notes, the brick—is this because I threatened them with the police? I doubt the police would have done anything, even if I had reported it."

"But maybe they finally realized you've no intention of selling, and they're trying to frighten you out."

Siobhan looked startled, and then angry. She picked the last agent's letter out of the bin. "I'm going to give these buggers a piece of my mind."

"Wait a minute. Alex has ways and means. It'll be faster to let her dig about. Before things escalate any further, let's see if we can find out why they're so desperate for this place." Kate took the letter from her and slid it into her purse.

"So this can't be a coincidence?"

"According to James, the official police line is there are no coincidences."

Their conversation was interrupted by Siobhan's phone.

Kate walked into the studio to give her some privacy. With the sun was streaming in through the windows, she couldn't imagine anything terrible happening here, but in the short time since the funeral, the island had become dangerous, and it was enough to make her wonder if she was somehow responsible.

"That was Winifred." Siobhan was standing in the doorway. For a moment, she didn't speak. "It's Hannah."

"What about her?"

"She's dead."

CHAPTER 23

It wasn't until David saw Dr. Marcus's blue Volvo parked in front of Sutherland Hall that the reality of Hannah's death hit him. He began to weep.

Hannah had been in his life since he was seven. She'd been the closest thing he'd had to a mother. At first being part of the Sutherland family seemed too good to be true, especially once he realized what he'd been missing all his life. But they'd loved him, even Hannah in her own way. She truly believed he could do anything he put his mind to—and she made him believe it too. If she hadn't, he might not have pursued his art with such determination, might not have fought so hard to become successful. Both driven by stubbornness, he and Hannah were more alike than either of them would ever admit. But while his tenacity had served to advance his career, it had also kept them apart for much of their lives.

His unfounded suspicion about Hannah's part in Emma's death had come from a place of resentment, a feeling that should have been abandoned a long time ago. After his discussion with Kate, he'd decided to ask Hannah's forgiveness so they could share what little time they had before her mind was lost to him forever.

But it was too late. They'd both run out of time.

Grabbing a tissue from his pocket, he dabbed at his eyes and blew his nose.

Simmons opened the large oak door and waited for him to step inside. "Mr. David, such a terrible thing. Come in, sir. They're in the drawing room."

He wiped away the last tears as Sophie rushed toward him. "Oh, David, what will we do without her? What will we do?"

"It's all right. I'm here," and he put an arm around Sophie.

Jane sat on the sofa with her head bent, murmuring quietly to herself in prayer. Sophie inclined her head against David's chest.

Marcus came into the room, pulling his stethoscope from about his neck. "Her heart just stopped. It was very peaceful."

David hugged Sophie. "You see? She just drifted away."

"She's with God now," Jane whispered.

"Yes, she is."

Sophie looked up at Marcus. "I checked on her earlier, but I thought she was sleeping. I should have tried to wake her up, shouldn't I? If I'd tried to wake her up, she'd still be alive."

"You musn't think that way," and David held her tighter.

"It wasn't your fault, Miss Sutherland. She died sometime during the night," Marcus tried to reassure her. "Her heart was just too tired to go on."

A blessing, thought David, *given her mental condition.*

He probably wasn't the only one to have this thought.

Sophie sniffled. "She was the best of us, wasn't she, David?"

"Yes, dear. The best."

—

Siobhan put the truck into gear and honked at a peahen to get off the road.

"Why are we going up to Sutherland Hall?" Kate asked.

"To offer our condolences. And to snoop around. Don't you think the timing of Hannah's death is highly suspicious?"

"She was over eighty and not in the best of health. She could have gone at any time."

"Stop being so bloody logical." Siobhan stepped on the gas, and the truck surged forward. "You're the one who just gave me the big lecture on coincidences, so add this to the list. It's a bugger of a coincidence that the one person who might have known the identity of Emma's killer has just died."

—

Having been away from Sutherland Hall for decades, David was reflecting on how strange it was that he was here for the second time in a week. It was both comforting and disturbing to find nothing in this room had changed—the oversized armchairs stuffed with horsehair, pie crust side tables with long-leafed plants, ancient antimacassars placed over the backs of chairs and the sofa, even though there was no use for them in a house of women. He felt as if he was in a museum—no, a mausoleum.

His sketches and paintings, and bits and pieces of china he'd given his sisters as Christmas and birthday presents still took pride of place in the room. The squat English bulldog and a pair of matching brown horses, and then there was the antique Moorcroft vase he'd bought with some of the proceeds from his first major sale. Hannah had kept everything. But the homey familiarity of the room was overshadowed by the ghosts of arguments with Hannah, arguments that were never resolved, that had served to separate them for almost twenty-five years.

His thoughts were interrupted as Marcus entered the room followed by Jane and Sophie attired in black. The sisters settled themselves on the sofa.

The large brass knocker fell twice, echoing through the front hall.

"Miss Galway and Miss Fitzgerald," announced Simmons a moment later.

Kate entered first and gave David a sympathetic look. She'd obviously forgiven him his angry outburst yesterday. Siobhan followed, her red hair wild and curly. He thought with some irony that she reminded him of a banshee, a herald of death, although her powers of prophecy had failed miserably today.

Kate extended her hand toward the sisters. "Miss Sutherland

and Miss Sutherland, please accept our condolences for your loss."

Jane clasped her hand, more for the sake of good manners, David thought. "Thank you, Miss Hewitt, Miss Fitzgerald. But I'm afraid we're a house in mourning and are not receiving visitors today."

Jane looked up at the sound of Simmons shuffling into the room. Simmons stood quietly with an envelope in her hand, an envelope David instantly recognized as Hannah's pale apricot stationery.

"Yes, Simmons?" Jane said.

"Sorry to disturb you, ma'am." She fingered the envelope nervously and then held it out toward David. "I was in Miss Hannah's room, laying her out, and I found this on the floor beside her bed."

Jane stood and held out her hand. "Well, give it to me," she said as Sophie muffled a sob.

Simmons hesitated. "Pardon, Miss, but it's addressed to Mr. David."

David was genuinely stunned. He thought he'd be the last person Hannah would have wished to communicate with. "Me?"

"Yes, sir," and Simmons stepped forward with the envelope and the pewter letter opener from the library.

David hesitated. His name was printed on the envelope. *Please don't let her last words be unkind.*

"Well, open it, David," Jane said.

He slit the envelope, acutely aware everyone was watching and waiting. Inside was Hannah's familiar handwriting, just as strong as he remembered:

Please understand what I have done has been for you, and I will never stop loving you, my angel. And when you remember me, think of one who loved not wisely, but too well—and forgive me, my dearest and best love.

Hannah

"What does it say, David?" Sophie pressed him.

"It's nothing, dears." He folded it up and put it in his jacket pocket. "Just some of Hannah's ramblings. Let's try to remember her as she was before the illness."

Siobhan stepped up to David and whispered in his ear. "What does it really say?"

David excused himself, inviting Kate, Siobhan, and Marcus to join him outside for a breath of fresh air. Standing on the front drive, he gazed over the green lawn and handed Siobhan the note. She read it aloud while he stuffed tobacco into his pipe.

"What does she mean 'what I have done has been for you'?" Siobhan asked. "Does this have anything to do with Emma?"

David looked at Kate, but she was staring at the note. Using a tissue from her pocket, she carefully took it from Siobhan. She pointed to the top edge. "Look at this. It's torn, different from the others. This paper originally had four deckle edges, you know, that feathery effect. And this page is smaller than standard notepaper. Someone tore the top off a larger page to remove whatever was written there. Also the letter is written in fountain pen while David's name is printed on the envelope in ballpoint. I'm no handwriting expert, but these appear to have been written by two different people. Someone placed this beside Hannah's bed to make us believe she committed suicide."

"Miss Galway, aren't you letting your imagination run away with you?" Marcus asked.

"I was married to a detective for twenty years and my daughter is a barrister. If I've learnt anything from them, it's that it's people without imagination who are susceptible to being tricked. This is a suspicious death, Dr. Marcus. We must inform the police."

David wondered if it was Kate's obsession with Emma's murder that made her suspect foul play. "You're saying Hannah was murdered."

"Almost certainly."

But Hannah never left the house, David wanted to say. *Who'd want to murder her?* Even during their worst arguments when he wanted to be rid of her once and for all, he could never see himself taking her life. "But why?"

"Because she saw Emma's murderer."

CHAPTER 24

The early morning ferry was disgorging its passengers from Porth Madryn. It had been less than twenty-four hours since Hannah Sutherland had been found dead. The news that the police had been called had swept across the island, and a crowd of curious onlookers gathered to watch two men in dark suits step onto the wharf. Kate was encouraged to see they weren't in uniform. That meant the Porth Madryn station was taking the matter seriously and had sent detectives. They would spend the rest of the morning questioning the sisters and visiting the scene of the alleged crime. Kate was disappointed that a forensic team hadn't accompanied them, but it was an expense they probably weren't prepared to risk until they were convinced it was a homicide.

But Kate didn't need any convincing. Hannah Sutherland had been killed because Kate had dredged up the past. If Hannah's death was even partially her fault, she had a responsibility to stay and help find her killer.

At noon she headed down to the pub with Siobhan in tow, hoping to pick up any gossip about what the police had learnt. The place was packed. Flo moved from table to table, delivering food and attempting to chat about the weather and the state of people's gardens, but the only thing on the islanders' minds was Hannah.

Siobhan was in mid-bite when she put her burger down, wiped cheese sauce from her mouth, and stared. "He looks tasty," she purred, waving a finger at a young man standing at the bar. She wasn't the only one to notice. The women in the room were alternately whispering to each other and brazenly staring.

Kate turned to look. He was quite attractive, and with his angular features, he could have been a model for the cover of a bodice-ripping romance novel. But the more she stared at him, the more Kate felt she knew him from somewhere.

"Siobhan, he's young enough to be your—Byron Finch."

At the sound of his name, the young man looked up, startled, as if he'd been caught doing something he shouldn't. "Miss Galway?"

"You know him?" Siobhan asked as Kate made her way to the bar. "Introduce me."

"Byron, are you a police detective?" Kate asked. She'd always thought he'd end up in a career where he could exploit those natural good looks.

"Miss Galway, are you back on the island?" He looked uncomfortable, as if he didn't quite know what to say to her. Perhaps that was because the only conversations they'd ever had were about essays and test results.

"Just visiting."

Kate could feel the eyes of every woman in the room upon her. Her status on the island was soaring. "How long have you been with the force?"

"Four years. You inspired me. Or rather, the stories of your husband did. I'm attached to the Porth Madryn station, and I let them know I was interested in CID. I'm not really a detective. Still in uniform." He looked down at his suit as if he felt uncomfortable being on the job without the authority a uniform afforded. "But this case is a great opportunity for me to learn firsthand."

"That was a lucky break."

A flicker of a grin passed over Byron's face, and he leaned in close to her. "Let's just say someone's recovering from a recent surgery that makes it hard to sit through an interrogation—actually to sit through anything."

Kate raised her hand to indicate no further details were necessary.

"They asked me if I wanted to accompany Detective Sergeant

Jenkins, and I jumped at it. And before you say anything, I realize I'm mainly here as a dogsbody. But it's still a great opportunity, and I have to start somewhere."

"Where are you staying?"

He pointed to the ceiling, indicating the rooms above the bar.

"Why don't you come over for dinner tonight, and we can catch up." It would be a chance to pump him for information.

Siobhan, who had obviously been listening to the conversation, stepped up beside Kate. "Are we having a guest for dinner?"

Siobhan flashed Byron her best Cheshire cat smile. Kate gave her a disapproving look. It was going to be a long evening.

"We'll let you get back to work," and Kate grabbed Siobhan by the arm and dragged her away. Kate threw some money on the table, Siobhan gathered up the last of her chips, and they headed for the door. As they left the pub, they walked straight into Gwynie Morgan.

Without skipping a beat, Gwynie announced, "Can't stop, Kate. Sorry," and continued walking, dismissing her with a wave.

Kate followed. "You're avoiding me."

"No, I'm not," but she looked like she might break into a run at any moment. Instead she power-walked down the road.

Kate hated being dismissed. It was like when she spent ten minutes explaining to a student why it was important to do their homework, and they'd just shrug, tilt their head, and say, "whatever." Gwynie had just 'whatever'd' Kate, and Kate was not best pleased.

"Obviously hiding something," Siobhan observed.

"But what?"

———

Angelica drew up in front of Sutherland Hall. She looked into the rear-view mirror to check her lipstick and then reached for the bouquet of lilies resting on the passenger seat. Easing herself out of the car, she smoothed her black silk dress and repositioned the long white scarf so that it cascaded down her back.

She had to keep in the remaining sisters' good graces if the art institute was going to get the go-ahead. Jane and Sophie were now feeling vulnerable, so perhaps the building could be renamed The David and Hannah Sutherland Art Institute in honour of Hannah's patronage of David's career. Or at least that's how she'd spin it. Sophie would be delighted with such a fitting memorial to her sister. Behind the gruff exterior, Jane was quite protective of Sophie. If Angelica could convince Jane to approve the project for Sophie's sake, well, Hannah's death could turn out to be a godsend.

"I've come to pay my respects to the family," she announced when Simmons answered her knock.

"I'm sure they'll appreciate you calling, Miss Lynley."

Angelica always felt uncomfortable around Simmons. Angelica had the distinct impression that in spite of Simmons' polite words, she was looking down her pointed nose at her. It didn't help that even in her serviceable flat shoes, Simmons towered above her. Angelica distrusted tall women. Not only did they attract all the attention, but there was an unspoken assumption that they thought they were better than everyone else. On more than one occasion, Angelica had taken great pleasure in putting some lanky tart in her place.

In the drawing room, the sisters sat like Victorian relics in black bombazine.

"Miss Lynley." Sophie rose to meet her. "How kind of you to come."

Jane acknowledged her presence with a nod.

Angelica wanted to press the flowers into Sophie's arms, but Simmons intercepted them. Suppressing her irritation, Angelica grasped Sophie's cool hand in hers. "I had to come and tell you how truly sorry I am."

Angelica expected to be offered a seat, but the invitation never came. She sat anyway.

"Is there anything I can do to help you at this trying time?"

"The Sutherlands look after their own," Jane said, a little too sharply.

And look where it's gotten you, Angelica wanted to throw back, but her face remained a mask of concern and sympathy. "I understand, but please don't hesitate to call on me."

"Thank you, but David is taking care of everything," Jane replied dismissively.

"And where is David?"

"With the Reverend Larkin seeing to," and Sophie lowered her voice, "you know, the arrangements."

Jane made an impatient noise. "The funeral, Sophie. The good Lord takes us all in His time, and there's no reason to speak as if it's something distasteful. God has seen to it that Hannah is finally at peace, and we should be thankful for that."

Sophie folded her hands. "Yes, Jane."

Angelica waited a minute for the emotional dust to settle. "I understand she died in her sleep. It must be very comforting to know it was a peaceful passing," Angelica said with all the sincerity she could muster. "I've also heard the police are on the island, but surely it has nothing to do with Hannah."

"It could be murder," Sophie whispered.

At this, Jane drew herself up. "Family business, Sophie, family business. Kindly remember that."

Simmons brought the lilies into the room in a large cut crystal vase.

"We're forgetting our manners," Sophie said. "Would you like a sherry?"

That was Angelica's cue to leave. The sisters' sherry wasn't up to the standards of a refined palate such as hers. "I'm afraid I should be going. I don't want to intrude any longer. I just wanted to offer my condolences."

"Thank you for coming, Miss Lynley," Sophie said quietly.

Jane grunted. "Simmons will see you out."

CHAPTER 25

DS Rhys Jenkins had Constable Finch set up an incident room in the island community centre. Hardly what he was used to, but beggars and all that. They'd compiled a list of people to interview who, Jenkins believed, might know something about Hannah's death or had been at Sutherland Hall within the last few days. Jenkins' personal opinion was that the whole thing was a tremendous waste of time, instigated by some middle-aged schoolteacher who thought she knew about policing simply because she'd once been a copper's wife. His wife, Dilys, knew better than to interfere with his job, but that would explain why the Galway woman was divorced. The whole thing seemed to rest on the edge of a piece of paper. It wasn't a lot to go on, but the place was pleasant enough and young Finch seemed eager to take advantage of Jenkins' years of experience. Hell, they were even paying for him to stay at a pub.

At home, Dilys had been at him to paint the upstairs. He was in no hurry to go back to that. Since everyone on the island had known Hannah Sutherland, it could conceivably take a week, possibly more, to interview everyone connected with the case. Then he'd have to confirm everything to ensure accuracy, submit reports, and of course socialize with the natives to build their trust. That would involve being a presence at the pub every night, buying a few rounds on the old expense account, perhaps a few fishing trips. *Yes,* he thought contentedly, *this investigation could turn out to be a very lengthy process.*

—

Byron sat across the dining table from Kate, tucking into a large portion of apple crumble and looking very official in his black suit. Siobhan was running through her repertoire of seductive moves—tilting her head, coy looks, the precise placement of food between her lips—to get his attention. Kate had never understood the attraction of younger men. The saying *young enough to be her son* was literally true in Byron's case. She wanted to kick Siobhan under the table and tell her to act her age, but she doubted it would make any difference.

"What did you and the sergeant get up to today?" Siobhan looked at him, doe-eyed over her wine glass.

"I shouldn't really say, Miss Fitzgerald."

Siobhan looked taken aback. She obviously wasn't expecting that.

"Byron," Kate began, "the reason we're interested in Hannah's death is we think it may have something to do with the death of my Aunt Emma."

He gave her a sympathetic look. "Oh, Miss Galway, I'm sorry."

"Oh no, it was a long time ago." Kate refilled their wine glasses. "The inquest said it was suicide, but my mother believed it was murder. She tried to get the police to reopen the investigation, but there was no new evidence. Hannah Sutherland recently revealed she'd seen Emma on a boat with someone just before she went missing. So I have a vested interest in you finding Hannah Sutherland's murderer because that person most probably killed Emma as well."

Byron was staring at her intently. "That's a pretty big stretch, Miss Galway. As you say, it was fifty years ago."

"Right now, Byron, it's all I've got."

He removed a flat black notebook and pen from his jacket pocket. "Tell me everything you know."

And Kate did just that—everything from the poisoned pie to David's vandalized car and her conversations with people on the island. She even brought out the corkboards. However, she didn't think it was her place to mention the threats against Siobhan, and Siobhan didn't bring it up.

When they finished, Kate took away the dessert plates and went to the sideboard for a bottle of brandy.

"I'm afraid you still have no evidence, Miss Galway," Byron said at last.

"Please call me Kate," she insisted. Otherwise it felt like they were back in the classroom.

Byron pursed his lips. "We used to call you Miss G among ourselves when you were our teacher. If that's okay with you..."

Siobhan looked at him from under her eyelashes. She was obviously tired of being ignored. She placed her hand on his. "Byron, we need your expert help. If there's any evidence out there, we—I—know you can find it."

He pulled his hand away. Siobhan looked like she wanted to chew the table.

"I'm not in charge of this investigation. As you observed, Miss G, I'm only the dogsbody." He smiled slyly. "Perhaps you should be wining and dining DS Jenkins instead."

Kate returned the look. He was just as clever as she remembered. "You and I can help each other, Byron. Jenkins is a little long in the tooth for a DS, so he either doesn't care about promotion or quite frankly he isn't very good at his job. Either way it leaves plenty of opportunity for a young, energetic police constable to impress the powers that be. We're prepared to share everything we know that might have something to do with your case. But in return, we'd like you to tell us what you discover to help us with ours."

"I'm not sure about the ethics of that, Miss G."

"Byron, I grew up on this island. When something happens here, everybody knows about it. But if they choose to keep a secret, there's no way you can crack them, especially if you're an outsider. Now, just how badly do you want to get into CID?"

He didn't look completely convinced, but his ambition to become a detective was his Achilles' heel. If he wanted her help to advance his career, he couldn't risk turning her down. He reluctantly shared what he'd learnt interviewing the Sutherland sisters earlier that day.

"Just so I've got it straight in my mind, let's go over what we know," Kate said. "Hannah routinely went to bed at nine o'clock. Sophie gave her a sleeping tablet and her heart medication with a cup of hot cocoa. The medication was kept in a secure cupboard to which Sophie had the only key. Then Hannah was locked in her room to stop her from wandering about. But the night she died, she was resisting going to bed. Toby was in the kitchen eating his dinner."

"Why was he there, and why was he eating so late?" Siobhan asked.

"It wasn't that late," Byron replied. "It was just gone half past seven. They'd been trying to get Hannah into her room early because she'd tired everyone out earlier, and they wanted some peace and quiet. Toby had been busy with something in the garden and wanted to finish, so Miss Simmons suggested he eat in the kitchen to save her having to take his dinner tray down to his cottage. Anyway, Hannah was fond of Toby. She thought he was one of her students, especially on days like this."

Kate took over. "So the sisters said if Hannah went to bed, Toby would bring up her cocoa, and the two of them could have a chat. That calmed her down. Simmons put the cocoa on a tray and sent Toby up. Sophie met him in Hannah's room, gave Hannah her tablets, watched her take them, and left the two of them talking. When Toby came down twenty minutes later, he said Hannah was asleep."

"And still alive?" Siobhan asked Byron.

"Siobhan, Toby wouldn't kill Hannah," Kate said.

"We have to keep an open mind. Everyone is a suspect until we catch the perpetrator," Byron insisted.

Siobhan turned away from Byron and gave Kate a quick *So there!* look. This time Kate did kick her under the table.

"Are you going to interview Toby?" Kate asked.

"Yes, but we understand he has no relatives on the island."

"He was orphaned on the mainland as a young lad. His foster father was an older man, a gardener, who nurtured his talent for growing things. After his dad had died, the Sutherland sisters took him in."

"He appears to be developmentally challenged, so we wondered if you could be present when we interview him."

"Of course, but I've no experience with Toby's condition."

"That's all right. It's procedure to have an appropriate adult present. We'll talk to him sometime tomorrow afternoon. I'll come by for you."

"Other than Toby, what's on the agenda?" Siobhan asked.

"We'll be talking to you two, of course."

"Us?" Siobhan seemed genuinely surprised.

Kate, on the other hand, was expecting it.

"You were attacked in the Sutherland garden a week ago. The two incidents might be connected."

Kate folded her hands in front of her. "You're working under the assumption it could be murder?"

"There were no suspicious fingerprints on the alleged suicide note or the envelope. However, Miss Sutherland's body was taken to Porth Madryn, and we're awaiting the toxicology results and post mortem report. Until then we're treating it as a suspicious death, and yes, we do believe there may be a connection to some recent events."

He stood up. "We'll see you here, Miss G, at nine o'clock, and you, Miss Fitzgerald, at ten. Thanks so much for dinner, Miss G. You keep feeding me like this, and I'll be tempted to adopt the vegetarian lifestyle."

He straightened his tie and brushed something microscopic from his pants.

"Byron, you know you don't have to dress up to come over here."

But he shook his head and stood tall, as if fighting the urge to snap to attention. "A police officer must always project an official image."

"Since you're going back to the pub," Siobhan said, walking him to the door, "you wouldn't mind giving a girl some police protection, would you?"

Byron managed a reluctant smile. "Of course not."

As he opened the door, Siobhan turned back to Kate and with exaggeration mouthed *Don't wait up*.

CHAPTER 26

Kate had been awakened by Siobhan slamming about, first in the bathroom, then in the kitchen. It ended with the thud of the front door. From the sounds of it, last night's mission had been unsuccessful.

Needing to clear her head before Byron and Jenkins arrived, Kate set out on a quick walk around the harbour. Most of the boats had gone out to sea, and the sky was filled with birds expertly hovering on currents of air. All she could hear were incessant squawks and waves skimming over the beach. She found herself slowing to match the pace of the island.

When she was on the mainland, she walked quickly, purposeful, easily irritated by anyone who meandered or blocked her way. Walker's Rage, she called it. But here, instead of her surroundings blurring past in her haste to reach her destination, she was actually noticing things around her, like a tourist who stops at every building, garden, or public monument to take in the details. Except she wasn't someone new to the island. This had been her home for seventeen years, and many a summer after that. So why should it suddenly hold such an attraction for her?

Was there some part of her that wanted to come back? But her life was on the mainland. There was Alex, of course, but also her doctors, hairstylist, dry-cleaners, season tickets to the theatre, cinemas, museums, and a wonderful health food store within walking distance of her flat.

She realized she hadn't included friends in that list. The trouble with having friends who were teachers was that the best you could hope for was to socialize during breaks or at lunch in the staff room, or to gather for drinks at the end of term. For the most part, they were all so busy preparing lessons and marking there was no time for extended get-togethers. The strange thing was that even though they'd known each other only a few weeks, Siobhan Fitzgerald was quickly becoming her best friend.

Up ahead, Gwynie Charlton was standing in front of the pub talking on her phone. Kate wondered if she could sneak up on her before Gwynie found yet another excuse to avoid her. But it was too late. Gwynie had seen her and was walking away.

"Sorry, Kate, but I need to finish this call."

But this time Kate followed her. She used her teacher voice. "Lady Charlton, you're obviously hiding something, and I'm not the only person to make this observation. Now we can do this with me shouting at you, or we can go somewhere quiet."

Gwynie said good-bye to whomever she was speaking with and allowed Kate to catch up.

Gwynie's face was hard and resigned. "I have nothing to hide, but I do have important things to do."

You're not the only one. "I wanted to ask you if you can remember anything unusal that was happening on the island that could have led to Emma's murder?"

Gwynie let out a deep sigh. She seemed almost relieved by Kate's request. Perhaps she'd been expecting another line of questioning. "No, nothing."

She shook her head rather too quickly as if about to make a break for it before Kate could ask anything else.

But Kate wasn't prepared to let her off that easily. "What was your relationship with David Sutherland?"

Gwynie blinked. "I didn't have one."

"But you were at school together. Weren't you friends?"

Her face relaxed. "Oh, that's what you meant."

"From what I hear, a lot of girls were attracted to David back then. Were you?"

"Not my type," she returned rather too quickly.

Kate kept pushing. "All the same, I've seen the film of the pub party. You couldn't take your eyes off him. And you didn't look best pleased that he was lavishing all his attention on Emma."

Gwynie's face was taut as if she was trying very hard to control herself. "Look, Kate, Emma was my friend. I didn't want her to get hurt. David was pressuring her to—you know. If she wasn't pre-pared to give him what he wanted, there were plenty of other girls who would. I don't know what you think you saw, but I was looking out for her. Now, if you'll excuse me..."

Kate was fairly certain that everything Gwynie had just told her was a lie, but she let it go for now. "One more thing. Where were you on the day Emma disappeared, say about five and seven o'clock?"

Gwynie looked up at the cloudy sky as if searching her distant memory. "I believe I was taking a walk with Rupert Gooley over by the community centre. Gooley was sweet on me, and we'd just started dating. It wasn't common knowledge, but we thought we'd give it a try, see if we could make a go of it."

Before Kate could say another word, Gwynie announced, "Now, if that's all, I really do have other things I need to be getting on with," and she turned and walked away.

No, Kate thought, she wasn't buying any of what Gwynie had told her. While Gooley was a sweetie, if Gwynie had her heart set on David Sutherland, she wasn't going to settle for Rupert Gooley. The look on her face in the pub party wasn't concern for Emma's well-being. It was jealousy pure and simple. She looked as though she'd do anything to get Emma out of the way.

—

DS Rhys Jenkins sat on the sofa in Kate's cottage with Byron beside him. She'd heard James talk about interrogating suspects, but she never thought she'd be on the receiving end. That line from the Monty Python sketch "Nobody expects the Spanish Inquisition" kept running through her head. But she kept reminding herself it would just be information gathering. She was helping the police with their inquiries. But wasn't that what they told everyone to convince them to go quietly to the station?

Byron had his black notebook at the ready, while Jenkins sat back. Jenkins had undone the top button of his shirt and pulled his blue and beige striped tie, wrinkled and puckered, to one side to get it out of the way. At least James, when Kate could get him into a suit, wore it better than Jenkins. Jenkins was the kind of man who would look slovenly even if you put him in new clothes. What was it someone once said about Dylan Thomas—he looked like an unmade bed? Jenkins was more like an untidy sofa, but it gave him the appearance of a man who coasted through life, ducking any responsibility. Anyone else might have been on guard against Byron's youthful enthusiasm, afraid of the competition, but not Jenkins. He seemed quite happy to let Byron do all the work.

Kate resisted the temptation to reach over and brush what looked like toast crumbs from his jacket.

"So, Miss Galway," he finally said, "you returned to the island for your grandmother's funeral. She must have been quite old."

Kate was aware she'd been insulted, but she doubted Jenkins realized what he'd just said. "One hundred and one."

"Well, she had a good innings then."

Given his squat build, Jenkins looked more a rugby man than a cricketer. Kate hoped he wasn't going to talk in sports clichés for the rest of the interview.

"Tell me about the last time you saw Hannah Sutherland."

"It was the day we were attacked in her garden."

"Ah yes, we've heard about this from the deceased's sisters. I'd like to hear your version of the events. When was this?"

"A week ago—last Sunday."

"And who attacked you?"

"We don't know. It was dark."

"I understand Siobhan Fitzgerald was with you."

"That's correct."

"So you and Miss Fitzgerald were in the garden of Sutherland Hall. Approximately what time was this?"

"Sometime just before eleven."

"A social call, was it?"

Kate looked at Byron and, knowing what was coming, he lowered his eyes. "No, Siobhan and I were digging for a tea tin we'd seen Hannah bury in the garden earlier that day."

Jenkins' look indicated that even though Kate was confirming what Jane and Sophie had already told him, he still wasn't sure if people were having him on. He leaned forward. "And why were you digging up a tea tin in the middle of the night?"

"DS Jenkins, even on Meredith, eleven o'clock is hardly the middle of the night. But that aside, we thought it might contain some evidence into the murder of my aunt."

Jenkins glared over at Byron. "There's been a second death? Finch, why wasn't I told?"

"It was fifty years ago, sir."

Kate was impressed with Byron's ability to keep his voice steady and calm, masking the irritation he must have felt at Jenkins's implied accusation of incompetence.

Jenkins leaned back. Painfully aware he'd made a fool of himself, he directed his anger toward Kate. "Regular Miss Marble, aren't you?"

Kate resisted the temptation to correct him.

"Did you report the attack?"

"No."

"Why not?"

"We have no law enforcement on the island. We handle things ourselves."

Jenkins' eyebrows descended and knit themselves together. "I hope that doesn't mean you take the law into your own hands. The police force doesn't hold with vigilantism."

This conversation only reinforced the intelligence of Kate's decision to work with Byron. He was obviously the brains of the outfit.

"What are you implying, DS Jenkins? That we convene secret

courts in the pub at midnight, pass judgement in dark hooded cloaks, and then throw the offender from the highest cliff..." She purposely left the sentence hanging in order to allow the image to work its way into Jenkins's brain.

After a few more questions, it had become apparent even to Jenkins that Kate's connection to Hannah's death was tenuous. He terminated the interview, which was perfectly fine with her. She was prepared to co-operate—James had instilled that into her—but she didn't want Jenkins meddling in her investigation. If she needed police assistance, she had Byron.

—

Siobhan hated coppers at the best of times—all authority and brass buttons and doing things by the book, everything black and white. All things which Siobhan hated and had resisted all her life. Besides this, Jenkins was a first-class wanker. To top it off, he kept staring at her breasts.

God knows what he was thinking about doing to her, but he was having trouble keeping focussed on his questions. "Miss Fitzgerald, do you have any idea...uh, any idea why...I mean, what Miss Sutherland was burying in the garden?"

Siobhan didn't buy that bollocks story Jane had fed them and was convinced whatever Hannah was burying was somehow linked to Emma's death. There was just one thing she needed the police to do for her.

She had to choose her words carefully. "If she was burying money or jewellery, it could've been a strong motive for her murder," and she looked directly at Jenkins.

"Go on." He was hooked. She just needed to reel him in.

"It's no coincidence we were attacked, and then only days later, Miss Sutherland was murdered. I don't know anything about policing—I leave that up to you trained professionals—but I'd be willing to bet there's a connection there."

Jenkins' eyes, in their fleshy folds of fat, had grown steadily larger. When Siobhan had finished, he turned to Byron. "Finch, call for reinforcements. We're going to dig up that garden."

Byron's pen hovered over his pad. He looked directly at Siobhan with his penetrating steel-grey eyes as if he'd sussed exactly what she was up to and had no intention of letting her get away with it. "Sir, wouldn't it be prudent to wait for the results of the lab work? The chief put a rush on it. It should be back tomorrow."

Bugger! Whose side was this guy on? Siobhan might have to re-think their relationship.

"Best not waste costly resources," Byron added.

Jenkins' eyes flickered as if the act of thinking was a real strain. "Miss Fitzgerald, we should wait for the results of the lab work before we do anything," he said decisively. Then he turned to Byron.

"But put the lads on standby, just in case."

Siobhan smiled. *Got him.*

CHAPTER 27

Sophie sat in the drawing room with Jane and David as DS Jenkins revealed the results of Hannah's blood tests. With high concentrations of heart medication found in Hannah's blood and the fraudulent suicide note, there was now no doubt Hannah had been murdered. Jane quietly listened and then thanked the sergeant for coming to tell them. David stared at the carpet. It was almost lunchtime, and Sophie wondered if she should offer tea and biscuits but said nothing.

"Hannah's with Mother and Father," Jane said with quiet authority after Jenkins had left, "and we can bury her in consecrated ground."

Sophie couldn't bear to look at her sister. For once in her life, she wanted to lose control and scream at Jane that dear Hannah had been murdered, and all Jane cared about was where they were going to put her body. Someone had come into their home, gone into Hannah's bedroom, and killed her. None of them was safe in their beds.

But Sophie knew ranting and raving wouldn't do any good. Jane would clutch her cross and tell Sophie to control herself. So Sophie did just that and went to look out at the back garden. Yet it was hard to relax with half a dozen people in white coveralls tramping through the house, examining doors and windows, rummaging through drawers and cupboards, looking under beds, tipping out boxes. Strange men would be touching Sophie's underthings.

Toby sat with Simmons in the kitchen in tears at what the people with hoes and spades were doing to his beautiful plants. Simmons attempted to calm him with a soothing voice and cups of hot chocolate. Chocolate was the only thing that settled him when he got himself into a state.

Sophie couldn't bear it any longer. Hannah had been responsible for restoring the garden after that terrible summer when all their plants died, and now it was being destroyed again.

David came up behind them and announced he was driving back to his studio.

Sophie looked up into David's tired face and wondered if he blamed her for Hannah's death. "I'm so sorry," she said.

He looked at her curiously. "What for?"

"I can be such a scatterbrain sometimes. What if I forget to lock the cupboard? Is that where the murderer got the tablets? If it was my fault, I'll never forgive myself, never," and she pressed a handkerchief to her mouth.

Jane came over and took Sophie in her arms, something Jane had never done, even when they were children.

"Not your fault," she whispered. "Not your fault."

Jane released her and turned to gaze out the door.

"I can't bear to watch this any longer," Sophie cried. "David, please take me away from here."

David went to fetch her coat.

"Don't let them touch the roses, Janey. Hannah did so love the roses," Sophie said, her voice catching.

They left Jane, her hands clasped behind her back, standing on guard.

—

James had spent the whole morning answering the damn phone, forced to listen to irritating voices demanding overdue reports and statistics. The hell of it was nobody was offering him the information he needed in order to get everyone else off his back. Policing at his level was all paperwork and damned little investigation. It was on days like this he wished he'd stayed in uniform.

The telephone rang, and he blew a long stream of air though his lips, hoping to release the tension. "Chief Inspector Hewitt," he barked into the receiver.

"Bad day, Dad?"

He was relieved to hear Alex's voice. "Sorry, sweetheart. The suits are circling."

When complaining to his barrister daughter, he always managed to forget she was now one of those predator suits, getting in the way of him doing his job. He knew it was just a matter of time before he faced Alex across an interview table with some sleazy pimp or drug dealer. "How's your mother getting on with her investigation?" and he put strained emphasis on the word 'investigation' to show his disapproval.

"Oh, I'm all right, thanks for asking." She sounded upset. "If you're so worried, call her. Remind me again why you two went to the trouble and expense of getting divorced."

Yes, he definitely wasn't looking forward to meeting her across that table, having to resist calling her "young lady" in a patronizing tone and telling her off for threatening to report him for the harassment of a pedophile or rapist. As a little girl, he'd been able to tell her anything, even things he was unsure of, and she'd happily believed him. Those days were long gone.

"She's fine, Dad. Hannah Sutherland died and there are two coppers on the island, so she can't get into too much trouble."

James looked at the photograph of the three of them at Alex's graduation ceremony. They'd been divorced for eight years, and he still had a picture of Kate on his desk. He'd told himself that like any couple with a child, they were bound together by Alex. But even after the divorce he'd rather have a meal with Alex and Kate than go through the hellish ritual of dating, of getting to know someone new, only to learn she was boring or clingy.

His chief had sent a group of officers to a stress course run by some pony-tailed psychologist who'd told them most people who went into policing had a need to control. Being a police officer was a socially acceptable way of controlling other people, but you can't control everything, he'd said. James decided that was bollocks. What was the point of having a life if you weren't in control? This guy's suggestion was to let go of the riverbank, and allow the current take you where you needed to go. James dismissed most of the course as useless psychobabble, but that image had stuck with him. Is that what a healthy divorce looked like? Theirs had been remarkably civilized. He thought that was what Kate had wanted—over and done with, no fuss.

But if he was honest, he'd never let go of his bank. Every time he heard Kate's ringtone, he worried it was news he didn't want to hear—not just about Alex, but about her as well. But he'd never told her. Then he really would have lost control.

"Tell her I'm still working on getting that information she asked for." He didn't know why he said that. He'd already told Kate there wasn't a chance in hell he'd be able to get hold of the files.

"You could tell her yourself, you know."

"I don't want to bother her." That sounded feeble. He waited for Alex's comeback.

"When did that ever stop you!"

Instead of responding, he changed the subject. "So are we still on for dinner tomorrow night? Dinner?"

"It's a date." She paused. "Unless one of us gets a call."

He sighed. "Yes, unless one of us gets a call." He put down the receiver. *And it'll probably be me.*

—

From her table by the window of The Sea Breeze, Kate could see people gathered outside the pub, impatient for the latest information about Hannah. Kate struggled with a craving for a toasted teacake. She was so focussed on the menu she didn't notice Sophie hurrying over to her table. "May I join you, my dear?"

"Of course."

"I'd rather not sit alone. People will insist on offering their condolences, asking questions, and I can't deal with any of it right now." She sat in a rustle of stiff black fabric. "Some awful people are digging up the garden."

The waitress came over with a second cup and quietly offered her sympathy. Encouraged by Sophie's order of a vanilla slice, Kate gave in to the teacake and poured out Sophie's tea.

"The tests say our dear Hannah was murdered," Sophie said at last. "I don't know if I should be relieved. Jane says now she'll be welcomed into heaven, that we can bury her in the Sutherland family plot. That's something, I suppose."

She took small sips from her cup. "It seems you were right about the letter, Kate."

This gave Kate no pleasure.

"Sophie, can I ask you some questions about Emma?"

"Of course, my dear, but I'm not sure how much help I can be."

"I've heard Hannah had a falling out with her at the school-end celebration. It had to do with the rumours about her and Alun Probert."

"A terrible business. Poor Mr. Probert felt it only right he leave the school. We lost a wonderful teacher."

"So the rumours were true."

Sophie vigorously shook her head. "Oh, my dear, of course not. It was completely unfounded."

Sophie sat back as the waitress delivered the cakes.

"How do you know?"

"There's no way Hannah could have had that kind of relationship with Mr. Probert," Sophie insisted.

"No way, because..." Kate prompted her.

Sophie leaned across her plate, putting herself in danger of getting icing on her chest, and whispered, "What I'm about to tell you, you must promise to keep to yourself. It mustn't get back to Jane."

She looked at the nearest tables to make sure no one was listening. "Hannah was keeping company with Felicity Lambert."

It took Kate a minute before she could actually say what Sophie's euphemism had implied. "You mean Hannah was a lesbian?" Kate had never heard even a whiff of gossip about Hannah's sexual orientation. "Are you sure?"

"No one had ever seen her with a man. Even Jane had a boyfriend once, in spite of her insistence that she wanted to take the veil. I kept company with a charming young man called Teddy. He was a botany student, but Father had decided that he'd never amount to anything, being interested in flowers. Well, Teddy became Dr. Theodore Bartell. His textbooks are used in all the best universities," she said proudly.

Sophie looked off through the window as if picturing this young student who had captured her heart so long ago.

In Sophie's silence, Kate cursed the father who had maintained such a hold over his daughters and in doing so had brought them so much loneliness. But she had to return to the topic at hand. "I'm sorry, Sophie, but I need to know more about Hannah. Why are you so sure she preferred women?"

"Hannah and Felicity—Fliss she called her—were friends before Fliss was hired at the school. She'd stayed with us at Christmas and for three summers. They were together constantly—long walks, swimming, trips to the mainland. Once I came across them in the woods down by the dell. They'd had a picnic. They were lying together on a blanket, and Hannah had her head on Fliss's shoulder, and Fliss was stroking her hair. I'd never seen Hannah so content, so comfortable with another person, and then I thought of Teddy, and I knew Fliss and Hannah loved each other. I'm sure Fliss came to the school so they could be together. And everything was fine for two years until this dreadful thing with Mr. Probert."

"So why did Fliss leave?"

"A few months ago when Hannah was having one of her funny turns, she let slip some of what happened. They couldn't take the chance they'd be found out. With the rumours about Mr. Probert, Hannah was being watched constantly. If her relationship with Fliss was made public, they'd both lose their jobs. She asked Hannah to go away with her, get a house together. But Hannah was so afraid of scandal, even that was too much to risk, and then there was Jane.

If Jane were to find out, she'd never speak to Hannah again. It's a sin in Jane's eyes, you see. So Hannah gave Fliss up. She lost the two people she loved more than anyone in the world—Fliss and David—and both out of fear." Sophie's voice was becoming louder, with an angry edge.

Kate felt uncomfortable probing into the private life of her former teacher, but for the sake of the truth, she pushed ahead. "What was she afraid of with David?"

Sophie looked curiously at Kate, as if the answer was obvious. "That something or someone would prevent him from becoming the man he was supposed to be."

"But Hannah never truly became the woman she was supposed to be, not if she felt she had to give up the person she loved."

Sophie looked down at her hands, still in their black gloves, and shook her head. "Father taught us value our place in society, to do our duty, and to protect our reputations. And in doing so, he took from us the courage to be who we truly were. That was why it was so important for David to become an artist, to do what we couldn't. Hannah didn't want his attachment to Emma to put that at risk. Each of us had given up any hope of living lives of our own, so we lived through David."

Kate placed her hand over Sophie's. The sisters' lives had been like so many others for women of their generation—lives of unfulfilled dreams. But what they never realized was that David's longing for Emma rivalled that of Hannah for Fliss and Sophie for Teddy. Just as their own father had inflicted a life of loneliness on them by doing what he thought was right, so Hannah had done the same to David.

"Sophie, why didn't Hannah testify at Emma's inquest?"

Sophie blew her nose quietly on a white linen handkerchief. "That evening Hannah came home and said I needed to keep a secret. She said she'd done something illegal in the eyes of the law, but the law was wrong. She asked me to trust that it was for the best and to promise never to tell Jane. Jane never lets anything rest, and she would have bothered Hannah until she learnt the truth. It was for our protection that we didn't know any more. Jane had been out most of the afternoon, so we told her Hannah had been working at the school until dinner."

"And you still have no idea what Hannah was up to?"

Sophie shook her head. "But it had nothing to do with Emma's disappearance."

"How do you know?" Kate insisted.

"When they discovered Emma's body, Hannah told me she'd seen Emma on a boat moving away from the harbour. But she was afraid if she testified, she'd be asked why she was there. Her loyalty, she said, was to the living. Nothing she could say would help Emma." Sophie stared into Kate's eyes. "I know in my heart my sister was not capable of murder."

"Did she ever tell you who was on the boat?" Kate held her breath and waited for Sophie to answer.

"No, I'm sorry. If I'd only known how important it was, I would have pressed her. But Hannah was so used to keeping secrets. Her whole life was a secret, so it was second nature to her." Sophie grew quiet and began to poke at the creamy inside of her slice.

"Sophie, I believe it's quite possible Hannah was killed by the same person who killed Emma."

Sophie pressed her hand against her chest. "Oh, my dear."

It was then the door flew open. Winifred stood in the doorway, the sun streaming in from behind her.

"It's Toby," she said, breathlessly. "He's just confessed to murdering Hannah."

CHAPTER 28

"How dare you!"

DS Jenkins was sitting in the pub with a ham sandwich and a bag of salt and vinegar crisps. A quiet lunch. Was that really so much to ask? Hell, he'd even sacrificed a well-deserved pint in case someone accused him of drinking on the job. And here was the bloody Galway woman bleating at him.

"How dare you interrogate that young man without me!" She stood in front of him like some spinster school teacher scolding a child. Just who did she think she was? The island had obviously been without a police presence for far too long.

Jenkins had heard about these small isolated communities—a law unto themselves, still living in the dark ages, full of superstition and pagan rituals. He'd transferred to Porth Madryn only a few months ago, and when the coppers at the station house learnt he was going to investigate an island death, they shook their heads and made *tsk, tsk* noises every time they passed. He'd heard the islanders were—well, eccentric, was the polite term—but he strongly suspected the truth was they were inbred to the point of lunacy. Maybe drawing out the investigation wasn't such a good idea. Even painting the upstairs had to be better than spending any more time with these people.

Jenkins dropped his sandwich onto the plate. He wished Finch was here. Finch seemed to know how to handle the woman. It didn't help that everyone in the pub was watching them—and no doubt taking her side. "What can I do for you, Miss Galway?"

"Why did you interview Toby without an appropriate adult present?" She continued to loom over him.

"I haven't interviewed him yet. He came to us and confessed."

"I don't believe that."

Jenkins ran his hand through what was left of his hair. It was shrill women like this who were responsible for his hair loss. "Toby Burridge came to me half an hour ago and said it was his fault Miss Sutherland died."

"That's hardly a confession," she glared at him.

"Finch is out looking for you so we can question him properly. You were supposed to be at home."

"I went out. There's a note on my door saying where I am."

She looked rather sheepish, Jenkins observed with some satisfaction.

"Have you arrested him?"

"No."

"Where is he?"

Jenkins jerked his head upwards. "Waiting in room number five. The landlady took him a sandwich and a fizzy drink. So you see, we aren't torturing or starving him, and he is not under arrest. We just wanted him somewhere we could keep an eye on him until we could find you. Now, if you'll let me finish my lunch, we can get on with the formal interview when Finch returns," and he took a bite to indicate their conversation was over.

"Can I speak with him?"

Jenkins waved his sandwich at her, a large piece of ham falling onto the table. "Be my guest." *Bloody woman!*

—

Kate turned her back on Jenkins and walked up the stairs. Having spent a career dealing with belligerent teenagers, she had no tolerance for bullies of any kind. What she saw in Jenkins was a man so incompetent he wouldn't hesitate to coerce a mentally challenged young man into confessing to get a result. After Jane and Sophie, Toby was the last person who could have murdered Hannah.

She knocked on the door of number five. Toby murmured a weak "hello." He was sitting on the bed, rocking slightly on the quilted cover and looking out the window, his drink and sandwich untouched. He turned to look at Kate. His face was swollen and red, and he was rhythmically pulling at his fingers.

"It's all right, Toby. Everything's going to be all right. I'm here to help you."

He looked up at her and leaned forward as if he wanted to run into her arms, but he held himself back. "I killed her, Miss Kate. I killed Miss Hannah."

Kate came over and sat beside him. He smelled of sweat and chocolate. "I don't believe that, Toby, not a good boy like you."

"Then why are they killing my flowers?" he wailed.

She dug into her purse and handed him a tissue.

He scrunched it in his hand.

"Tell me why you think you killed her, Toby. What did you do?"

"The tablets killed her. I gave her the tablets with the cocoa. I killed Miss Hannah," and he started crying in gulping, unrestrained sobs.

This time Kate put her arms around him. "It wasn't just one or two tablets that killed her. It was lots of tablets, and you know it's Miss Sophie who always gave Miss Hannah the tablets."

He became quiet as he thought about it.

"On Friday, how many tablets did Miss Sophie give her?"

"Two. But I told Miss Hannah to swallow them," he insisted. "She didn't want to. I told her to do it for me."

"But she always took two, right? One to make her heart better, and one to help her go to sleep," and she turned him toward her so she could look into his round, red face. She took another tissue from her purse and wiped his wet cheeks and chin. "So two can't have hurt her. This isn't your fault, and that's what we're going to tell the police."

"Will they leave the garden alone?"

"I don't know."

Toby touched Kate's head. His eyes watered up again. "I'm sorry you got hurt, Miss Kate."

Kate stroked his cheek. "It wasn't your fault, Toby. Not everything that happens in the garden is your fault."

But from the look on his face, he wasn't convinced.

—

When Kate came back into the pub, she found Sophie standing in front of Jenkins, glaring down at him.

"Detective Sergeant Jenkins, I would ask you not to interrogate my staff without my permission. I could have told you Toby was not responsible for my sister's death."

"I'm sorry, Miss Sutherland, but this is not the Middle Ages. I can question who I want with or without your permission. And I'll be the judge of who is guilty." He rose to his feet as Byron joined him. "Now, if you don't mind, we're going to take the suspect to the incident room. Miss Galway, are you coming?"

"I'll be accompanying Toby," Sophie stated, as if daring him to refuse her.

"You're not a solicitor, are you, Miss Sutherland?"

"Of course not!"

Kate was fairly sure Sophie hadn't caught the sarcasm in Jenkins' voice.

"You can be present, but only if you promise to sit quietly. Do I have your word?"

She didn't look happy about the condition but she nodded her agreement.

Byron joined them, and Jenkins told him to fetch Toby so they could get on with it.

—

Once the four of them had settled around the large worktable in the community centre archive room, Jenkins turned on the recorder and identified everyone in the room. He asked the same questions of Toby that Kate had. Toby was feeling better now and was able to focus on his answers. Kate kept hold of his hand, squeezing it whenever he hesitated, patting it approvingly when he said something Jenkins didn't want to hear. Every so often, Sophie opened her mouth as if to object to a question. Kate gave a slight shake of her head, and Sophie reluctantly narrowed her eyes and tightened her lips.

When, after ten minutes, it had been established Toby wasn't responsible for Hannah's death, Jenkins turned off the recording.

"So," Kate asked, "is Toby free to go?"

"For now. I may need to ask him some more questions. I'll come by later to get him to sign his statement. He can write, can't he?"

Just when Kate thought this man couldn't get any more ill-mannered and condescending. How she pitied his wife. Imagine waking up beside him every morning. But she kept her outrage to herself. "I'm sure Toby will be happy to answer any other questions, won't you, Toby?"

But he had more important things on his mind. "Will you stop digging up my garden?"

"We will keep digging until we find what we're looking for, young man!" snapped Jenkins, obviously angry he'd been cheated out of a quick result.

Toby's face grew red as if he was about to cry again.

Sophie pushed herself to her feet. "That's quite enough, Detective Sergeant. Toby and I will be going now. And if you don't like it, you can arrest me!"

Taking Toby by the hand, she marched him to the door, eager to get him away from the ridiculous man.

"Sophie, wait. I'll get Siobhan to drive you," Kate said.

"Please don't trouble Miss Fitzgerald. I'm sure she has more important things to do. Come along, Toby. You can walk me home." She placed her arm in his, and together they left the room.

Jenkins shook his head as he fiddled with the buttons on the recorder. "I'm surprised more of you people don't get killed."

Kate could control herself no longer. "Why you have been al-lowed to continue to serve on the police force is anyone's guess. But we are not the ignorant fools you think we are. We know our rights, and we will not be intimidated by the likes of you. Not only is my ex-husband a detective chief inspector, but my daughter is a barrister. If you continue to make libelous remarks about the people of this island, I will not hesitate to report you to your superiors. Is that clear?"

Byron hid behind his notepad, while Jenkins appeared to stare at the scratches in the table. "Yes, ma'am," was the reluctant response.

Byron looked up at her, and Kate could have sworn he winked.

CHAPTER 29

It was a long trek back to Sutherland Hall, and Kate doubted Sophie's ability to walk the whole way, despite her bravado. A quick call and Siobhan and the blue truck appeared, and they set out to find Sophie and Toby.

It was Kate who spotted Sophie at the church, sitting on a stone bench and leaning against the church wall. Red-faced, her chest rising and falling, she was fanning herself with a white handkerchief.

"Oh, how lovely to see you both, and Miss Fitzgerald's vehicle. I was so angry with that offensive little man that I quite forgot how long it would take to walk home. I'm afraid my legs aren't quite what they used to be."

She paused and quietly inquired, "Miss Fitzgerald, you wouldn't happen to have any whiskey, would you? Jane doesn't allow it in the house, and I do so enjoy a drop of the Irish, when I can get it. Purely medicinal, of course."

Kate wouldn't have been surprised if Siobhan had produced a hip flask, but she shook her head apologetically.

"Toby, are you all right?" Kate called over to him, his head down among the gravestones.

The events of the past few hours seemed to have been vanquished by his mission to rid the cemetery of its offending weeds. "Plants need to breath. Got to help the plants to breath."

"He's a good boy." Sophie watched him like a doting grandmother. "And what that lad doesn't know about plants. He not only does for us, he takes care of Mr. Faraday's gardens. Well, the beds by the house. It would take a whole team of gardeners to do it all. They had that, you know, in Mr. Faraday's time, a whole team."

"Do you still take care of the manor house?" Kate asked.

"Oh yes," Sophie was breathing easier now and proudly sitting tall. "The Sutherlands were entrusted with the care of the estate when Mr. Faraday was here. It's a duty each generation has carried out with the utmost dedication. Once a week Simmons does a walk-about to make sure everything is as it should be, and of course there's the Spring Clean, but you know all about that." Sophie laughed softly. "I read somewhere it takes a village to raise a child. Well, it seems it takes an island to clean a nineteenth-century manor house."

Even though it was hard work, Kate fondly remembered those weekends when everyone marched up to the manor, carrying buckets and brooms to clean and polish the great house, ready for the summer onslaught of tourists. It was a treat for Kate to be allowed into Artemis Faraday's world which was exactly as he'd left it in the mid-nineteenth century.

Against the advice of his architect, he'd designed the house himself—his vision of a grand English manor. It was the fantasy of an American who as a young boy had probably stayed awake well into the night reading gothic novels, believing them to be true depictions of contemporary British life. If only he'd read Jane Austen, perhaps the house might have had an elegant Georgian style.

But while the islanders looked upon both the manor and Artemis Faraday as eccentric oddities, the Sutherland sisters, as the direct descendants of the original estate manager and housekeeper, took Mr. Faraday and their duty to him very seriously. For four generations, they'd held the keys to the manor, guarding both them and Mr. Faraday's property with a ferocious dedication. But as none of the Sutherlands had children, their would soon die out. Who would inherit the keys to the kingdom then?

Kate and Sophie watched Toby teaching Siobhan how to identify weeds. Siobhan seemed genuinely interested.

"Sophie, remember we were talking about Alun Probert. Apparently, the rumours about Hannah and Mr. Probert got started because someone saw them in The Breeze. Do you know why they were there?"

"They were talking about Sami Sparrow."

Kate was surprised. "Sami?"

"Mr. Probert was quite impressed with Sami's aptitude for biology. I mean, she'd learnt an awful lot about plants from her father. Mr. Probert believed if she put her mind to it, she could go to university. He was asking Hannah's advice on how he should approach Clive about Sami staying on for another year to do her A-levels. The problem was she'd have to give up working in the gardens and devote all her time to her school work. He didn't think Clive would agree to that."

"From what I've heard, I'm sure he wouldn't."

"That man made that poor child's life a misery."

Here was yet another life unfulfilled because of an overbearing father. At last Kate said, "When was the last time you saw Emma?"

"Oh, Kate, it was such a long time ago. I can't quite remember. Definitely not the week before she disappeared. I twisted my ankle, you see. Fell into a badger hole, or was it a rabbit hole? No matter. Jane insisted I stay off it for a week. She really was quite the ministering angel—cold compresses and all my meals on a tray."

She paused. "Now, wait a minute," and she poked at the air with her finger. "Jane told me something about Emma. It was Thursday. Thursday was the butcher, the day I went to Porth Madryn to buy meat. Jane didn't trust the housekeeper—it was Morag Potter then. Jane thought Potter had a bit of a thing for the butcher, and she was afraid he might be taking advantage and pawning Potter off with cheaper cuts. After that, Jane insisted I get the meat myself, but I couldn't go that week because of my ankle. Jane went instead. Jane's much better with salespeople."

Kate could well imagine Jane's wrath against anyone who dared to take advantage.

"When she came home, she said she'd run into Emma."

"Are you sure you don't mean Saturday? Emma was on the mainland the day she disappeared."

Sophie shook her head. "No, it had to be Thursday. Fruit and veg on Wednesday morning—half-day closing, remember—meat and fish on Thursday, and dry goods every second Friday. Jane is very regular in her habits. She takes after Father in that regard."

"Do you have any idea what Emma was doing on the mainland?"

Sophie shrugged. "That's all I can remember, I'm afraid. If you want to know anymore, you're going to have to ask Jane."

That was a conversation Kate wasn't looking forward to.

—

Siobhan loaded Sophie and Toby into the blue truck, leaving Kate to walk back to her cottage. While it was tempting to rush up and question Jane, Kate felt the destruction of the garden and Toby's confession had caused the sisters enough upheaval for the day.

On the way back, she was debating continuing on to the pub. She'd only eaten a teacake since breakfast, and she was suddenly hungry. But any chance of lunch had to be postponed when she found David waiting on her doorstep.

She invited him inside.

He settled himself on the sofa, a basset hound expression on his face. Hannah's death had obviously hit him harder than anyone would have thought, and Kate was afraid their conversation the other night had made it worse.

"Everyone's talking about how you stood up to Jenkins in the pub," he said. "I wanted to thank you on behalf of the family. Not just for Toby, but for your suspicions about the note. If it hadn't been for you, Hannah's death might never have been investigated."

She passed David a glass of whiskey. "I'm glad I was able to help."

"Sophie said at the dinner party Hannah mentioned seeing someone with Emma just before she disappeared," David said. "It was her murderer, wasn't it?"

He threw back half of the whiskey while waiting for her to confirm his suspicions.

"I believe Hannah saw Emma's killer, and Hannah was murdered to keep her quiet."

David looked shocked. "So does that mean the murderer was someone at dinner?"

"Not necessarily. You know how information spreads across the island."

"But why didn't Hannah say something before now? It might have saved her life and brought Emma's killer to justice."

Kate said nothing. It wasn't her place to share what Sophie had told her in confidence.

"Tell me about the vandalism," she asked him. "The morning we discovered your car, you said it had happened before."

"It had to have been five or six times. And then there were the notes with words made up of letters cut out of magazines."

Just like Siobhan's notes. Could it be the same person, or do all psychopathic nut jobs cut letters out of magazines?

"Despite the clichéd presentation, the messages were quite nasty. They said vicious things about my wives—they were working as prostitutes, explicit sexual details about what they were doing with other men, horrible stuff. I couldn't hide the damage to the car, but I never shared the letters with them."

"Did you call the police?"

"They set up a file, but there were no forensics. They assured me there was no evidence that whoever was doing this was a threat. I suppose today it might be taken more seriously. Maybe I should feel flattered I had a stalker." He attempted an amused look.

"Did they stop when you got divorced?"

David thought for a moment. "Yes, although there was still the odd letter and damage to my car even then."

"I'm no psychologist, but if I had to hazard a guess, I'd say this was the work of a jealous woman—or man—hoping to destroy your marriages, in fact any relationship you were having."

"Then you should feel flattered it's happened again." He obviously saw the disapproving look on her face. "Look, if this person really wants me, why haven't they approached me?"

"How do you know they haven't?"

"I think I would have noticed."

"Not necessarily."

How could he be so cavalier toward what was obviously a threat?

"Well, there's no use me getting upset about this. It'll stop soon enough. It always does. Let's have another drink," and he held out his glass, "and talk about something else."

She poured them both a refill.

"What are you planning to do with the cottage?" he asked. "You could always move back here. You know the saying—once an islander, always an islander. Everyone comes back eventually, like a homing pigeon. I'd use the spawning salmon metaphor, but I for one am well past it. And it would be most ungentlemanly to presume to speak for you."

Only David could use the word ungentlemanly and sound neither patronizing nor pretentious.

"I don't know. It would be a real upheaval to move back. You know what it's like when you get to a certain age. You get into a comfortable routine."

"Give it some serious thought. If you're anything like me, cities don't hold the attraction they once did. Too loud and busy and full of young people with mobiles not watching where they're going."

Putting his glass down, he reached over and touched her shoulder. "I'd like you to stay. I'd like to think we could be friends."

He looked into her face as if studying her before beginning to paint.

Starting to feel uncomfortable under his gaze, she said, "David, who do you see when you look at me. Is it me or Emma?"

"I wondered how long it would be before you asked that question. All right, if you want the truth, I see both of you."

His eyes softened, making him appear vulnerable. "You have her Wedgwood blue eyes, and there's something about the shape of your mouth. That doesn't mean I can't appreciate you for who you are. But yes, there is something familiar, something comforting about being with you."

While she had no romantic aspirations with regard to David—and she might possibly be the only heterosexual woman over the age of forty on the island who could truthfully say that—Kate didn't want their friendship to be compromised by David's desire to reconnect to Emma through her.

"I'm not Emma, David. We share some DNA, but that's all."

He nodded, somewhat reluctantly, she thought.

"Look, I've heard something disturbing about her, something I don't want to believe, but I have to look into."

David was still watching her closely, which made it even harder to get the words out.

"Do you know if Emma was involved with anything illegal?"

CHAPTER 30

After dropping off Sophie and Toby, Siobhan made her way down to the pub where she listened to the islanders take delight in repeating the story of how Jenkins had made a fool of himself over Toby. Even Flo had to concede the island would breath a collective sigh of relief once the man left. In her desire to catch what was left of the afternoon sun, Siobhan took her drink outside.

Walking along the wide strip of beach was Byron, his face flushed. From the length of his stride, he looked as if he was trying to walk something off. Maybe Jenkins had found a way to blame him for the loss of a quick result, so Byron could do with someone to talk to, a comforting shoulder or some other body part. Siobhan abandoned her glass and ran down the path to the beach.

It had to look like an accidental meeting, so she slowed her pace as she rounded the corner and came into sight. His head was down, like a schoolboy looking for shells in the sand. It made him look innocent and very appealing.

"Constable Finch, what a surprise."

He looked up at the sound of her voice.

Siobhan stared into his grey eyes.

"Oh, Miss Fitzgerald." His skin had become even rosier, dare Siobhan hope, from his excitement at seeing her.

"Look, I heard all about this afternoon. And let me assure you, no one on the island blames you in the slightest."

"Thank you, ma'am."

How was she to break through his detachment? First it was his insistence on addressing her as Miss. Now ma'am. "Please don't ma'am me. You make me sound like the Queen, and she's positively ancient."

Siobhan would have felt better if he'd at least acknowledged her joke, but he remained infuriatingly official.

"As you wish, Miss Fitzgerald."

This guy was a tough act. She'd never had to work this hard before.

"Listen, Byron, maybe we got off on the wrong foot. Why don't you and I meet up later and have a quiet dinner at The Breeze? Then if there's anything you need to know about the island or the people, I can fill you in."

He seemed to have trouble looking her in the eye. He kept staring over her shoulder, leading her to wonder what was so interesting behind her. "That's very kind of you, Miss Fitzgerald, but I liaise with Miss G."

Siobhan stepped closer. What would he do if she tripped and fell against him? Surely, he wouldn't let her fall, and once he was holding her, well...

"Byron, this investigation must be very stressful. It would do you good to relax a little. Why don't you come to mine, and I'll cook you something. What about a steak? I know how you men like your meat. A little wine. Put your feet up. Watch a film. The police force can't expect you to be on duty all the time."

She thought she saw a waiver, a flicker of weakness.

But then he seemed to stand taller, as if a steel bar had suddenly been shoved up his bum. "Thank you for your kind offer, Miss Fitzgerald, but if you don't mind, I believe we should keep our relationship professional. Good day." His hand came up as if to touch the brim of his missing police cap. Then he stepped around her and resumed his walk.

Bloody copper! He was damn lucky he wasn't wearing a uniform because nothing would give her more pleasure than to knock his cap right off his head.

Instead, she ran to the sea, kicking at the frigid waves lapping over her feet, then stomped up and down as hard as she could. But no matter how hard she tried to drive her heels into the wet sand, it didn't make her feel any better. Now she had to walk home in soggy shoes.

—

David stared at Kate, a disbelieving grin on his face. "Emma do something illegal? Never. It's just ridiculous. Who's been saying these things? Frankly, I'm surprised at you, Kate," and he pointed at her with his glass. "Not only listening to vicious gossip, but spreading it."

"I'm not spreading it. I'm asking you as one of her closest friends."

He kept shaking his head, denying her words.

"David, it doesn't mean I believe it. I don't want to believe it. The hardest part of all this may be having to face the fact that she wasn't the person I thought she was when I was three years old. But if I'm going to get to the truth about Emma's death, I have to look at everything, no matter how unpleasant. And even you have to admit that if she was involved in something criminal, well, it's a possible motive. And there's another thing. Emma had a Porth Madryn bank account with almost £800."

David's face hardened, and he gripped his glass as if he would crush it.

"Please don't break my grandmother's best crystal."

He handed her the glass and collapsed back into the sofa.

"I'd like more than anything for there to be an innocent explanation for the bank account," Kate said. "Were you giving her money?"

"Me?"

"A vacation before you parted company. Some money toward her education. I don't know."

Hiding his face in his hands, he mumbled from behind his palms. "Emma would never do anything wrong. Why would she? And if she did, she'd tell me."

Not if she felt betrayed by you. "David, while you and Emma were together, did you ever have a falling out, a breakup of any kind?"

"Not again, Kate. We've already talked about this. All couples disagree."

"But could there have been something more, something she might have regarded as disloyalty a betrayal?"

David's lips grew tight over his clenched teeth. "I loved her, and I would never have done anything to hurt her."

But behind his expression of outrage, Kate thought she detected embarrassment.

"Is this Smee again?" he asked.

How could she ever hope to break through everyone's defences? Damn, she'd been so arrogant to believe she could uncover the truth. This wasn't a university research paper on a dead poet. It was about someone she'd known and loved, and people who could get hurt if secrets were made public.

"David, I—" but Kate was interrupted as Siobhan stomped into the house, her face as red as her hair.

"Bloody man! Bloody, bloody man! He's obviously gay!"

Kate looked up, startled at Siobhan's dramatic appearance.

"Oh bugger, I'm sorry."

Suddenly everyone was in motion. Kate scrambled off the sofa, and David strode to the door where he grabbed his coat and scarf.

"I'll just be hiding back here," and Siobhan retreated to the kitchen.

David paused before opening the door. "Hannah's funeral is tomorrow," he said. "I hope you'll come."

"Of course. We both will."

He smiled. The door closed behind him.

Siobhan turned to face her as Kate walked toward the kitchen. "I just blurt out whatever comes into my head without considering the consequences. I have a history of embarrassing people, and for that reason I never get invited to formal social gatherings. You should know that if you're at all considering becoming my friend."

Kate stood in the kitchen doorway smiling.

Siobhan looked surprised and relieved. "I interrupted something, didn't I?"

"Yes, but not what you think. I was telling David that Emma might have been involved in something criminal."

Siobhan kicked off her shoes, wrung out her wet socks, and placed them all outside the back door.

"Bit early in the season for a paddle, isn't it?"

"Long story," Siobhan said in a tone that made it clear she didn't want to talk about it. "What's this about Emma and something criminal?"

Siobhan listened as Kate told her about Feebles' conversation without mentioning him by name.

"And there's something else. You know those nasty letters you got? David has been getting them for years. The same thing—letters cut out of magazines."

"You think they're from the same person?"

"Maybe. It was the whore reference in yours that got me thinking. David's letters contained sexual comments about the women he was with at the time."

"Damn!"

"What?"

Siobhan looked reluctant to continue the conversation. "When we first met, David and I had a…well…a friends-with-benefits relationship."

Siobhan, the tattoo and clay-splattered overalls, and David Sutherland, Italian suit, silk tie, and handmade shoes. Kate just couldn't put the two of them together. "That's why you're so defensive of him."

"I really respect the guy. And it's not like we were ever in love. It was strictly casual. If one of us was at a loose end or wanted some company, we'd go to an exhibition, a film, grab dinner and talk about how the work was going. And often as not, we'd end up in bed. It was over long before I moved here. Nobody knows, and I want to keep it that way. I'm not ashamed of what we did, but you know how the island likes to gossip. It would be awkward for both of us if it got out."

"I won't breath a word. I promise." *Besides, who'd believe me?* Kate thought.

"I don't regret it. You should know I never regret anything."

"Anything?"

"Well, maybe those red platform shoes I bought six years ago. But on the whole, no." Siobhan took a deep breath. "You must think I'm disgustingly self-indulgent."

"I don't think that." Well, maybe just a bit, but that was tied up with Kate's envy of Siobhan's ability to so easily embrace the choices she made.

"I go on instinct. I tend to do whatever I want in the moment, but I always make sure no one gets hurt, and that includes me. I really do try to conduct myself with some sort of integrity, but I also grab life by the bollocks. So yes, I had a sexual relationship with David Sutherland. We both wanted it, so we went for it."

"I'm not judging."

"No, but your opinion is important to me, and I can't say that about many people." Siobhan looked almost bashful.

Kate gave her a look of genuine affection. She remembered her own initial attraction to David, those striking good looks that still excited Fiona.

"You know, Fiona would probably have a fit if she ever knew about you and David."

There was Siobhan's sensuous laugh again. "Oh, I don't know. I think she'd beg me for all the steamy details."

"And speaking of steamy details, you and Byron. Nothing going on? Is that why he's gay?"

"Either he's gay or I'm past it. If I have a choice, I'll take the first over the second."

Kate realized that for the first time in Siobhan's life a man hadn't seen her as sexually desirable. She'd run straight into the brick wall of middle-age, and it had hurt. It was a place where every woman eventually finds herself, but there was no way Siobhan was going to age gracefully. She was going to have to be dragged, kicking and screaming.

Before Kate could offer any advice, the phone rang.

"Hi, Mum. Sorry, this is going to have to be short and to the point. I'm off to a client meeting, but I've got some news, and I thought it would be faster to call than email."

"What have you got?"

"I managed to dig up the name of the person who wants Siobhan's cottage."

Kate waved to Siobhan. "Alex knows who wants to buy the cottage." She tapped the speaker icon so Siobhan could listen in. "Who is it?"

"The property agent is acting on behalf of Bella Casa, an interior design company and Italian furniture importer. Bella Casa is a division of a London architectural firm."

"Why would an architectural firm be interested in an island cottage? Who are these people?"

"Anton Lynley and Associates."

Kate looked over at Siobhan.

Siobhan's mouth fell open, and she pounded the wall. "Bloody Angelica!" She stalked into the living room, presumably to pour herself a large drink.

"Mum, I need to talk to you about Dad."

"What's wrong?"

"Is the speaker off?"

"Yes."

"Sorry, it's not about Dad, but I don't want Siobhan to hear this, not yet. I don't want it all over the island until we can decide what to do about it."

This whole cloak and dagger routine wasn't like Alex at all. "Now you've got me worried."

"I called the architectural firm and spoke to the receptionist. Thought I'd try to pump her for some more information. I told her I was calling in regard to some property on Meredith Island. When she heard the name, she said we must be very excited about the new project."

"What new project?"

"Their firm has been commissioned to design an arts centre. And it's huge—a three-storey building, with a gallery, gastro-pub, and shop, and a floor of artists' studios. And that's just for starters. There's a six-storey hotel with a convention centre, more shops, and an ultra-expensive restaurant in the works."

"But someone can't just build without the island's permission," Kate struggled to keep her voice down. "This is ridiculous. Where's it going?"

"The other side of the harbour. They're planning to tear down the community centre, the lifeboat station, the cottages. It'll destroy the island." Alex sounded as disgusted as Kate felt.

"Alex, are you absolutely sure about this?"

"Don't take my word for it. Ask David Sutherland."

"What's David got to do with it?"

"Mum, this atrocity is going to be called The David Sutherland Art Institute."

CHAPTER 31

Kate couldn't accept that David would have anything to do with the art complex. It just didn't seem to be his style. However, from what she'd heard about Angelica Lynley, this sort of project would be right up her street. But how did she think she was going to get the islanders' permission to use the land? Kate still needed to speak with Jane about the time she saw Emma. Perhaps she could get her take on the art complex as part of that conversation.

To be honest, Kate had been putting off the visit. She was a little intimidated by Jane's severe clothes and tight lips. That and her hands, which were always held firmly clasped in front of her, reminded Kate of a dour mother superior. But if she had anything to add to the investigation, Kate had to face her.

She didn't want to ask Siobhan for yet another ride and then have her wait in the truck, so Kate decided to take Lilian's scooter. Luckily, it was still sitting in the garage, its red paint and helmet covered with a thick layer of dust. It obviously hadn't been ridden for a long time. A can of petrol was in the corner of the garage. Once the tank was filled, the scooter started on the second try.

In no time at all, Kate was sitting in the Sutherland drawing room across from Jane who was perched on the edge of the sofa. "So, Miss Hewitt, are you still on this fool's errand?"

Oh dear, this isn't a good start, Kate thought. "Miss Sutherland, I'm simply trying to get an impression of what people remember about the last days of my aunt's life. Miss Sophie said you saw Emma on the mainland two days before she disappeared. It would help me a great deal—no, it would give me peace—to know what you saw."

Kate thought she saw Jane's chest rise and fall quickly with an inaudible sigh. "Very well. What do you wish to know?"

"Where did you see her? What was she doing?"

"I had just placed our order with the butcher. His boy was supposed carry the basket down to the ferry, but he was out on a delivery, and it would be half an hour before he returned. I had some time before meeting him at the harbour, and St. Mary's Church was on the way, so I thought I'd stop in for some silent contemplation. That's where I was going when I ran into Miss Galway coming out of Mowbray's Antiques. I felt it only courteous to say hello. I asked if she'd bought anything nice. She said she'd been looking for a birthday present for her sister. I wished her good-day."

Jane broke eye contact with Kate. "I hesitate to tell you the rest of the story as it casts me in a poor light, but it is my burden to bear. You did ask for the truth."

"Yes, Miss Sutherland, I did."

Jane clasped the cross about her neck. "Well, when Miss Galway was leaving the store, she had some money in her hand, a considerable amount of money as far as I could tell, and she was counting it. She seemed shocked and uneasy that I'd seen her. And since she wasn't carrying a package—well, to be blunt, I didn't believe her story about buying a birthday gift. I'm ashamed to say I went into the store to ascertain the truth. I told the man behind the counter that I was a neighbour of your aunt, and she'd told me about the present for her sister. Since I also was purchasing a birthday gift, would he tell me what she'd bought so as to avoid buying something similar. It's a sin to lie, Miss Hewitt. I'm fully aware of that, and I have no excuse. I have since prayed many times for God's help to conquer this deficiency in myself."

God might see it as a failing, but Kate was quite thankful for Jane's 'deficiency'. With her ingenuity and her ability to lie with such conviction, she'd make an excellent detective.

"The owner appeared confused and said I was mistaken. Your aunt hadn't been shopping. She'd sold him something, but he didn't tell me what it was. He said Miss Galway had explained to him that her grandmother had recently died and the family was forced to sell some of her possessions to pay for the funeral expenses."

Jane stopped as if waiting for Kate's reaction, but Kate said nothing.

"I'm sorry if this offends you, Miss Hew—Miss Galway—but as I knew this simply wasn't true, the only conclusion I could draw was that your aunt had stolen whatever it was she'd sold. Where else could she have gotten something valuable enough to sell?"

The silver vinaigrette. Was that the next item to be sold? But it hadn't belonged to the Galways. Could Emma have taken it from someone else, perhaps the Sutherlands?

Kate stood up and thanked Jane for her time.

"I'm sorry," said Jane. It was said with a greater measure of compassion than Kate had ever heard her use before.

It wasn't until she was half-way home that Kate realized she'd forgotten to ask about the art institute.

—

Kate came home by way of the harbour to see if she would catch a word with Gooley. She wanted to corroborate what Gwynie had told her earlier that day. As luck would have it, the Gents were just mooring Smee's boat. Quentin Feebling looked up and waved at her.

A few minutes later, they approached Kate and the scooter waiting on the wharf.

"Good to see the old engine up and running," Feebles said. "Care for a drink, lass?"

"Maybe later. I'd like a quick word with Rupert, if you can spare him."

Gooley looked apprehensive.

"I'll see you inside, lads," he said to the others.

Kate waited until they were alone before she spoke. "Can I ask you about Gwynie Morgan?"

"Oh, aye." It was said with some resignation.

"Rupert, were you and Gwynie together at the time Emma disappeared?"

"Well, lass, if Gwynie remembers us together..." He looked out over the open sea, as if afraid to make eye contact.

"She led me to believe you two were a couple."

At first, he looked like he thought she might be making a joke. But he must have seen her serious expression because he pulled back from whatever he was about to say.

"If she says so."

Kate shook her head. "Rupert, you were always a terrible liar."

He said nothing.

"Remember when I was preparing for my A-levels, and I asked you to take me over to the mainland? I'd missed the early morning ferry, and I needed to get to the Porth Madryn library. You made up some excuse about why you couldn't take me. You had that same expression on your face."

"You were meeting a lad, an older lad," he said as if that explained everything.

"A library is hardly a hotbed of teenage seduction. He was a second-year university student who was preparing me for my geography exam, and he was helping me to draw up a list of universities to apply to."

"You had no da, so we had to protect you."

Kate didn't know whether to yell at him or kiss him. "So were you or weren't you with Gwynie?"

He looked down and rubbed at the dry skin on the palms of his hands.

"There's that look again," Kate barked in frustration. "God damn it, Rupert. People have to start telling me the truth. If I don't find Emma's murderer, I'll never be able to move back to the island."

And there it was. What had been simmering below the surface, what had kept her from making the commitment everyone wanted her to make. The argument she'd trotted out to David and Alex, and even herself—that she was too attached to her life on the mainland—had simply been an excuse. The real reason was fear, fear that she couldn't trust the islanders, that she'd be constantly wondering if someone she passed on the road, shared a drink with at the pub, danced with at a celebration could have been her aunt's murderer. She now knew without any doubt that she had to solve Emma's murder if she ever wanted to return. And the longer she spent here, the more she wanted to come back.

She forced herself to focus on what Gooley had said, or not said, about Gwynie. It was obvious her alibi had been a lie. But why? And what else had she lied about?

"Rupert, was Gwynie dating David?"

"Dating?" He emphasized the word. "No."

"Was he seeing anyone other than Emma?"

"How am I supposed to know? We didn't travel in the same circles, him and me. Still don't."

Gooley looked like a man who was desperate for a drink. Kate wasn't going to get anything more out of him, so she waved her hand to indicate he could join his mates in the pub. But he didn't leave. Instead he stared at her. At last he said, "You look just like her, you know."

"So everyone keeps saying."

Gooley started to walk away but then stopped. "I was on the mainland."

—

Siobhan had run out of jam. Her favourite afternoon treat was biscuits smeared with a thick layer of jam, any jam. The sugar kept her energy up and her creativity flowing. Luckily she still had her key to Kate's place.

Walking into Kate's front hall, she was immediately hit with a greasy, burnt smell. Smoke was rapidly filling the kitchen, and it seemed to be coming from a large pot on the stove. But before she could reach it, the oil exploded onto flames. Instinctively she backed away. *Keep calm*, she told herself. All she had to do was smother the flames with the lid.

Oven mitts. She had to protect her hands with oven mitts.

Siobhan jerked open drawer after drawer until she found a pair. By now her hair was sticking to her hot face, and the mitts were hampering her efforts to push her hair out of the way. Please don't let her head go up in flames.

She held the lid in front of her like a shield and banged it down on the pot. She dragged the pot off the burner, careful not to spill the contents, and turned off the heat. It wasn't until she opened the back door and gulped in the fresh air that she realized she'd been holding her breath the whole time.

She was hot and sweating, and desperate for a drink. She was just helping herself to a whiskey when Kate came in the door.

"Where's the smoke coming from? What's that smell?"

Siobhan swallowed the whiskey in one go. She took Kate by the hand, led her into the kitchen, and raised the lid on the pot. "Look, I can understand. You were rushing off somewhere, and you've had a lot on your mind. It could have happened to any of us."

"I didn't do this," Kate said, staring into the pot.

"It's all right. I caught it in time."

"No, you don't understand," Kate insisted. "I really didn't do this. This pot is full of oil. I'm fifty-three years old. I don't deep fry anything!"

Siobhan wandered into the hallway, climbed up on a chair, and snapped the top off the smoke alarm. "The battery's missing."

"Lilian would never have taken the battery out without replacing it," Kate insisted.

As Siobhan climbed back down, Kate came over and put her arms around her.

Siobhan could feel her shaking, so she hugged back. It felt good. "Bloody hell, the house was supposed to burn down, and you were supposed to go back to the mainland. If I hadn't been here..."

"Why are you here?"

"Ran out of jam."

Kate laughed, and Siobhan started to relax. "I think I know how you felt when they broke into your place."

"We have to report this to Byron." Siobhan couldn't believe she was saying this. "And no, it's not just an excuse to see him again, and yes, I know I'm being hypocritical because I didn't want to report it when it happened to me. I obviously take better care of my friends than I do of myself."

"We'll have to work on that."

Kate examined the back door, "The lock's been broken. As for reporting it, I doubt the police will be able to do anything."

"What about fingerprints?"

"Whoever did this probably wore gloves," Kate said. "And even if they didn't, that door is covered in fingerprints from almost everyone on the island. Besides, you know what Jenkins would say."

"'Typical middle-aged woman. Hot flashes muddled her brain. Probably forgot she left the pot on the boil.'"

Kate gave her friend a sideways glance. "That came into your head rather too easily."

Siobhan tapped the side of her head. "To outsmart the enemy, you have to think like the enemy."

"You know why this happened."

Siobhan knew all right. It felt exciting and dangerous at the same time. "We're getting close."

CHAPTER 32

Kate sat in the island church wearing an outfit she'd cobbled together. The Sutherlands didn't hold with the island custom of bright colours at funerals, and Kate hadn't packed anything suitable. Black made her look washed-out, and she had neither the time nor the inclination to make a trip to the mainland to buy an outfit she'd never wear again. Her only recourse was to improvise, pairing her black trousers with Lilian's navy beaded cardigan. The cardigan smelt of the lavender sachets scattered in Lilian's dresser drawers. It was like having her grandmother's comforting arms around her.

The church wasn't large enough to hold the entire island population, so latecomers were forced to stand outside and peer through the windows. In spite of whatever people may have thought of Hannah, the whole island had turned out to see her off and dressed appropriately. This included Siobhan who sat pressed against Kate on the hard, wooden pew in a black knit dress, a gold belt resting on her hips, and knee-high black suede boots.

Flo, subdued in dress and makeup, struck a sustained chord on the organ. It was the signal for everyone to stand. From the back of the church came the haunting sound of a single voice. Retired opera singer Elspeth McEwan, who had sung at Lilian's funeral just two weeks earlier, sang Fauré's "Pie Jesu" as Hannah's ebony casket slowly made its way down the aisle. David and Marcus were among the pallbearers. Sophie and Jane followed and took their places in the front pew. In her straight black dress with a large silver cross resting against her chest, Jane might have been mistaken for a nun from a progressive order. Sophie wore a full stiff dress that crunched when she walked. A large-brimmed hat was balanced atop her head, draped in a patterned black veil, making her look like an Edward Gorey caricature. She looked terribly sad.

The funeral was a fitting tribute to Hannah Sutherland. The congregation, led by the Reverend Imogen, sang traditional hymns. Jane read an appropriate passage from the Bible, while Sophie recited a Shakespearean sonnet. Not "No Longer Mourn for Me When I am Dead," which would have been the conventional choice, but "Shall I Compare Thee to a Summer's Day?" Rather than focus on Hannah's death, Sophie wanted the islanders to remember her sister as vibrant and alive. Elspeth performed several more classical numbers. Then people came forward and spoke of Hannah's inspirational teaching.

Simmons sat in the row behind the Sutherlands. Toby was absent. Kate assumed he was doing his best to repair the damage inflicted on the garden by the forensic team who, according to Byron, had found nothing.

When the congregation bent their heads in prayer, Kate turned to look toward the back of the church where Byron and Jenkins were standing, their hands behind their backs.

"We always make a point of attending the funerals," James had once told her. "It's common courtesy to pay our respects to the family of the victim, but it's also interesting to see who turns up."

"But surely the murderer isn't stupid enough to come to his victim's funeral?"

"If they know the victim, they do. Otherwise they'd be conspicuous by their absence. But mostly it's a convenient way for us to meet people who were acquainted with the deceased and observe their reactions."

But there were no new faces here.

Kate felt a sharp jab in her ribs from Siobhan, and she turned back to find Angelica Lynley standing in front of the altar, sharing her anguish at the loss of Hannah.

Siobhan shifted about uncomfortably. "Damn woman always

has to be the centre of attention."

Angelica had been at it for several minutes now and showed no sign of winding down.

Fiona, who was sitting directly in front of Kate and Siobhan, turned and whispered, "My Billy used to say it was women like her that drove men into the priesthood!"

Siobhan's explosive laugh quickly morphed into a sputtered cough. Angelica glared at Siobhan but quickly regained her focus—and apparently got the message. "And so, I bid a heartfelt adieu to my beloved friend Hannah Sutherland."

One more hymn and some official words from Imogen, and they all drifted out to the graveside. After the internment, David broke away from his sisters and came to greet Kate. "Thank you both for coming, I hope you'll come back to the house for some refreshments."

"We'll be there," Siobhan said affectionately.

—

For many of the islanders, this was the first time they'd set foot in Sutherland Hall, and Kate observed they were wandering about the place like tourists broken away from their tour guide. In their exuberance, they were pointing and commenting on the artwork and furniture, the leaded glass windows and beautifully manicured lawns, their curiosity overwhelming their sense of propriety. It was also evident from the way they tucked into the food they were enjoying being at a function where someone else was providing the nibbles.

Siobhan stuffed a salmon canapé into her mouth. "These are really quite good. Try one. Oh, sorry, forgot," and she scooped another one from a passing tray. "I'll have yours."

Julian and Flo were in attendance, mingling rather than serving, and Kate wondered if Julian was going to lead the traditional island toast. Probably not. It didn't seem to fit with the tone of the gathering somehow.

A waiter with more than a passing resemblance to a young Johnny Depp stopped in front of Siobhan who grinned and exchanged her empty whiskey glass for a full one.

"This is a funeral, and you're flirting with the waiter?" Kate said in a disapproving tone.

Siobhan looked surprised at her reaction. "Yes."

"Don't you think it's inappropriate?"

"It's not my funeral. But if it were, I'd want people to have a good time. Go on, give it a try."

"I'm going to find Byron." Before Siobhan could make a comment, Kate added, "To see if there have been any new developments."

Siobhan emptied her glass and looked around for another waiter. "You go work. I'll just stay here and enjoy myself."

Kate needed to get Byron alone. He and Jenkins had been joined at the hip during the service, but here they'd split up and were circulating, listening in on people's conversations. At least Byron was making some effort to be sociable. Carrying a glass of fizzy water, he smiled and exchanged small talk. The older women were treating him like a son or grandson, reaching to brush a piece of lint from his jacket or straighten his tie, while the younger women gave him flirtatious glances over their drinks. Byron had the ability to put people at ease, and that was a great advantage in getting them to talk. On the other hand, Jenkins was a shark, constantly circling, waiting for someone to make a mistake, so he could take a lethal bite.

"You look so handsome, Constable," Drucilla Cragwell fussed. "Your mother must be very proud of you."

"Thank you, ma'am, she is."

Kate gently took Byron by the arm. "Excuse me. I need to talk to Constable Finch for a minute."

"Just make sure you return him."

Kate wanted a quiet place to talk and so steered Byron into the hall and toward the library. But there were voices coming from behind the door.

"You're such a hypocrite!" snapped an older female voice.

"Please, Gwynie, no more." This voice was David's, but it was hard to tell whether he was angry or simply weary. "In case you haven't noticed, we're at my sister's funeral, so please try to show some respect."

Gwynie responded with a long shrill laugh. "You're one to talk about respect after how you betrayed Emma."

Kate gripped Byron's arm.

"I never betrayed Emma," David insisted.

She laughed again, but this time it was deep and earthy. "As long as I live, I'll never understand the ability of men to ignore the significance of their sexual infidelities. Did that night mean so little to you?"

"We were both drunk. It was sex. I loved Emma."

"Loved her so much that you took my virginity without a backward glance!" Gwynie's voice was getting louder.

So Kate had been right about David's indiscretion.

There was silence. Then David spoke softly. "We both decided it was a mistake."

"No, you decided it was a mistake." Gwynie was still shouting.

"It was a long time ago. Why bring it up now?"

"Because it was Hannah who had to clean up after you. All their lives, those uptight, upright spinsters have been flaunting their family honour, your family honour, while the great and noble, the respected Hannah Sutherland arranged for your baby to be terminated."

"You lying bitch!" David shouted with a malice Kate didn't think he was capable of.

Kate looked at Byron. He put his hand on the doorknob.

There was silence, and then David spoke. "You were really pregnant?"

"For eleven weeks and three days." Gwynie's voice had gone soft with remembering. "I told Hannah. I told her because I stupidly believed she'd compel you to marry me. I said I'd let everyone know that you were the father, that the Sutherland name would come to stand for a sexual rogue who impregnated young girls. But if you married me, I'd go to Paris with you. We wouldn't be back for years, so we could say the baby had been premature.

"But I underestimated Hannah. She didn't rant or rage or yell at me. She just talked quietly. The first thing she told me was that marrying you was out of the question, so I was to get that out of my head. Then she reminded me I was a schoolgirl, and schoolgirls with babies were shunned by society, ruined. It would reflect on me much worse than on you if this were to get out. People always blamed the woman. Then there were my parents to think about. You were just sowing your wild oats, being Jack the lad." Her voice took on a sarcastic tone. "Men were weak, she said. Men couldn't be trusted. As a woman, I should've been strong enough for both of us, kept control. She convinced me having a termination was the best thing for me. She arranged it. Even travelled with me to the mainland."

That's what Hannah was doing the afternoon she saw Emma's killer. Terminations were illegal then. Hannah had told Sophie to trust that what she had been doing was for the best. But for whom?

"No! Hannah would never have done that." David was struggling to believe it.

Gwynie laughed again, but this time it was tinged with sadness. "She would have done anything for you. She murdered our baby to protect you. It's not much of a jump to believe she murdered Emma."

"Or you murdered Emma out of jealousy."

There was a loud crash from inside the room. Kate jerked the door open. A large blue and white vase lay in pieces at David's feet.

Gwynie looked at Kate and Byron, a look of uncertainty slowly washing over her face, not knowing how much they'd heard. She turned back to David. "You'll excuse me if I can't pray for Hannah Sutherland's soul."

She brushed passed Kate and Byron as she left the room. "I've got to get off this accursed island."

By now, the crash and Gwynie's angry voice had attracted a

crowd in the hall.

"You hypocritical bastards!" she shouted at the islanders. "I always thought you had more guts than this. You talked about what a rotten cow she was behind her back, yet you all make a public exhibition of pretending you're sorry she's gone."

There were several small gasps and a muted sob Kate assumed had come from Sophie.

Angelica stepped forward, a faint smile on her face. In some perverse way, she was enjoying this spectacle. "That didn't stop you from dining here last week. Who's the hypocrite now, Lady Charlton?" she said, with the emphasis on 'Lady' a sarcastic singsong.

Gwynie planted herself in front of Angelica. "Go to hell, you pretentious old tart!"

Despite her previous bravado, Angelica took a few steps back to shield herself behind Julian.

Gwynie grinned. "You don't think we recognize mutton dressed as lamb when we see it? You've done nothing but social climb since you arrived here. Oh, and do share with everyone your plans to turn the island into some grotesque tourist attraction to boost your monstrous ego. We're fed up to the back teeth with your flash yacht and your rich dead husband. You were nothing before you married him. At least prostitutes have the decency to be honest about what they do."

She walked toward the front door, leaving Angelica sputtering.

Byron left Kate's side and stepped in Gwynie's way. "I'm sorry, Lady Charlton. I'm afraid I must insist you not leave the island. We need to speak with you."

Kate had to find a way to be part of that conversation.

"If you insist, Constable, but let's make it as soon as possible." Gwynie turned and stared in Angelica's direction. "I still have a husband waiting for me at home."

Jenkins pushed his way to the front of the crowd. "Finch, is there something I should know?"

Byron snapped to attention. "Just about to update you, sir."

Jenkins walked over to Byron, as if he had been in charge all along. "Good man. Lady Charlton, we'll see you in the morning," and he opened the door for her to leave.

People began to murmur among themselves. Siobhan came up to Kate, an empty glass in her hand and a curious look on her face, waiting to be filled in on what she'd missed. Angelica steadied herself against Julian, while Simmons appeared with a brandy. People made sympathetic noises and gestures, and Sophie was offered a chair. Jane paced about, probably working off the anger she felt it inappropriate to display. Nothing was said, but Kate was quite sure if Jane had anything to do with it, neither Angelica nor Gwynie would ever set foot in Sutherland Hall again.

—

The air was damp and Gwynie pulled her jacket tighter. She'd only been walking for ten minutes and was already regretting the decision to make her own way back to the pub. It would take close to an hour in the chilly afternoon air, but she had no other way of getting back. She'd come with the doctor, and he'd stayed behind. Besides if anyone offered her a ride, it would turn into a cross-examination, and she was going to get enough of that from the police.

She could hear a car, probably someone leaving. Damn, they were going to stop and ask if she wanted a lift. No doubt it would turn into a cross-examination, and she was going to get enough of that from the police. But her feet and ankles were throbbing from her high-heeled shoes. She hadn't expected to be walking on these terrible roads. Still, a little pain was preferable to intrusive questions or platitudes of sympathy.

If only it were Hugh's Mercedes behind her. It was their one ostentatious sign of wealth, and damn, it was comfortable. Hugh would pull up beside her, roll down the window, and whistle. "Hey, Old Girl, looking for a little company?"

It was a silly joke between the two of them. He'd started calling her Old Girl when she stopped dyeing her grey hair.

"Think you can keep up, Old Man?" she'd throw back, and then he'd laugh, a laugh that still knocked her sideways. And then she'd call him *cariad*, because that's what he was, her one and only love.

That's why she could never tell him about David or the termination because if she did, she'd never hear that laugh again. The only way to ensure her indiscretion remained a secret was to sever all ties with the island.

Religion had never been very important to her when she was younger, but Hugh was a devout Catholic, and she'd converted when they'd married. Every time she stepped into the confessional, she wanted to tell Father Joseph, to blurt it out before she could stop herself, but she never could. Deep in her soul, she knew neither God nor Hugh could ever forgive the murder of an innocent.

Damn and blast! Why did she tell David? She'd had no right to take it out on him. The poor sod hadn't even known about the baby. They'd both been responsible for the conception, but it was she alone who'd been responsible for its death. So many times she'd wished she'd given it away, become one of those mums whose adult child suddenly appears one morning on the doorstep, a fully-formed human being with her eyes and David's artistic bent, wanting to get to know and love her. But she'd been afraid, and it was her fear Hannah had recognized and exploited. So Gwynie had conveniently disposed of her baby, flushed it away.

The car engine revved higher, as if speeding up. What sort of an irresponsible idiot drove like that? That's what the island got for not having any traffic laws or police. At least, she was walking on the right shoulder of the road, well away from any cars coming up behind her. She wondered if the islanders were still up there talking about her.

Gwynie heard the car tires scream. She turned to catch a glimpse of the driver but caught only a dark shadow as the car swerved toward her. Without thinking, she jumped into the ditch and heard the dry twig sound of her ankle snap as everything went black.

CHAPTER 33

Immediately after Gwynie's dramatic exit, the islanders stood in small groups whispering about what to do next. They were torn between staying to show support and leaving so as not to cause further embarrassment. Some wanted to question Angelica about her project, but she cut them off by announcing she had a sick headache which necessitated lying down upstairs with a sedative Marcus fetched from the bag in his car.

While Siobhan was still eager to confront Angelica about the annoying offers to buy her cottage, Kate managed to restrain her by pointing out that while Siobhan might relish the idea of adding yet another insult to the injury Gwynie had hurled at Angelica, two public outbursts in as many weeks would only reflect badly on her. Besides, the sisters shouldn't have to go through any more distress. It seemed the others shared this sentiment. There was a general consensus that there had been enough excitement for one day, and it was time to withdraw to the pub. People began to say their good-byes.

Siobhan waited until she and Kate set off in the blue truck before pressing her friend for all the details she'd overheard behind the library door. But just as Kate was getting to Gwynie's revelation, Siobhan started to slow down, craning her neck to see out the side window.

"What's wrong?" Kate asked.

"There's something down in that hollow, something grey. It could be an injured gull." Siobhan pulled the car over.

By the time Kate got her seat belt off and the door open, Siobhan was down in the ditch feeling for a pulse.

"Over here, quick. It's Gwynie. She's still alive," Siobhan announced. "Fetch the blanket under the passenger's seat. We need to keep her warm."

When Kate returned, she saw blood had caked Gwynie's grey hair. Her body was twisted, and her ankle lay at an unnatural angle, already puffed and discoloured.

"I don't think we should move her," Siobhan said as she unfolded the blanket. "If she's broken something, we could make it worse. Call Marcus on my mobile. It's in the glove box."

As they waited, Siobhan stayed with Gwynie, periodically checking her breathing. She was still unconscious. The islanders making their way down from Sutherland Hall were congregating on the road.

It took Marcus only a few minutes to arrive. His initial assessment was a broken ankle and probable concussion. Gwynie was strapped into a neck brace, loaded onto a backboard, and placed in his estate car which served as the island ambulance.

As Marcus drove off toward the hospital, and scooters and pedestrians began to disperse, Kate turned her attention toward Siobhan who was brushing mud off her bottom. "You're very good in an emergency. It was sheer luck you spotted her. Although perhaps the Reverend Imogen would say someone was looking out for her."

"It was her hair I spotted. If it hadn't been me, someone else would have found her."

"Well, don't downplay your role in all this. You did a really good thing today."

Siobhan acknowledged Kate's praise with a faint smile. They climbed back into the truck, but rather than start the engine, Siobhan sat staring at the ditch. "She could have fainted, or tripped and lost her balance, or been frightened by an animal crossing the road—a complete coincidence after what had happened up at the hall. But what does your copper ex-husband say about coincidences?"

"Exactly."

—

Less than two hours after the accident, DS Jenkins was leaning against the bar at the Filly. The sound of the approaching medical helicopter had summoned curious islanders to the harbour. The tide was out, and the wide strip of beach made an excellent landing pad. Through the front window, Jenkins watched four men carry Lady Charlton on a stretcher and secure her inside the helicopter. The gossip in the pub was that upon hearing of Gwynie's accident, her husband insisted she be transferred to a hospital close to their home where she'd get the best of care, and he and the boys could stand vigil at her bedside.

The doc was probably relieved, Jenkins thought. It didn't look like his ramshackle hospital could handle anything more than an ingrown toenail. Besides, if anything had happened to his wife, good old Sir Hugh wouldn't hesitate to bring the full force of his stable of lawyers down on the doc's neck.

Jenkins was eager to interview Gwynie as soon as possible, but he wasn't sure if the chief would approve of him leaving the island. There was nothing to indicate her accident was anything more than an old lady falling off her pins and knocking herself out. But as Finch had informed him, Lady Charlton believed Hannah Sutherland had pressured her into terminating a pregnancy many years ago, and if she was as angry as Finch claimed, perhaps she still felt strongly enough to seek revenge.

Seven of the islanders, including the landlord, had pushed some of the tables together and were discussing with exaggerated gravity whether or not to hold a dressing up contest. For a place where there was no cinema or rugby team, and only one pub, dressing up was probably a big deal.

He drained his pint—his fifth, or was it his sixth? It didn't matter. The case had ground to a halt and him along with it. Just his luck! He'd finally found a suspect, and she'd just been whisked off the island. But there was no evidence. So unless he could get her to confess... But then her high-priced lawyer would get a Harley Street doctor to testify she wasn't in her right mind due to the head injury. Faced with yet another bollocking from the chief, he'd given himself long overdue permission to work his way through the pub's beer list.

He pushed his empty glass across the bar and ordered another pint from Flo who was beginning to look more and more attractive as the afternoon wore on.

But she wasn't refilling his glass. "Sergeant Jenkins, don't you think you've had enough?"

He'd bloody well decide when he'd had enough. But he said nothing. She didn't deserve his anger. Besides, it wasn't her he was angry at.

"You don't look very happy. It must be a very difficult job you do." Her eyes, accented with smoky eye shadow, showed sympathy and sincerity, with none of the ridicule so many other people chucked at the police.

Since her warm eyes reminded him he hadn't seen his Dilys in several days, he allowed himself to tell her. "You have no idea. My prime suspect in the Sutherland murder just flew away."

She took a towel and started to polish glasses. "What are you going to do?"

"What can I do?"

"What does your heart tell you to do?"

If anyone else had tried talking to him about his heart, he'd have thrown off some sarcastic comment and walked away. But he didn't do either of those things. What he didn't tell her was that he wanted to prove to the chief he wasn't a washed-up copper. He knew his career had been far from exemplary—that was the phrase used at his last personnel review. The general consensus was he didn't handle people well, so they kept sending him on bloody useless courses. Well, he'd show them.

"Solve this bloody murder."

"Good."

"When's the next ferry?"

"The early morning run is at seven."

He slammed the bar with the flat of his hand. "Make up my bill for tomorrow morning. I'll be checking out."

He'd crack this case wide open. He shouldn't leave the island—after all he was in charge—but once he came back with a result, all he'd get would be a talking-to. His initiative and a result would overshadow any other disciplinary action. Besides, he'd leave Finch in charge. What could happen?

—

Rupert Gooley had purposely chosen the table next to the Queen Victoria Celebration Committee who were holding an emergency meeting to decide whether to cancel the festivities just two days away. In all its history, the celebration had never been cancelled. Not even rationing and the threat of bombing during the Second World War had stopped it. In fact, the celebrations held during the war were reputed to have been some of the best. So why all the fuss, Gooley wondered. Did people think it was in bad taste to have fun so soon after two deaths? Gooley certainly couldn't see Lilian wanting the festivities cancelled, and Hannah—well, who cared what the Sutherlands thought.

For the longest tradition on the island, the population more than tripled with mainlanders coming year after year for the celebration. It was the unofficial start of the tourist season, and while islanders often whinged about strangers being underfoot all summer, everyone benefited from the money made renting out beds, conducting tours of Faraday Manor, or the increase in sales at Craggy's and the island art shop. Gooley gladly put up with city folks spreading their towels all over the beach when it meant that with the additional beer sales Flo and Julian were able to put on a free Christmas bash for the whole island. Gooley, along with Feebles and Smee, earned more than a few extra quid themselves from conducting sightseeing tours around the island. There wasn't much to see, but city folks seemed to be willing to pay to look at anything they couldn't find in their own back gardens. Then there were the day-long fishing trips where they never seemed to catch anything. As long as there was enough booze, they didn't complain.

But Gooley had another reason for wanting the celebration to go ahead. He was in the running to win the Queen Victoria Challenge, the award for the islander who presented the best interpretation of the old queen herself. A perennial favourite, he'd won the last four years in a row, and he was buggered if he was going to miss out on number five.

After several more rounds of whiskey, one which he himself sent over—much to everyone's astonishment—the committee unanimously adopted Julian's proposal that the celebration go ahead and be dedicated to Lilian and Hannah.

An audible cheer came from Gooley.

—

After everything that had happened that afternoon, all Kate had wanted was a drink and a soak in a hot tub, but she'd only gotten as far as the drink. Sitting in the waning light, she'd been wondering if Gwynie was supposed to have died in that ditch. Unable to reach any conclusion, she finally worked up the energy to get off the sofa.

She checked her phone, which had been turned off during the funeral. A voice message was waiting. Damn, it was her editor.

"Kate, it's Ursula. I realize it hasn't been long since your grandmother's funeral, but I'm phoning to remind you about your deadline. If there's a problem, please let me know."

She tapped the erase button. Ursula could wait.

She was halfway up the stairs when there was a knock. *Not now,* she grumbled. Why couldn't everyone just leave her alone!

"Kate?" It was Quentin Feebling.

Against her better judgment, she came down and opened the door.

"Quentin, what can I do for you?" she said, sounding irritated.

He stepped into the hall, somewhat reluctantly, she thought. "The cat seems to be out of the bag, Kate."

She didn't know if she should offer him a drink, but she ultimately decided against it. She didn't want to encourage him to stay, especially if he was going to speak in vague generalities again.

He noticed her hesitation. "You remember what we talked about on Friday."

"Gwynie was David's indiscretion." She didn't tell him she'd already figured it out.

"Aye, and I was the one who told Emma about it." He had that regretful look on his face again.

"Don't feel bad. After all, Emma told you she didn't care what David got up to."

It didn't look like he felt any better.

"Uncle Quintin, there's something I have to ask you. Did Emma ever mention how she was going to pay for her living expenses once she moved to the mainland? Were my grandparents going to help her out?"

"They could pay for her tuition, but nothing else. Even sharing with Fiona, she was going to have to work for the money for books and lodgings and such. I didn't have much, but I offered her what little I'd managed to save. But she told me not to worry. She had a plan. But maybe she wouldn't tell me what it was, and that got me worried she might get herself into trouble." Quentin hesitated for a minute. "What you have to understand about Emma was that she was smarter than any of us. But she knew it, so she thought some of the rules shouldn't apply to her."

"Entitlement," she said. She'd never seen that in Emma, but then why would she?

"She wanted to be able to focus on her studies, thought she deserved that. Problem was the more people praised her, the more she figured she was special."

"You loved her."

"Aye, for my sins. She was so clever and beautiful. If anyone deserved to be treated special, it was her."

Kate slumped down onto the stairs. She wasn't sure how many more disturbing things she could bear to learn.

"I'm sorry, lass. Do you have any idea what she was up to? With her brain, it'd have to be something clever."

"Quite the opposite, Quentin." Kate rubbed at the ache in her temples. "She was stealing antiques and selling them on the mainland. Jane Sutherland caught her coming out of a shop with a handful of cash the week she died."

"Emma thieving? No." Feebles violently shook his head. "Jane's making it up. None of the Weird Sisters liked Emma."

"I'm afraid it's true. I found Emma's bankbook, and she had a lot of money put away."

"You don't think she was going into people's cottages."

Kate covered her eyes. "I hope not. How could I ever look anyone in the face again?"

"Now, lass, no one will blame you for any of this. We have the greatest respect for your family. You can't be responsible for the actions of someone who died when you were just a wee thing." He squeezed himself down beside her on the stairs, threw his arms around her, and hugged, a fishy bear of a hug that was over too soon.

"I think I secretly hoped if I learnt what happened, I could get closer to her, understand who she was, and now I have. The expression *be careful what you wish for* was created for this moment," she sighed.

He was looking at her with soft, wet eyes, as if he felt as sorry for her as she felt for herself.

"Don't worry, Quentin, I'll be all right. Really."

"Aye, if you're sure."

"I'm not sure of anything anymore."

He stood to leave but kept his gaze fixed on her. "Hannah Sutherland knew who killed Emma, didn't she?"

"Yes, she did. And she took it to her grave."

—

David sat collapsed on his sofa, staring at an empty whiskey bottle. Before he'd left the reception, he'd done the responsible thing and arranged for Angelica, groggy from Marcus's tablet, to be taken home. He'd tucked Jane and Sophie up in bed—Sophie with a brandy and Jane with a cup of chamomile tea—and fought the urge to go over to Kate's to try to explain Gwynie's outburst. It would involve defending his betrayal of her aunt, and for that, he had no excuse. He'd been young and drunk and at the mercy of his hormones, hormones already ignited by Emma. He was ashamed to say he barely remembered the details.

But he'd paid an enormous price. He'd fathered and lost the only child he would ever have, a child he never knew he wanted until now. Looking back, he realized there had been unspoken agreements with Olivia and Rachel that they wouldn't have children. It was probably no accident he'd been attracted to women who were singularly focussed, women whose lives were devoted to being successful. Work hard, play hard, and neither included cleaning up puddles of sick or changing dirty nappies.

Perhaps it had been his own childhood that had made him think he had nothing to offer a child, that he would have been a terrible parent. But is anyone truly prepared when a child comes along? Maybe all he needed was to hold his baby, soft and warm and smelling of powder, to know this little thing needed his protection.

But Gwynie had killed the only child he'd ever have. He could never forgive her for that, and he could never forgive Hannah her arrogance for believing that once again she knew what was in his best interest. It seemed her life had been devoted to chipping away at him bit by bit.

The photograph albums, which normally lay neatly stacked behind the glass doors of the bookcase, were scattered across the low table in front of him. He hadn't looked at them in years, but tonight he was searching for something, something he'd misplaced, something he hadn't even known had gone astray.

He'd always been driven to paint, and yes, he truly believed the universe, or God, or whatever, had wanted him to do that, otherwise why had he been given this talent, the commitment, and God help him, Hannah, to push him at every opportunity. After all, he could just as easily have been born into a family of coal miners a hundred years ago and died of some horrific lung disease at the age of forty. But while he'd had a highly successful artistic career, his personal life had been a royal cock-up.

As he turned page after page of the albums, it was as if he was looking at someone else's life. And it had been such a shallow life. The photographs, first black and white, then colour, appeared posed and artificial. He and Hannah, smiling; he and Olivia, smiling; he and Julia, smiling. Then there were the group shots at receptions, first nights at the opera, his own show openings. Slightly out of focus people in the background, well-dressed but anonymous, who knew little about art, who came up to him and pressed their hands into his, saying something vaguely complimentary, the gallery owners hoping for a sale, and his agent calculating his cut.

There he was—David Sutherland, the show. The forced smile, the expensive suits, the well-dressed wives, the rich, middle-aged art groupies. But where was his real life?

Olivia was always down at the gallery—preparing for a show, mounting a show, selling a show, soothing clients' brittle egos. Rachel was rehearsing, performing, recording, on tour. David's schedule was no better. He could understand why the most enduring celebrity marriages were with people with ordinary jobs or no jobs at all. But it's a lot to ask of another person, to become a satellite orbiting a star, and maybe that's why people like him should never marry, and why he hadn't had a serious relationship since Rachel. Didn't someone once say the muse is a jealous lover? She demands you sacrifice everything for art.

He pushed the albums to one side, toppling them off the coffee table. Well, from where he was sitting, it had been just too damned much to sacrifice. If he'd known fifty years ago this was how it would be and how much it would hurt, he would have gladly gone down that sodding coal mine.

CHAPTER 34

The irritating sound of the alarm jerked Kate out of bed at half past seven. Two coffees later, she was sitting at the dining room table, her laptop open in front of her. She couldn't put off her editor any longer. That meant making an early start and keeping at it for the rest of the day.

It had finally dawned on her that her procrastination was due to something much more profound than simply avoiding the boredom of smoothing out clunky bits of exposition and checking continuity. She'd been struggling with a pivotal point of her plot. A former servant, Molly, returns to the estate where she'd once worked and had fallen in love with the earl's eldest son. Now dressed in opulent clothes, adopting an upper-class accent, and calling herself Lady Charlotte Cavendish, Molly is welcomed by the earl as an honoured guest. Unaware of her true identity, the son is attracted to her strength of character and independent spirit, renouncing his rakish lifestyle. Together they save the estate from ruin.

But could someone actually reinvent herself to the point of being unrecognizable? Was it plausible? If not, the book might as well be scrapped. On the other hand, did plausibility really matter? It was popular fiction, not great literature. It was enough that her readers bought into the fantasy. Besides, if you can believe a woman can change a man's character, you'll believe anything.

Kate knew the only way she was going to finish the editing was to give herself an incentive. Marathon marking sessions for school had been rewarded with a mint toffee every fifteen minutes, so a trip to Craggy's was in order.

But she couldn't find her house keys. After the incident with the boiling oil, she was more determined than ever to lock the door when she was absent from the house. She'd checked all the usual places, but the keys were nowhere to be found. To be sure she checked all the usual places once again, knowing she'd already checked them.

She'd had a bath after Quentin had left. Maybe she'd thrown them on the top of the dresser. But wouldn't she have noticed when she got up this morning? She checked anyway. No luck. On a hunch, she leaned over and stared down at the space behind the dresser. There they were, caught on the top of the skirting board.

Dragging the heavy dresser from the wall made enough room for her to crouch down and grab the keys. But as she did, a piece of skirting board fell loose, exposing a gap in the wall. There was something stuffed into it, something that looked like a piece of tissue paper. She tugged it out. Wrapped in the paper was a heavy black key. It looked medieval—not that Kate knew what a medieval key looked like. Still, it conjured up images of an ancient stone building with thick oak doors embellished with black cast-iron hinges and latches. But what did it really open? And more importantly, why had Emma hidden it?

Kate slipped it into her pocket and set out for Craggy's. As she came to Siobhan's house, she paused. She considered checking in on her friend. Siobhan had slept in her own bed last night, buoyed by her anger toward Angelica. She'd assured Kate if anyone dared to disturb her, she'd go after them with the tire iron she'd placed within arm's reach and a war cry worthy of Boudica.

—

Siobhan was sitting in her truck outside Angelica Lynley's house. Surrounded by meadow, it was a modest little cottage, close to Sutherland Hall, and one of the few that hadn't been renovated. At first Siobhan wondered why Angelica, with all her vast resources, hadn't turned it into some over-the-top mansion with white columns, plaster lions, and gargoyles—a temple to bad taste—but it was probably only rented. The blasted woman was waiting to get her hands on Siobhan's place.

Siobhan stomped up the walk and knocked at the door. Her knock was loud and forceful, the result of having worked herself up in the truck. She was ready for anything Angelica threw at her.

What she wasn't prepared for was Angelica's welcoming expression. "Miss Fitzgerald, what a pleasant surprise. Do come in."

Angelica was quite short when you got up close to her, like a porcelain figurine, dressed in a powder blue twin set, pink and blue plaid pencil skirt, and pearls. Did women actually dress like this just to sit around the house?

Angelica made herself comfortable on the sofa, her feet demurely crossed at the ankles. Siobhan decided to stand, having heard that the height difference would make her more intimidating. "It's about Bella Casa."

Angelica seemed to grow smaller, if that were at all possible. She looked down at her hands. "Oh, so you know about my little secret?"

"Is that what you call it? You broke into my home, left nasty notes, and vandalized my art." Siobhan hadn't thought she would get this angry quite so soon, but a floodgate had opened. "Last night was the first time I've been able to sleep in my own home in more than a week. The only thing that got me through the night was knowing I was coming here to tell you exactly what I think of you and reporting you to Constable Finch."

"Oh, Miss Fitzgerald, I was just as shocked about what happened as you were. Please believe me when I tell you I had nothing to do with any criminal activities in your home. Yes, I will admit I asked my estate agent to reach out to you about selling your cottage, but that's as far as it went."

She paused, as if swallowing a sob rising in her throat. "I lost my dear Anton two years ago. And believe me, I couldn't sleep a wink for months after he died. I lived with my parents before we were married, and so went from the security of their home to his. I'd never known what it was like to live alone. I do so admire you modern women who are able to do that, but mine was a more traditional upbringing. After my darling Anton passed, I was terrified to be by myself in that big house. I would never want any other woman to go through that."

She patted the cushion beside her, indicating her visitor might be more comfortable if she sat. Still concerned about giving her any advantage, Siobhan chose an armchair and reluctantly lowered herself onto the soft cushions.

"You see, my Anton is the reason I wanted to buy your house. We came here many years ago on a holiday, and we rented that cottage, your cottage. Anton fell in love with it and always said when he retired, we'd come back and buy it. I even have a picture of it upstairs in my bedroom. I can show you if you'd like."

Siobhan shook her head.

"Anton loved that he could wake up every morning to the sound of the sea, and he did so want a garden to potter about in. The gardens in London are the size of pocket handkerchiefs."

Siobhan wasn't so sure she bought the grieving widow routine, but Angelica looked so small on that sofa that Siobhan couldn't imagine her creeping around in the dark, hurling bricks through windows.

"Living in your cottage would have helped me to feel close to him again. Please say you understand." She looked over with soft, moist eyes as if expecting Siobhan to forgive her.

But Siobhan wasn't finished yet. "Why couldn't you just ask me yourself? Why go through this Casa thing?"

"Bella Casa is a division of my husband's architectural firm. I'm like you, not the sort of woman who can just sit back and do nothing all day. So I started an interior design company. We developed a modern European aesthetic when most of the country was still mired in flock wallpaper and chintz curtains. I had the good fortune to be able to mentor some wonderfully creative young designers." She gestured to indicate the interior of the cottage. "As you can see, I haven't even begun to work on this place."

"No, you were hoping to get your hands on mine."

Angelica leaned forward and spoke softly, almost intimately. "I never meant to do anything other than offer you a fair price. I didn't come and see you myself because...well, to be truthful, I thought you might resist selling if you knew it was me. I must admit my agent was unnecessarily aggressive, and I shall chastise him severely for it."

She looked down at the carpet. "I know I haven't made a lot of friends here. I'm a woman who speaks her mind and that can put some people off, and perhaps my friendship with the Sutherlands has made people suspicious of me. It's just that they were so welcoming when no one else was, and I do so want to feel part of the community."

She looked up from under heavily mascaraed eyelashes. Under any other circumstances, Siobhan might have actually felt sorry for the woman. Siobhan stared her straight in the eye. "I'm not selling the house. I don't care how much you offer me. Do you understand?"

Angelica played with the garish diamond ring resting above a thick gold wedding band and said quietly, "You've made that perfectly clear."

Siobhan stood up, preparing to leave. "No more letters."

Angelica lifted up her hand as if swearing an oath. "No more letters."

"No more harassment."

Her hand stayed up.

Siobhan nodded to signal their conversation was over and let herself out. She didn't know if the story about Angelica's husband was true, but what she did know was Angelica could swear until she was blue in the face, and Siobhan still wouldn't trust her as far as she could throw her. And Siobhan had thrown bags of clay heavier than Angelica Lynley.

CHAPTER 35

Her pockets full of mint toffees, Kate stood outside Craggy's shop staring out at the sea. The reflection of the high morning sun shimmered like a piece of freshly polished gold against the dark water. On the beach, long-legged birds skittered to the edge of the water and, like children cautious of the cold, darted back and then dug in the sand, revealing the razor edges of broken shells. The more Kate watched, the more she saw the details of the sea and the sky as if she'd never really seen them before.

When she was young, Kate had been in too much of a hurry to stop and just look. Too busy chasing gulls, searching for shells, retreating to her secret places among the rocks, but never just sitting and watching the rhythm of the waves, the changing colours. Is that why the island was mostly populated with older people? You had to reach a certain point in your life to appreciate the quiet things, the stillness. You had to wait until everything you believed was important—ambition, money, ego—burnt away, leaving only simplicity and clarity. Kate could do with some of that right about now.

"You look tired, my dear," said Fiona as she and Winifred approached, bulging shopping baskets in hand.

Kate must have looked quite distressed because Fiona hooked her arm through Kate's. "Don't let this business with Emma get you down. You know, the one regret she had about our plans to leave the island was that she was going to miss you growing up. She loved you so very much. Don't let what happened stop you making plans for your life. Emma wouldn't have wanted that."

Kate stared into Fiona's soft eyes and suddenly felt incredibly sad. Fiona hugged her and tears started to run down Kate's face. She forced a smile—more for Fiona than herself—while reaching for a tissue from her pocket. Her hand touched the large key.

She dabbed at her eyes, and then presented the key to Winifred and Fiona. "Emma had this hidden in her room. Do either of you recognize it?"

They both shook their heads.

Kate slipped it into her purse and felt about for the vinaigrette. "What about this?"

Fiona touched it gently. "It's lovely."

But there was no sign of recognition from either of them.

Kate was disappointed, but it was too much to hope that either object would be identified by the first people to see it.

"I noticed you signed out some films from the archives," Winifred said. "Did you find anything of interest?"

"I'd completely forgotten about those," Fiona said.

"Do you know who shot the film?" Kate asked.

"I do," Fiona was excited to be able to contribute. The other two waited for her explanation.

"When he left, Mr. Probert gave a camera and three rolls of film to us students to make some motion pictures of the island. He said the island needed to be preserved, *an historical record*, he called it. The girls made a film about the boys playing football—well, it was mostly the boys with their shirts off!" Fiona smiled self-consciously. "We let Sami shoot the party in the pub."

Kate remembered how the camera had been focussed on Emma and David. Maybe after the way Emma had befriended her at the school-end celebration, Sami felt close to her, wanted to be her friend. "When was the party?"

"About a week or so before Emma died."

"Who shot the garden competition?"

"Oh, that was Feebles, Gooley, and Smee."

"I've seen the poster in the archives," Winifred said. "It was only held that one year and never again. What happened?"

"Sabotage!" Fiona announced with a sinister tone.

"That's rather melodramatic," Winifred chided.

"No, I think she's right. The film shows gardens full of dead plants."

But Winifred would have none of it. "Then it was obviously some sort of disease."

"That only affected the plants that were in the competition?" Fiona had a 'so there' look Kate had seen Siobhan make. "And only those gardens Clive Sparrow worked on?"

"That's why he was yelling at the end of the film," Kate said. "The boys must have accused him of being involved. But surely Clive wouldn't risk destroying his own business."

Fiona shrugged her thin shoulders. "Some people wanted to give him the benefit of the doubt, said it might have been an honest mistake like using weed-killer instead of fertilizer. But he swore he'd done nothing wrong. Whatever it was, he lost a lot of business. The Sutherlands for a start. To their credit, Lilian and George didn't desert him. But he was left with only a few customers, and that just wasn't enough. He had to beg for work on the boats to get by. It wasn't long after that he fell ill and had to leave the island."

"Peregrine Tully had said it was a strange old summer," Kate said. "I can see why."

They nodded their heads in agreement. When it was evident that they had nothing else to offer, Kate said, "Thank you, ladies. I think I'll go check on David. Enjoy the rest of the day."

Fiona grabbed a quick hug, and she and Winifred walked in the direction of The Breeze. Kate continued past the harbour toward David's studio.

Three loud knocks on his door brought no reaction. Her face pressed against the front window, staring between the half-drawn curtains, she could see him stretched out on the sofa. He was still in the clothes he'd worn to the funeral, and an empty whiskey bottle lay on its side on the carpet. Open photograph albums littered the floor.

"David," and she pounded on the window. *Oh God, what if he's had a heart attack?* But he began to move, slowly, like an overturned tortoise trying to right itself. "David, are you all right?"

His hands waved in the air, signalling to her to come in. The door was unlocked, and she pushed inside and ran to the sofa. "David, please say something."

He stared bleary-eyed at her, his hair sticking out at the side. "Kate, you always manage to always see me at my worst, yet you keep coming back. Maybe I should marry you."

She kicked the bottle out of the way and pulled him to an upright position. "I'm making you coffee."

"Lots, since you're going to the trouble," he called to her in the kitchen, "and I was joking about the marriage proposal."

"I know."

They were soon sitting side by side, each blowing over a cup of hot coffee.

"Are you sure you don't want anything to eat? Some dry toast?" she asked.

He pulled a face, making the corners of his mouth and his eyebrows droop down. "Maybe later. I was planning to sneak away to London today," and he attempted a sip from his cup. He pulled back as if the coffee had burnt his mouth but then forced himself to take another mouthful. "It wasn't so much the others. It was you I couldn't face. I couldn't bear for you to learn I'm just like every other man on the planet, and I betrayed the woman I loved for meaningless sex."

"Don't worry about me. It must have been an awful shock to learn about the termination." Kate poured more cream into her coffee. "Do you want to talk about it?"

David said nothing. She wasn't surprised. The realization that he could have had a very different life must be disconcerting.

The morning sun began to fill the living room. The only sounds disturbing the quiet of the house were the sharp, indignant squawks of the gulls and fragments of conversation from people passing outside.

Kate looked down at the photograph albums. One was open to a series of pictures of a younger David. In his youth, his movie-star good looks had made him attractive in a conventional way, but his face now had a depth of character that was missing in these earlier pictures.

In many of the photos he was flanked by an elegant woman with rich brown hair, wearing a double row of gold beads and an expensive evening suit.

"Is this one of your wives?" Kate pointed to the pictures.

He laughed for the first time. "You make me sound like Blackbeard!" He leaned forward to see where she was pointing. "That's Olivia."

He'd told her his wives had reminded him of Emma. There was a superficial resemblance. "And is this your exhibition?"

He pulled back the plastic covering the page, peeled the picture off its sticky backing, and squinted to read the note written on the back. "September 18, 1983, Galbraith Gallery, London. This was the year before we separated." He handed the album back to Kate.

Although David was smiling at the camera, there was a sadness in his eyes. What had Siobhan said about his art—there was a shadow, a darkness in his paintings? All the same, it was hard to stop staring at this beautiful couple. David must have been in his late thirties, and Olivia at least five years younger. Their practised smiles did an excellent job of hiding the cracks in their marriage.

Kate's eye was drawn to the blurred figures behind David and Olivia, all with their faces turned toward the pictures on the walls—all except one, a woman with sharp features. Kate looked closer. The mystery woman was smiling, posing for the camera as if she were connected to the couple. She looked familiar.

"Did you know the people at the opening?"

David was looking better, his eyes brighter, less puffy now he was upright. He shook his head and snorted. "My agent sent out the invitations. I was just supposed to turn up and smile and try not to insult too many of the punters."

Kate searched the other pictures from the exhibition. There was the same woman, still smiling into the camera. Kate held up the picture to David and pointed. "What about her? She seems to be in an awful lot of pictures."

But David brushed it aside.

"Do you mind if I take it? I promise to return it."

He waved his approval. "Take the whole damn lot."

The wave felt like a dismissal. But she wasn't finished.

She told him about Jane meeting Emma at the antique shop and Jane's suspicions. Kate slowly withdrew the silver vinaigrette from her bag and offered it to David. "Does this look familiar?"

"No, should it?" He took it from her and checked the hallmarks. "It's a nice piece, but it didn't come from Sutherland Hall. Where did you find it?" He handed it back.

"It was in a box of Emma's things in the cottage."

Then Kate took out the large key. "What about this?"

He stared closely at it. "The head is different, but it looks like the front door key for Faraday Manor."

"How do you know?"

"This part that goes into the lock. As a child, I imagined it looked like a face. See the square nose and chin, and the bit at the bottom, a beard. Where did you find it?"

"This was in Emma's things as well."

It hadn't been the Sutherlands Emma had been stealing from. It was Artemis Faraday.

David made the connection too. "Oh no," was all he said.

"I'm afraid so. Remember the bankbook I found?"

David closed his eyes as if in pain. "It must have been the time she came for tea. I insisted Hannah invite her. The manor keys were, probably still are, hung on hooks in a kitchen cupboard. Emma must have taken the key, had it copied on the mainland, and returned it when no one was there."

He seemed to shrink into himself, and he rubbed his hands over his face, as if hiding from her. When he looked up, the white stubble was conspicuous against his red skin. "Our family takes the protection of the manor very seriously. For someone to steal using the key that was in our keeping, under our protection—Hannah would have been so angry. But I still swear Hannah didn't kill Emma," he said with real conviction.

"No, she didn't. But it was someone with just as much to lose."

—

Toby had just finished his breakfast in the kitchen. It was finally quiet in the house. It was good to be quiet. There'd been too much noise with the police and Miss Hannah's party.

Miss Sophie had said he could go to Miss Hannah's funeral, but he hadn't wanted to. The angry policeman might've been there. And he didn't want to see Miss Hannah in a box. That wasn't right. So he stayed to save the garden.

His plants had been lying on the ground, sad and limp, but most of them still had the roots attached. He'd replanted them quickly to make them live again. He'd done that for Miss Hannah.

Now full of bacon, eggs, and all the trimmings, he shoved his feet into his boots. His grandmother said a gentleman guides his feet into his boots, but he always shoved them in, especially when he was in a hurry. And today he was in a hurry.

From the kitchen window, he'd noticed one of the white rose bushes was leaning, like the picture of that funny tower Miss Sophie had shown him. He must've done a bad job with that one.

"The soil needs to be tight," that's what Bert always said. Bert knew everything about gardening. "But not too tight. Plants are like people. They need room to breathe." Maybe a peacock or a badger had come and dug in the garden. But what would a badger want with his roses?

His feet had settled deep into his boots by the time he reached the bush. He had to do a good job with Miss Hannah's roses in case she was looking down from heaven. That's where Miss Jane said she was, and since God can see everyone from heaven, Miss Hannah can too.

Pushing down into the soil with his spade, Toby lifted the plant. It came up easily, but hidden among the roots was an empty bottle, like the one Miss Hannah's tablets came in. Did Miss Hannah bury the bottle? Maybe she didn't only bury tea tins. The policeman had been angry when he thought Toby had hurt Miss Hannah. He didn't want the policeman to be angry, so he reburied the bottle.

CHAPTER 36

Julian sat at the old oak desk in the sitting room at the back of the pub, sipping a brandy and listening to the Rolling Stones. For some reason, the drink and the music made the VAT calculations go quicker. He was just about to belt out a particularly impassioned chorus of "Satisfaction" when the music died, and he turned to find Flo standing by the stereo and Jane Sutherland in the doorway.

"Sweetie, Miss Sutherland would like to speak with you," Flo said gently.

To say Julian was speechless was an understatement. He'd never seen any of the Sutherland sisters in the pub and was convinced he never would. It took him a moment to find his voice. "Of course, Miss Sutherland. Can I get you a drink?"

Jane was clutching her purse, and Flo had to take her arm to guide her to a comfortable chair. "Perhaps a nice cup of tea," whispered Flo.

"No, thank you," Jane replied without looking up. "I need to speak to the Father without interruption."

Any other woman would have felt insulted, but not his Flo. She understood completely and left the room, closing the door behind her.

Julian came over and sat on the sofa facing Jane's armchair. He leaned forward, his elbows resting on his knees. "Miss Sutherland," he began, "you know I'm no longer a priest. If this is a religious matter, I'm afraid I can't—"

"Does God forgive all sins, no matter how terrible?" Jane interrupted him, still gripping her purse. Julian was sure that under the black gloves, her knuckles were white.

He was suddenly thrown back into a role he hadn't occupied for some time. "Well, if someone truly repents in their heart, then yes, God is all forgiving. But surely this is something you should be talking to the Reverend Larkin about."

Imogen was his friend, and he didn't want her to think he was speaking out of turn. Jane looked him full in the face. "Father, I need to confess something. Can you give me absolution?"

Clearly something was worrying her, and he had to tread gently. "Miss Sutherland, I really think you need to speak with the Reverend Larkin."

Jane reached for his hand and gripped it, tighter than he thought she was capable. "She can't forgive me, Father. Only you can forgive me."

He felt uncomfortable letting Jane proceed. "Please let me call her for you."

She jerked as if she'd been slapped. "No."

"Miss Sutherland, I can't help you. The church doesn't allow me to grant absolution."

She released his hand and collapsed into herself. "Then there's no hope for me. I'll go to hell, and I'll never see Hannah or Father again."

"You mustn't think that way. You're a good and devout woman. Surely whatever you think you've done can't be as bad as all that, and I'm certain God has already forgiven you."

An expression Julian could only describe as complete desolation came over her face. "But I can never be sure."

"I'm sure," and he was. Julian had left the priesthood after realizing God's love was no longer enough, that he could never be satisfied without earthly love, the love of a woman. But that didn't mean he'd lost his faith. If anything, it was stronger than ever. After all, God had sent him Flo.

Jane rose to her feet.

"Would you like me to call Miss Simmons to collect you?"

"No, thank you. I'd rather no one knew I was here. I'll go out the back way. I want to visit Hannah's grave."

At the sound of Jane's leaving, Flo came into the room and placed her hand on Julian's shoulder. "Is she all right?"

Julian sighed and took her hand. "No, *cariad*, I don't think she is."

—

"Now there's a sight you don't see very often," Siobhan announced.

"What's that?" Kate asked.

"Jane Sutherland walking up the road." Siobhan turned away from Kate's front window and settled herself on the sofa.

"I'm sure the Sutherlands walk up roads and across lawns and down stairs just like the rest of us. I suspect, on occasion, they even go to the bathroom."

"Thanks for that disturbing image!"

"Did you manage to have a word with Angelica?"

"She admitted setting her agent on me, but nothing else. Her excuse was that she and her husband had planned to retire to my cottage, and she wanted it to remember him by."

"Do you still think she was involved with the break-ins?"

Siobhan tilted her head. "She's a rich, stuck-up, manipulative bitch, but she's a five-foot, seven stone, seventy-year-old manipulative bitch. The break-ins probably had nothing to do with her." She grinned. "Maybe it was one of my many rejected lovers."

"It'll take a while to narrow down the suspects then!"

Siobhan threw a cushion at her.

"Do you remember our discussion about Emma's bank account? I'm affraid she was stealing things from the manor and selling them to Porth Madryn antique shops." Kate explained how David believed Emma had copied the key.

"I'm so sorry."

"Feebles said she wanted to be free to concentrate on her studies while she was at university. It's no excuse, but the more fuss people made over her—the more pressure she felt she was under to succeed." In spite of everything she'd learnt, Kate still felt the need to defend her aunt.

"You're right. It's no excuse." But it was said gently. "Are you any closer to figuring out who the murderer is?"

"There's just one piece of the puzzle left. Could you and Byron help keep an eye on people at the Queen Vic Celebration tomorrow? Make a note of anything suspicious?"

"I'm not sure Constable Finch will be any too pleased to be working with me."

Kate had to ask. "Tell me if I'm being too personal, but is Byron the first man you've been unable to seduce? You know it doesn't work that way for the rest of us."

Siobhan wrinkled her forehead and squinted her eyes, as if she was struggling with a concept beyond her comprehension.

Kate had to be careful how she phrased her next sentence. "You know, Siobhan, there comes a time in a woman's life when she's not as attractive to men—younger men—as she used to be, and that can be very liberating, if approached in the right way."

Siobhan leaned forward. "I know what you're trying to say, and I appreciate it. After all, I've come to look on you not just as a trusted friend, but as the older sister I never had."

Not so much of the older, Kate grumbled to herself.

Siobhan sat back. "And while your insights are valuable, and I'll give them consideration when the time comes, the simple truth is that Byron Finch is gay."

———

After Siobhan left, Kate finally had a chance to study David's albums. Collecting the pictures of the mystery woman from his openings spanning over thirty years, she dealt them out like a pack of cards so that they covered the surface of the dining table in chronological order. She added a picture from her corkboard.

Siobhan, David, and Hannah had all seen a resemblance between Emma and Kate. Now that she knew what she was looking for, Kate saw someone familiar in David's pictures. The woman had a different hair colour and style at each event. She might even have had a new nose or a facelift. But she couldn't disguise how she stood, how she held her head, her expression.

Kate scanned the pictures into the computer and outlined her suspicions in an email to Alex. It was up to her daughter now. If Alex didn't come up with the answer Kate was hoping for, she didn't know what else to do. She'd talked to everyone who'd known Emma, looked in all the places that might yield some insight into what had happened that summer. If only her mother and grandmother were still here, could have told her what they talked about over the dinner table, the secrets only family shared. It wasn't fair all that had died with them before being put somewhere safe, like a diary locked away in a box.

And then Kate remembered. The special box.

She climbed the stairs and stood in the doorway to Lilian's room. The sheets were still on her bed, the fluffy duvet that was always spotlessly white. Kate hadn't had the heart to remove them. Not yet. Kneeling down, she pulled out the wooden box her grandfather had made for their important papers when he and Lilian were first married.

She ran her fingers over the carved lilies, the smell of lemon oil where Lilian had lovingly polished it to look its best, even though she was the only one who ever saw it.

As a child Kate had often asked to see inside it but was told that it was full of special papers that couldn't be replaced. She now knew it contained the history of the family—birth and wedding certificates, even school reports.

Lifting the lid, she stared at the papers all neatly laid out. She longed to spend the afternoon reading everything, getting lost in the memories.

But she forced herself to focus on the task at hand as she slowly and carefully removed each piece of paper, putting aside anything to do with Emma. At the bottom, there was an envelope addressed to her mother. Of all the things she expected to find, she couldn't have anticipated this—Emma's post mortem report. Her mother must have ordered a copy, but why wasn't it with her notes? Winifred had said that George had wanted the family to put Emma's death behind them. Had he hidden the report away before Miriam had a chance to look at it? But why not destroy it? Was this his and Lilian's last connection to Emma, a connection they couldn't bring themselves to sever?

It was hard to imagine that only a few weeks before Emma had been enjoying herself at the pub party. But it hadn't been all fun, had it? David had stomped off when she wouldn't leave with him, when he couldn't have her all to himself. Why had Sami filmed their argument? She'd also filmed Gwynie Morgan's interaction with David. Did Sami know about the one-night stand? Replaying it in her head, Kate now saw the film as intrusive, with so much of the camera's attention focussed on Emma and David.

She began to read the report. Sea water was found in Emma's lungs, consistent with drowning, blunt force trauma to the head, the wounds a combination of peri and post mortem. There was no way to determine if the perimortem wounds occurred immediately before or while she was in the water. No sexual interference. There was nothing here that Kate hadn't already learnt from her mother's notes from the inquest.

To see something so personal as her aunt's death laid out in an official document like that sent a shiver through Kate. This woman with such plans for her life and people who loved her had been reduced to an object on a metal table. A stranger had cut her open, looked inside her, studied her naked body. And with all their education and experience, they still got it wrong. They all got it so terribly wrong.

What is it you're hoping to find? James had asked. At the beginning, it had been something to magically appear to solve the mystery of Emma's death. But now it was anything to confirm what she suspected was the truth. All that was missing was a motive.

What if Kate had got it wrong too? From the beginning, she'd been focussing on Emma, what she'd done to make someone want to kill her. But what if it wasn't about Emma?

Maybe it was David.

What if David Sutherland was the reason Emma had to die?

CHAPTER 37

The Queen Victoria Celebration was in full swing by the time Kate stepped onto the beach the next morning. It was just as wonderful as she remembered it. An imposing papier mâché statue of Victoria dominated the festivities, surrounded by white canvas marquees sheltering tables of sandwiches and cakes, tea, sherry, port, and lemonade, all safely placed above the tide line. Multicoloured deckchairs were scattered about to rest legs and ankles, weary and aching from the effort of walking on sand in heavy trailing dresses and high-heeled shoes, and for those who were feeling the effects of too much sun and port.

The harbour was crammed with the boats of visitors who had sailed over from the mainland that morning. The rest had crowded onto the ferry, their lace and ribbons flapping in the warm, salty breeze.

As she walked along the sand, Kate was surrounded by a profusion of Victorias, lace parasols resting on their shoulders. Young women had adorned themselves in pastels or white, richly accented with sashes of red or royal blue. The middle-aged were resigned to black, taking some consolation in being able to recycle major parts of their costume year after year. The older portrayers were lacy, buxom, and bejewelled—and still in black. Occasionally one of the more inventive of the islanders, and Kate's personal favourites, would explore alternative forms of Her Majesty. There was the art deco Victoria, the surreal Victoria, and of course the never to be forgotten—or repeated—cubist Victoria. However this year most people had chosen traditional interpretations.

Decked out in a dark grey morning coat, fuchsia waistcoat, false moustache and sideburns, Dr. Marcus tipped his top hat in Kate's direction. "Good morning, Kate. How's the head?"

While Marcus's outfit was typical of most of the men on the beach, there were more than a few cheeky ones strutting about in black jackets, kilts, and sporrans as Her Majesty's special friend, Mr. Brown.

If she'd been in costume, she'd have been inclined to bob a curtsey. "Good morning, Dr. Marcus. The head has healed quite nicely, thank you."

"Glad to hear it. Enjoy the day," and he bowed and walked on.

People began to look skyward, smiling and pointing, as kites appeared in the sky, their dazzling shapes and colours floating above the beach and out over the sea. Kate was particularly attracted to a group of birds with flowing tails of green and yellow swooping above her.

"Not dressing up this year, Kate?"

David stood beside her in his Sutherland tartan kilt, puffing on his pipe. In her comfortable cotton shirt and pants, Kate did feel a trifle underdressed. Most women who weren't costumed had chosen flowery summer dresses and spectacular hats that wouldn't have looked out of place at Ascot.

"Not this time. Though I more than made up for it as a child. I drove my mother and Lilian to distraction by demanding my dresses and hairstyles be exactly like the pictures I'd researched at the Porth Madryn library. I won three of the under sixteen competitions, so it all paid off in the end."

He grinned. "Why, Miss Galway, are you suggesting the end justifies the means?"

"It does when you're eleven."

Offering Kate his arm, David guided her through the crowds.

"David, do you know anything about this building project Angelica Lynley is involved with?"

"Quite honestly, I try to avoid the woman as much as humanly possible. She seems to have attached herself to my sisters, but I can't stand her."

"Can someone use your name without your permission?"

"Ah, you're referring to The David Sutherland Art Institute. My lawyers are already on it. Look, she can come up with all the plans she wants, but there's no way the island is going to allow something like that to be built. For one thing, she doesn't own the land."

"Neither do we. Legally, it belongs to Faraday's descendants."

He squeezed her hand reassuringly. "And therein lies our salvation. She'll have to battle her way through mountains of government red tape and paperwork going back over one-hundred and fifty years in two countries. We'll all be dead long before she secures permission to build. And on the off-chance she does, I'll make it my personal mission to tie her up in court for the rest of her life. I don't think we need to worry about Angelica Lynley."

He cleared his throat. A swoop of glittering fish kites caught their attention, and they stopped to look. "Look, Kate, I'm afraid I haven't been completely honest about my relationship with Emma."

He didn't wait for her to respond, but continued as if afraid that if he stopped, he'd lose his courage. "A few days before she died, I asked her to go away with me. For months, I'd been telling her I loved her, hoping she'd eventually be swayed by my persistence, but if Emma taught me anything, it was that you can't force someone's feelings. At first, every time I said, 'I love you,' she'd smile politely. Later it became a look of sympathy at the bloody fool I was making of myself." He looked down at the pipe in his hands. "You see, Emma loved something much more important to her than I could ever be."

"What was that?"

"Herself. I know Quentin blames me for ruining things for the two of them, but he didn't stand a chance with her any more than I did. Emma wanted a university degree and the kind of life it could buy her, a life she couldn't get on the island. I'm sure that's why she wanted the money. Living with me in Paris might have initially held out some appeal, but then what? She needed to be someone in her own right. When I finally worked up the courage to ask her to come with me, I knew what her answer would be. But I had to ask, just in case there was the slightest possibility she'd say yes."

"And what did she say?"

David's head shook slightly. "Nothing at first. Then she laughed as if at a joke only she understood and said, 'Why would I want to do that?' It was so condescending, and I'm afraid I got angry. I grabbed her wrist and held on so she couldn't leave. I still hoped there might be some way I could convince her."

He looked into Kate's face, perhaps expecting shock or disgust, but she said nothing. While she disapproved of David's behaviour, she was ashamed of Emma's.

He continued. "But then I saw so clearly what we'd become. This was our relationship—me forcing her to listen when it was so obvious she didn't care. All the time my hand was gripping her wrist, she just stood there, like she was humouring me, pitying me, me at the mercy of my emotions, begging her to give up her dreams and ambitions. When I let her go, she just walked away. In that moment, I knew not only that I'd lost her forever, but that I'd never had her."

"The disagreements you two had at the school-end celebration, the party in the pub…"

"That was more of the same."

"But when I visited you at your studio—the picture, the way you talked about her…"

There suddenly came an expression on his face which could have been either a smile or the beginning of tears. "We all remember Emma the way we want to. I pathetically wanted to believe she was a sweet, lovely young woman I would have married if she hadn't tragically died. When Emma passed away, we reinvented her as innocent and pure and perfectly formed. For George and Lilian and Miriam's sake—and even for Emma's sake—that's the Emma the island chooses to remember."

And for my sake as well, Kate thought. It took a lot of courage for a man like David to admit his failings. "Thank you for being honest with me. I know it couldn't have been easy."

He looked relieved. "It was a lot easier than I thought it would be. And as someone recently told me, I need to let go of the past."

They'd reached the canvas marquee where Fiona and Winifred were bustling about tables of food, pouring tea and offering ginger cake topped with clotted cream. Kate accepted a couple of cucumber and cress sandwiches from Winifred and left David chatting to the ladies while she went in search of a glass of sherry.

Some of the men had started a game of football at the far end of the beach and young women were gathering in hopes of a glimpse under a flying kilt. Every so often an appreciative howl would arise at a particularly revealing play. Siobhan in a skin-tight black jumpsuit tended goal for one team, while Byron was in the opposite net.

"A beautiful day," a voice purred beside Kate.

Kate looked over at Angelica, dressed for the occasion in a lemon-yellow trouser suit. "What quaint customs you islanders have," Angelica said.

"To someone who's always lived in London, I suppose we do appear quaint, as you put it. But I'd rather be here than at some stuffy cocktail party."

"I don't suppose teachers and policemen get invited to many cocktail parties."

"No, we're a very humble people. Rather like fishermen and gardeners."

Angelica was silent for a moment and then announced, "Kate, I've come across something that might help in your investigation—some old papers and photographs that were in my cottage when I moved in. They're on my yacht, if you'd like to take a look."

"Why don't you donate them to the island archives? I can study them there."

Angelica gave her a smug look. She obviously wanted to take this opportunity to show off her yacht. "It won't take a minute, I promise you."

"Where are you moored?"

"On the other side of the harbour. I thought it would be safer there with so many boats coming to the island today. You can't trust strangers to show consideration for other people's property, can you? I've a motorboat that will take us to the yacht, and I guarantee you'll learn something very interesting."

The wind suddenly shifted, a little cooler now. Kate wished she'd brought a cardigan.

Siobhan and Byron were still engrossed in the game. David was deep in conversation with the Reverend Imogen and Dr. Marcus in front of the drinks marquee.

Angelica was walking away, slowly, as if expecting her to catch up. Kate looked over at Fiona and Winifred. Winifred was squinting in Kate's general direction, her hand shading her eyes.

Kate waved.

Angelica stopped and turned toward Kate. "Coming?"

"Right behind you."

—

During the short trip to Angelica's yacht, Kate gripped the side of the small motorboat, the spray bouncing off her hands. Angelica expertly pulled alongside the yacht, and Kate secured the boat and climbed up the ladder.

While she didn't have an eye for this sort of thing, Kate's first impression was that Angelica's yacht looked quite expensive, or perhaps excessive was a more appropriate word, seeing as it had been built to sleep at least six people. On the stern deck was a white table and a padded bench, the site, no doubt, of cocktail parties and elegant dinners with Angelica playing the part of the glamorous hostess.

"There's someplace special I want you to see."

"What about the papers?"

"Be patient. It won't be long now."

They set off for the far side of the island, a barren landscape with high cliffs. If anything sinister had happened to Emma, this is where it would have happened, away from people's eyes. This is where Emma would have been pushed into the cold sea.

—

A roar went up from the crowd as Siobhan blocked a goal. She'd decided that there was no way she was going to give Byron the satisfaction of winning.

Damn, her mobile was ringing. Most of her team appeared to have wandered off to Julian's table to celebrate the save—a spontaneous time-out. Siobhan pulled the phone out of her cleavage and looked at the display. It was a corporate name she didn't recognize. "Hello?"

"Siobhan, is that you?"

"Who's this?"

"It's Alex. Kate's Alex. Mum must have left her phone at home. Do you know where she is?"

Siobhan scanned the beach to see if she could spot her friend. "It's the Queen Vic Celebration. We're all on the beach, but I haven't seen her."

"It's really important I get in touch with her. I think I know who killed Emma."

When she heard the name, Siobhan gasped, but it made perfect sense. It also meant she was going to have to ask Byron for help.

—

The yacht rounded a bend and came upon a tall rock face pitted with dark caves. According to island lore, they'd been hiding places for pirates' loot plundered from ships unfortunate enough to have been caught in the surrounding waters. The insides of the caves were hollows of shadow and staring into their depths was like looking into empty eye sockets. A cold spray misted Kate's face, and she clung to the metal railing to steady herself against the sense of dread building up inside.

Angelica slowed the yacht. The engine cut out, and the boat rocked from side to side, waves from its wake slapping against the cliff. She emerged from the cockpit, shutting the door behind her, and walked slowly to the stern, the sun glinting off her gold sunglass frames.

Leaning against the railings, she stared out toward the island. "I haven't been here for years."

Kate tensed. "Welcome home, Sami."

CHAPTER 38

Siobhan knew Kate was in trouble and time was of the essence, but everyone seemed to be moving in slow motion. They all piled into Smee's boat—Siobhan, Byron, and the Old Gents. Feebles and Gooley were throwing off the mooring lines while Smee tried again and again to coax the engine to turn over.

Byron cleared his throat. "Mr. Smee, how many drinks have you had?"

Smee turned abruptly and came close to Byron. Siobhan wasn't sure if his face was red with outrage at the comment or irritation that the motor wouldn't start. "Listen, lad, I've been drinking longer than you've been drawing breath, and I'll decide if I'm in any fit state to handle a boat."

"Bloody hell, Byron, we have to rescue Kate," and Siobhan punched his upper arm. "Stop being a tight-arsed copper, and let the man drive."

Byron kept his composure. "It's Miss G I'm thinking about. A sober man can react quicker in an emergency."

Gooley, dressed as the Golden Jubilee Victoria, in black taffeta, clouds of lace, and a blue sash emblazoned across surprisingly sumptuous breasts, stepped up and placed a gloved hand on Smee's shoulder. "I'll drive her, old son."

"You?" Siobhan said, as if doubting Gooley would be any more sober than Smee.

Gooley put out his hands to show they were completely steady, not even a quiver from the froth of lace encircling his wrists. "Sober as a judge. Always like to keep a clear head for the competition."

Smee took a deep breath. "Be gentle with her, lad."

Gooley positioned himself in front of the wheel and turned the engine over.

———

Kate had expected Angelica to flinch, but she didn't. She didn't even look in Kate's direction. "I wondered how long it would take before you figured it out."

"I can understand why you wanted to reinvent yourself. No child should have to endure what you did."

Angelica turned to face her with such vehemence that Kate took a step back to brace herself. "My father was an evil son of a bitch. Oh, he never laid a finger on me. He didn't have to. But he could never forgive me for what my mother had done. He was determined I wasn't going to turn into the sort of woman she became." She spit out the last words.

"So you decided to destroy him. The Island Garden Competition. You poisoned the plants so your father would get the blame."

"But he only became angrier, more controlling. With the business failing, I suggested we move to the mainland. But the bastard refused. He was an island man, born and bred. He wouldn't leave, so I couldn't either." She sounded so miserable.

"The thing my father never understood was that in spite of everything he did to prevent it, I turned out exactly like my mother. I wanted a man to love me, to rescue me. I wanted David Sutherland. But there was no one to teach me how to be the kind of woman he could love."

"Emma tried, didn't she? Did she encourage you to dress up for the school-end celebration? I saw the pictures. You were pretty."

Angelica smirked. "It was ironic, really. She had no idea she was helping me to catch David's eye. But it didn't work. He only had eyes for her. I went to the Porth Madryn library every Saturday to learn what to do. I read books, books where women find their soul mate.

They all said if a woman is patient and constant in her love, in time the man will love her too. So I waited. I waited so long, but David never came to me." Her body seemed to collapse in on itself, her shoulders rounded. She looked down at her empty hands.

Kate went cold. How could she reason with a woman who'd used romance novels as an instruction manual for her life?

"Then my father's health failed, helped by some toxic herbs that found their way into his food." Her face lit up as if proud of the part she'd played in his demise. "I put him into the foulest shit-hole nursing home I could find and left him to rot in his own piss."

She looked out over the open water. "When I left the island, I left Sami Sparrow and everything she was behind. I took my middle name, Angela, made it sound sophisticated. Then I put myself through secretarial school by taking any job I could find, no matter how degrading."

Her voice became softer. "The woman I lodged with had always wanted a daughter. She enjoyed teaching me how to dress, do my hair and makeup. Thanks to her I eventually got a job at an art school. I was able to educate myself about David's world so I could talk intelligently to him.

"When my father finally died, I sold his cottage to Old Alred. I didn't get much—nobody wanted to live on an isolated island back then—but it was enough to invest in some designer clothes, a few pieces of expensive jewellery. I made myself beautiful, like the women in the books, like the women who surrounded David. I went to his openings, found out where he lived, and waited on the street for him. But he never so much as looked at me."

Her face showed such sadness and humiliation that Kate felt the stirrings of sympathy for her. But Kate swallowed them down. She couldn't allow her feelings to distract her. "But you married."

"For money. Nothing else."

Kate expected tenderness, but the tone in Angelica's voice was one of disdain.

"We were married thirty-eight years. Thirty-eight years he adored me, bought me anything I wanted—sports cars, a London flat, holidays in the world's most beautiful cities. This yacht. And when my husband crawled on top of me, I closed my eyes and imagined he was David."

She paused and smiled almost wistfully. "You mustn't think badly of me, Kate. You know what it's like for us women. Once we've found our one true love, we can't settle for second-best. With David, I knew it was just a matter of time. I'd be at one of his art openings. He'd look at me across the room. Our eyes would meet. And that would be it. I'd leave Anton, and David would leave his wife, because in that moment, we'd know we were supposed to be together forever."

Her face grew dark and ugly. "But no matter what I did to myself, to David Sutherland I was invisible."

"Is that why you wanted to get rid of Siobhan? Because she was friends with David?" Kate asked. James had always said the trick with mentally unbalanced people is to keep them talking. It delays them acting.

"Friends? Don't pretend you don't know what's been going on. I'm sure that whore has bragged about seducing my David. They've been at it for years. When she moved here, I thought it was over, but he followed her. They can't keep away from each other. She has to go."

Was Angelica seriously prepared to kill Siobhan because she thought she and David were still having an affair? And was she responsible for the death of Hannah? Once Angelica confessed to murder, there was no going back, no telling what she'd do.

Kate breathed deeply to steady the waver in her voice. "And Hannah? Why did she have to die?"

Angelica stared at Kate with genuine surprise. "Hannah? I didn't kill Hannah. The woman was as daft as a brush. What would be the point?"

"Then Gwynie."

"Ah, Gwynie. You see, Gwynie was the only one—other than yourself—who saw through my disguise. 'Mutton dressed as lamb.'" There was a laugh and a defiant toss of her head. "That's rich, calling me a prostitute. She dropped her knickers for David without a second thought when she had the chance."

Angelica took a moment to straighten her hair. "But I never touched her."

"You pretended to take a sedative and lie down in one of the upstairs bedrooms. You took the car keys from the kitchen, slipped out the back door. The garage is far enough away from the house that you could drive out onto the road without anyone seeing you."

Angelica looked genuinely impressed Kate had figured it out. "As much as I'd love to take the credit, Gwynie's injuries weren't down to me. All I had to do was steer the car in her direction and the stupid woman jumped into the ditch and knocked herself out."

Kate took a step forward. "Then tell me. Why did you kill Emma?"

CHAPTER 39

Siobhan stood on the deck of Smee's boat, the wind and salt spray hitting her face. She was trembling but she wasn't sure whether it was from fear or the cool wind. "Faster," she urged Gooley.

"There's only so fast she'll go, m'dear," a black lace fan hung from his wrist and banged against the steering wheel. "She's built for cod. She's not built for speed."

"She'll be firewood, if we're too late," Siobhan shouted over the roar of the waves and the engine.

Byron stood beside her. She hoped he couldn't see her shaking.

"Don't worry, we'll get there," he said calmly.

But will we? she wondered. In that moment, Siobhan thought if she put her head against his shoulder, he wouldn't step away. He might even put her arm around her. But for the first time since she'd clapped eyes on him, the thought of seducing Byron Finch was no longer uppermost in her mind.

— \

Kate was half expecting Angelica to deny responsibility for Emma's death, but she didn't. She didn't look shocked or taken aback. She said nothing.

"This is about David. You're obsessed with him," Kate finally said. "You followed him around London, used your husband's position to get yourself invited to his openings. You were stalking him."

The realization hit her. "It was you who vandalized his car."

"He always had such poor taste in women. They were never good enough for him." Angelica's words became a whining bleat. "He could have had me."

"That's why you're building the art centre. You're trying to buy his affection."

"It will be a monument to my beloved David. It's the least he deserves."

"But David doesn't care about things like that."

"You know nothing about him, nothing," Angelica snarled. "I'd do anything for him."

"Including taking someone's life?"

Kate thought she saw a glimmer of remorse come over Angelica's face.

"I'm sorry it had to be Emma." Her regret almost sounded genuine. "She was good to me. We could have been friends. But David chose her, so it had to be done. Besides, she was pregnant."

Although incensed by Angelica's casual attitude, Kate was determined to keep calm. "You killed her because you thought she was pregnant?"

The look on Angelica's face was that of someone who was convinced her actions were completely justified. "David would have married her. He was like that— the Sutherland duty, that ridiculous need to always do the honourable thing. And I would have lost him forever."

"I have a copy of the post mortem report. There was no mention of a pregnancy. Why in God's name did you think she was pregnant?"

Kate hadn't meant to shout. She braced herself, in case Angelica decided to attack.

But Angelica simply shook her head. "You're lying. She was coming out of the medical centre. She said she'd just learnt something that would change her life forever. She was so happy. She'd obviously been told she was pregnant. She was going to be David's wife, have his children. They were going to be together for the rest of their lives."

Kate couldn't control her anger any longer. She no longer cared if she set Angelica off. She was confident she could overpower her on size and age alone.

"You stupid woman! She was at the medical centre to pick up something for my grandfather. And her news was she'd just received her final acceptance to university. David begged her to go away with him, but she turned him down. She wasn't interested in David. She was leaving the island. Why couldn't you have just waited a few more weeks?"

"Then it was her own fault. She should have told me what it was."

Angelica had obviously spent a lifetime rationalizing and justifying her actions, convincing herself it was Emma who was to blame. Nothing Kate could say would convince her otherwise.

"What did you do?" Kate had to know.

Angelica started to strut, as if she had been waiting to tell this story all her life. "It was surprisingly simple. I'd just returned on the ferry and was working in your grandparents' garden. Your grandmother took Emma out for tea. While the house was empty, I typed the note on their typewriter and left it in Emma's room under her pillow. They wouldn't find it until it was over.

"Getting her to come with me was almost as easy. For someone so intelligent, she was naively trusting. When she came back, I got her alone and told her I'd seen you and her sister stranded on the rocks around the back of the island. We had to rescue you before the tide came in. She wanted to get help from some of the others, but I convinced her we didn't have the time. We took my grandfather's boat."

Dear God, Emma died because she thought I was in danger. What kind of monster uses someone's love for a child to lure them to their death?

Angelica paused and looked back out over the water toward the caves.

Kate wanted to scream, to cry, to hurt her for all the pain she'd so casually inflicted on Kate's family. And while the Galways had been left to pick up the pieces, to deal with the guilt and the loss, Angelica had gone on to a life of extravagance, sheltered from the consequences of her actions. It was time to pay. The only way to do that was for Kate to gather information. Angelica had to finish the story.

"It was right here, or maybe a little further along. Forgive me if I can't give you the exact location, but my mind was on other things. You see, I had to make sure she couldn't swim to the caves, so I hit her over the head with a rock."

Angelica turned around, as if curious to see Kate's reaction.

Kate forced herself to remain calm. "It was you who sent David off the island."

"He needed an alibi in case no one bought the suicide story."

"You poisoned my daughter."

"A little nudge to convince you to give up this silly notion and go home. If you want to blame anyone, blame Fiona. Such a lot of fuss and bother over something that happened so long ago."

"*Fuss and bother*! Is that what you call my aunt's death?" She took a deep breath. "And what about trying to burn down my cottage?"

"At least I waited until you were out. Given the situation, I showed considerable restraint. You know, I could have done something really nasty, something protracted and painful. I know all about plants, remember." She grinned. "Just ask my father."

Kate swallowed the words she wanted to spit at this mad woman. She drew herself up and tried to sound commanding, like when she had to break up a fight on the school grounds. "We're going back to the harbour."

A weary, almost condescending grin appeared on Angelica's face. "Oh I am, but not you, Kate."

Just how was Angelica planning to overpower her? Did she have a gun hidden somewhere in that designer trouser suit?

"I can't go to jail, not now. There's still so much work to do on the art complex. Only I can fulfil this vision. And then David will finally realize I'm the woman he's been looking for all his life."

"The woman David has been looking for all his life is Emma. When you killed Emma, David idealized her. You ensured he could never love anyone else—and that includes you." Kate took satisfaction in saying this.

Angelica took a step towards Kate, her fists tight, her face screwed into an ugly mask. "No, he will love me, he will," and she threw herself at Kate, fists pummelling her about the head, rings scratching Kate's face.

But instead of screams of rage, Angelica started to cry for help.

Kate was momentarily distracted, then grabbed her bony shoulders.

Angelica went limp, allowing Kate to shake her, and brought her hands up into a defensive position. "No, stop, please don't hurt me. Stop, you're hurting me."

Kate almost let her go, afraid she'd overestimated her opponent's strength, that the struggle might bring on a heart attack.

But there was a yell behind her, and someone rushed up out of the cabin and grabbed Kate from behind, strong pudgy hands wrapping around her chest, hot chocolate breath on her neck. "Don't! Stop hurting my nana."

"Toby, it's Kate. Let me go," she managed to say, breathless from the strength of his arms gripping her tight.

Angelica stood wringing her hands. "She tried to kill me, Toby. She tried to kill your nana. Get rid of the bad woman so she can't hurt me. Throw her into the sea."

Toby's sweaty arms still pinned Kate. She calculated she might be able to swim to the caves if she was thrown over the side, but she feared that was the least of her problems. What if Angelica knocked her out, as she'd done with Emma, or tried to run her over with the boat once she was in the water? Kate had to get Toby on her side. "You know me, Toby. I helped you when the police wanted to arrest you."

He held her fast but didn't move.

"Don't make me hurt her, Nana. I like Miss Kate," he whined.

"Listen to me." Angelica's voice was strong and insistent. "Remember what we talked about? If you do this for Nana, you can come and live with me in my house. You won't have to work in anyone's garden ever again."

"But I like the garden."

Angelica's face was red with impatience. "Shut up, and do what I tell you."

"I can't hurt Miss Kate. Please don't make me do it."

"Just throw her overboard and be done with it. Stupid moron!"

"Don't call me that," he pleaded.

Angelica obviously couldn't handle Kate on her own. She needed Toby's strength, but she was becoming more and more frustrated at not being able to control him.

"Just do what I say," Angelica barked.

"I can't," he said.

"Stop being so pathetic."

Toby's gasp became tighter as he grew angry. "Don't say that. Don't say that about me, Nana."

But Angelica had run out of patience. "Stop calling me that. I'm not your grandmother."

"You are, you are." He sounded desperate.

"No, she's not, Toby," Kate said evenly, hoping to defuse the situation. "She lied to you."

Angelica threw her arms up in the air. "This will teach me to ask for help from the island idiot!"

Toby released Kate.

"You're the idiot," he shouted.

Surprised by his outburst, Angelica took several steps back, knocking into the bench, and falling against the railing.

Toby rushed toward her. The force of his movement coupled with Angelica's imbalance tipped them both over the side and into the water.

Kate ran to the railing.

Angelica was struggling to hold onto Toby, grabbing at his

shoulders. It was obvious she couldn't swim. He was throwing her off as he flapped his arms about, frantically gulping in large mouthfuls of air. He couldn't swim either.

Kate called out to calm him, but he was in too much of a panic. She only had a few minutes to act before they both went under. There was no use her jumping into the water. Toby's agitation would drown them all.

Kate looked about for a lifebuoy. She'd just unhooked one when she heard the sound of a motor and someone shouting her name. It was a fishing boat, and Byron and Siobhan were waving from the stern.

"Angelica and Toby are overboard. They can't swim," and she tossed the buoy toward where Toby was still thrashing. Byron tore off his blue windbreaker and dove into the water. Toby was tiring, his face red from the exertion.

Kate could see the yellow of Angelica's trouser suit just under the water. "Byron, Angelica's going down."

As Byron got closer, Toby found a renewed strength and started to churn the water. Byron dove down, his white trainers kicking the surface, but Toby grabbed at his feet, desperate for help. Byron's head appeared, and he grappled with Toby's hands to break free.

A second splash and Feebles was in the sea, heading as quickly as he could to where Kate had last seen Angelica. Byron grabbed Toby around the neck and held his face above the water until they got to the buoy. Once he realized he wasn't going under again, Toby began to relax.

The sea's turbulent surface began to calm as they watched the place where Feebles had disappeared beneath the water. With each second, Kate became more anxious, praying Angelica hadn't claimed him. It was too much for her, and warm tears flooded out onto her cheeks. If it hadn't been for Toby, it could have been her down there, sinking into the dark depths, just as Emma had done.

Feebles' white head erupted through the surface as he gasped for air. "Couldn't reach her," he told Byron. "She's too far down."

Toby began to cry.

CHAPTER 40

It wasn't until Kate was sitting on Smee's boat that the reality of what she'd witnessed hit her. She began to shake uncontrollably. As they pulled away from the yacht, she looked back to the place where she'd last seen Angelica, her ash blonde hair and yellow suit, desperately trying to hold onto Toby. She, who had so casually taken another life, had in the end been desperate to live.

Byron, wrapped in a grey blanket and still dripping wet from his rescue of Toby, placed a bulky woollen sweater smelling of fish about Kate's shoulders. Siobhan sat with her, gently wiping away the blood from the scratches left by Angelica's ring.

As Gooley guided the boat back toward the harbour, Smee poured whiskey into some chipped enamel mugs and handed one to Kate. Byron sat with Toby, rubbing him down with another stained blanket.

"You're a man now," Smee told him, offering Toby a mug. "Take it."

Toby closed his eyes and gulped, coughing on the liquor.

Kate tipped hers back, barely feeling it go down. She'd watched someone die in front of her eyes. She didn't know how she could ever erase that from her mind.

"How did you know where I was?" Kate asked Siobhan.

"After Alex's call, I asked if anyone had seen you. Winifred said you'd gone off with Angelica."

"Alex?"

"She got someone to look into Angelica's past and made the connection. Winifred said you'd waved to her and then followed Angelica in the direction of the harbour. We noticed her boat was missing so we went looking for you. You suspected, didn't you? You waved to Winifred on purpose."

"I wanted to leave a bread crumb trail, just in case." Despite her safeguards, Kate shivered at how close it had all come to going disastrously wrong.

"Why didn't you tell me Angelica was Sami Sparrow?"

"I wasn't completely sure, so I dangled some bait in front of her to see if she'd take it. I mentioned gardeners in a way that might make her think I'd seen through her disguise. She jumped at it."

Siobhan looked over the edge of the boat at the dark water. "That could have been you down there."

She threw her arms about Kate. "Why didn't you tell me what you were doing?"

"No time. I acted in the moment." Kate grinned. "Hey, that's something you'd do!"

Siobhan smirked and then asked, "Why did you suspect it was Angelica?"

"My current novel."

Siobhan looked puzzled.

"A woman returns to the estate where she'd once worked as a servant and is able to pass herself off as a noblewoman. I'd seen pictures of David's art shows, spanning maybe forty years. There was one woman who kept appearing over and over, gradually ageing. When she was young, she vaguely resembled Sami, and later she looked more like Angelica. Gwynie recognized her too. That's why Angelica tried to kill her."

"That was who Hannah saw on the boat the day Emma disappeared."

Smee made another pass with the bottle, and Kate accepted a second shot. "She claimed she didn't kill Hannah."

Byron looked over. "Do you believe her?"

"She admitted to killing Emma and forcing Gwynie off the road, and she tried to get Toby to push me into the water. She had no reason to lie about Hannah."

Feebles' hand rested on her shoulder.

The harbour swung into view. Islanders and visitors alike were gathered on the wharf as Gooley guided the boat into the harbour. Assembled in their bonnets, bustles, and kilts, they looked like the cast of a 19th century costume drama.

It didn't take long to moor the boat. Toby scrambled onto the pier, helped by some of the men. A circle of cooing ladies descended on him and whisked him away, while strong hands helped Kate and then Siobhan out of the boat. Fiona and Winifred came close.

"Where's Angelica?" Winifred asked.

"You mean Sami Sparrow," Siobhan said.

There was a general gasp from those within earshot.

Byron had just climbed onto the wharf when Julian took him by the arm. "Constable Finch, you're needed up at the church."

In spite of being cold and damp, Byron immediately adopted an authoritarian stance. "What's the problem?"

"It's Jane Sutherland."

Kate turned at the sound of Jane's name.

"I'm afraid she's dead."

—

Julian had been the one to find Jane. He'd driven Marcus's car to the school to get some more chairs. On the way back, he stopped at the church. After Jane's visit the day before, he felt in need of spiritual guidance. As he walked through the graveyard, he found Jane, lying on the fresh earth of Hannah's grave, dressed in her best black, her arms folded over the cross on her chest.

Tucked under her hands was a letter, addressed to David and Sophie. Julian could guess what it said. He'd never seen anyone so troubled. She'd wanted to confess. She'd wanted forgiveness, and Julian hadn't been able to give it to her.

Drawing on his faith and the certain knowledge God would

understand the compassionate intention with which he performed it, Julian had administered the last rites. In her death, he'd granted Jane the absolution he'd been unable to give her in life.

—

When Kate and the others arrived at the church, they found Jane still lying on Hannah's grave. David's coat covered her, as if to keep her warm. David handed Byron the letter.

"She took an overdose of the same tablets she gave to Hannah." David's voice wavered. "She was able to get a second prescription by telling the specialist that Hannah had thrown the tablets away. Lately Hannah had been talking about some of the things she'd done when she was younger, how she'd arranged a termination for a student. Hannah was taking her private letters and pages from her diary and burying them. That's why Jane attacked Kate and Siobhan in the garden that night.

"In her letter, Jane asks for forgiveness—for hurting Sophie and I, for making it seem like Hannah had taken her own life. She was relieved in a way when the police realized it was murder, because it meant Hannah could be buried beside our parents. In her own misguided way, Jane had been trying to protect Hannah. She knew how proud Hannah was."

"Pride," Sophie cried out from behind David. "It's destroyed our family. How many more of us have to die for our blasted Sutherland pride?" and she collapsed against him.

David put his arm around her and continued. "Jane was a deeply religious woman, and she couldn't live with what she'd done. She believed suicide was a sin. But her action wasn't to escape punish-ment. It was a self-inflicted punishment, far more severe than any law could impose—to be separated from us for all eternity."

From under David's arm, Sophie saw the Reverend Imogen com-ing toward her through the crowd. "But that's not true, is it?" Sophie implored her. "Surely God won't punish Jane for doing what she thought was right, for trying to protect Hannah," and she gripped Imogen's arm.

Imogen took Sophie's hands in hers. "Jane was a troubled soul. If we can find it in our hearts to forgive her, I have no doubt God in His infinite mercy will do the same."

"Then we can bury her here beside Hannah and Father?"

"Of course we can."

People began to wander back to the beach to pack away the food, gather up the chairs, and dismantle the tables. The papier mâché Queen Victoria would be put away for another year.

Kate couldn't believe it was over, that she'd finally uncovered the truth about Emma's death. But how much closer was she to knowing Emma as a person?

Her first inclination had been to interpret her aunt's actions as motivated by arrogance. But Emma could just as easily have acted out of fear. She'd worked hard to earn her place at Cambridge. It was expected by everyone that she excel. If she failed, she was letting down not only her family but the whole island. Being the best and brightest on Meredith was one thing. But the prospect of being thrust into a world where everyone was just as intelligent, if not more so, as well as coming from economic privilege which allowed them to devote all of their time to their studies... That would have seemed daunting and terribly unfair. Emma must have been keenly aware that having to work as a salesclerk or a waitress would not only carry a social stigma to people whose friendship and acceptance she sought, but would also disadvantage her academically.

In a way, Faraday Manor and its possessions belonged to all the islanders. They tended and cared for them, and just possibly Emma had convinced herself that if her small share helped her to achieve what the islanders believed she could, then she had every right to take it.

But was Kate rationalizing Emma's behaviour? She would probably never know what had driven her to do what she did, to risk losing her parents' trust, Fiona's friendship, and the islanders' respect. But as much as it frustrated Kate's need for closure, it was something she would have to accept.

—

James stared at the framed photographs on the far wall of his office, most taken at police functions—retirements or station Christmas parties. Kate was in many of them, wearing that sexy red dress that made her tits look good. *Did she still have that dress?* he wondered.

She'd just rung to tell him they'd found Emma's killer. She'd been reluctant to give him any details. With that and the way she'd managed to side-step his questions, he'd concluded she'd been in some danger but had come through it safely. He didn't know whether to be angry or relieved.

He picked up the photo of Kate and Alex from his desk. Other people got divorced and moved on. It happened all the time. What was his problem? Eight years later and he should be able to stop worrying about her, stop wondering what she was doing out there on her own. Or if she was on her own. *Let go of the riverbank, my arse.* His finger tenderly touched her face in the photograph. This was one riverbank he wasn't prepared to let go of quite yet.

—

Kate had just hung up the phone when Fiona's head appeared around the front door. "Do you mind if I come in, my dear?"

"Oh, Fiona, please. I'm afraid I'm not in any shape to entertain." Then she realized how ridiculous that sounded.

"I won't stay but a minute." She thrust a tin into Kate's hands. "Just a few raisin buns. They're yesterday's, I'm afraid."

Only Fiona would apologize for day-old baking.

"To help with the terrible shock of today," and she lowered her voice as if someone might overhear. "Now these are all for you, my dear. Treat yourself. Don't feel you have to share them. I have nothing but admiration for Siobhan, but she can be a bit of a greedy guts sometimes."

She kissed Kate on the cheek. "I just wanted to thank you. They can all rest in peace now, and so will I," and she scurried back out the door.

—

Winifred had watched Fiona walk up Kate's path, carrying a tin. Dear Fiona thought everything could be put right with a bit of baking. Yet on the island, most things could. Winifred wanted to go over, but she'd leave it until later. The islanders were often supportive to a fault. It wouldn't do to overwhelm Kate. Best to give her some space.

Lilian would have been so proud of her. The island bred tough women, and Galway women were some of the toughest.

Winifred remembered the summer Kate brought baby Alex to the island to meet her family for the first time. They'd had a party in the back garden, and people stopped by and shared cake and drinks to wet the baby's head. They'd laughed, laughed at nothing and everything. Cradling this new little life in her arms, it seemed that for one afternoon, Lilian was able to forget the pain of losing Emma. That was how Winifred would always remember her.

—

Kate leaned against the stone wall looking down at the harbour. From the pub door, she could hear Julian announcing that Gooley had won the Queen Victoria Challenge Cup for the fifth year in a row. He would be graciously accepting congratulatory drinks for the rest of the evening.

Siobhan came up beside her. "All right?"

"I feel strangely calm now it's over."

The light from the pub reflected off Siobhan's hair, making it seem even fierier than usual. Siobhan briefly inclined her head against Kate's. "You're a good woman, Kate Galway. How did I end up with a friend who has so many morals? This will take some getting used to."

They stood and listened to someone tinkling away on the pub piano.

"There's something I need to ask you," Kate said. "When we were attacked in the Sutherland's garden, you said you knew karate. Do you?"

"No. Anything else?"

"Today in that black jumpsuit, who were you supposed to be?"

"Queen Victoria if she'd been in *The Avengers,*" Siobhan managed to say with a straight face.

Kate burst out laughing.

"I was trying to come up with a clever name for her. There was Emma Peel, you know, M. Appeal for the men. And Tara King. I was thinking of V. Appeal, Vicky Queen, Regina Something." She crumpled her face. "It didn't work, did it?"

"The puns might not have, but that outfit certainly did. I'm surprised you weren't beating the men off with a cricket bat."

"Speaking of men, does James know what you were up to today?"

"I called Alex and thanked her for alerting you to Angelica. She'd already told her father, so I had to call him. I was sure he'd either rant and rave about what a fool I'd been or threaten to come up and drag me off the island to somewhere safe. He surprised me. He was quite amiable. He even congratulated me on 'the collar.'"

"Does that mean you and him..." and Siobhan made some sort of undefined gesture.

"No. Every so often I think we're getting along so well that maybe we should give it another go. Then I realize the reason we're getting along so well is that we aren't trying to make it work."

Siobhan nodded.

"So are you and Byron friends now?" Kate asked.

"He saved Toby from drowning. That counts for something. I also have it on good authority our friend Jenkins is up to his neck in you know what for missing all the action. And since Byron was invaluable in helping to solve a murder and saving a life, well, who knows? We just might see a bit more of him on the island."

"Hopefully not in a professional capacity."

"I can always start knocking people off," and Siobhan left to join the others inside.

A mournful rendition of a traditional folk song filled the night sky. Kate recognized Smee's strong baritone voice.

The lights from the houses around the harbour stretched out over the water, undulating with the slow rhythm of the sea that had settled in for the night. Kate now understood why her family had never left the island. In spite of the day's events, she felt more at peace than she had for a long time.

A large warm hand gently came to rest on her shoulder. Quentin Feebling stood behind her. "Drink, lass?"

"No, I don't think so."

"You've had a terrible day. You know, no one would blame you if you went home."

She looked into his face, a face as serene and all-knowing as some ancient Buddha. "I am home."

"Aye, lass. You are."

She linked her arm in his, and they stood quietly and watched as the clouds blew across the pale spring moon and the stars rippled on the sea.

The End

ACKNOWLEDGEMENTS

It really does take a village to get a book into a reader's hands. No writer does it alone. *Diolch yn fawr iawn* for the support and care that these fabulous people took with this book and its sometimes fragile creator. You mean more to me than you'll ever know.

My Clarkson family, Joy, Ken, and Chris, who had the good sense to move to Wales when I was a child and welcomed me to Pembrokeshire each summer. It was during this time that I fell in love with the country and its people. If it hadn't been for them, Meredith Island would never have existed.

My grandparents, George and Alice Fitzpatrick, who believed I could do anything I set my mind to even when it was something different every time.

My family and friends who never once scoffed or laughed when I said I was a writer.

My publisher, Netta Johnson, who said such wonderful things about the book and supported me every step of the way. Because of her trust in me and the wonderful Stonehouse team, people now get to meet the eccentric people who live in my head.

Alison Layland, crime writer and translator, who is always there to helped me with the Welsh language. Any mistakes are my own.

Nicholas Rheinberg, Honorary Archivist, Coroners' Society of England and Wales who patiently answered my questions about post-mortems. Any changes I've made to serve the plot are entirely of my own making.

Joan Blackwood and Chiquita Philips, who showed exemplary

courage in reading the manuscript and offering valuable criticism.

Howard Shrier, Peter Robinson, Jill Edmondson, and Barbara Kyle whose insightful, thoughtful and practical suggestions helped me to craft the best story I could.

Caroline Duetz who keeps me focused and writing when I'm afraid I have nothing to say that anyone wants to hear.

Elisabeth Pomès who understands that creativity has many expressions and forgave me when I sometimes neglected my singing practice to do "writer stuff".

My favourite writers of all genres who teach me valuable lessons about writing every time I open their books.

To My Readers:

Please don't drive yourselves crazy trying to find Meredith Island on maps or the internet. It's not there. When I decided to write a mystery series, it was important to create a world in which I would enjoy the long hours I'd need to spend there.

There is a Welsh word—*hireath*. It's multi-layered with no exact English translation. It can be grief and nostalgia, homesickness, melancholy, and yearning, and as a result, people have different interpretations of its meaning. But most agree it's a longing for some place you haven't been for a long time, or to which you cannot return, or perhaps it never even existed; somewhere that feels like home but is out of reach.

I've felt this all my life without understanding what it was, that is until I found Meredith Island. It was then that I realized this place where everyone is welcome, neighbours are friends, and you're never without whiskey, tea, and home baking, is where I belong.

Enjoy your stay.

MORE ABOUT ALICE FITZPATRICK

Alice Fitzpatrick has contributed short stories to literary magazines and anthologies and has recently retired from teaching in order to devote herself to writing full-time. She is a fearless champion of singing, cats, all things Welsh, and the Oxford comma. Her summers spent with her Welsh family in Pembrokeshire inspired the creation of Meredith Island. The traditional mystery appeals to her keen interest in psychology as she is intrigued by what makes seemingly ordinary people commit murder. Alice lives in Toronto but dreams of a cottage on the Welsh coast. To learn more about Alice and her writing, please visit her website at www.alicefitzpatrick.com.